Wish Upon The Moon

By

Ellen Dugan

Wish Upon The Moon
Copyright @ Ellen Dugan 2022
Cover art designed by Kyle Hallemeier
Image: Adobestock: Andrey Kiselev
Legacy Of Magick logo designed by Kyle Hallemeier
Copy Editing and Formatting by Libris in CAPS

This is a work of fiction. Names, characters, businesses, organizations, places, events and incidents either are the product of the author's imagination or are used fictitiously. Any resemblance to actual persons, living or dead, events, or locales is entirely coincidental.

No part of this book may be reproduced, or stored in a retrieval system, or transmitted in any other form or by any means electronic, mechanical, photocopying, recording or otherwise without the express written permission of the publisher.

Published by Ellen Dugan

Other titles by Ellen Dugan

THE LEGACY OF MAGICK SERIES

Legacy of Magick, Book 1

Secret of the Rose, Book 2

Message of the Crow, Book 3

Beneath An Ivy Moon, Book 4

Under The Holly Moon, Book 5

The Hidden Legacy, Book 6

Spells Of The Heart, Book 7

Sugarplums, Spells & Silver Bells, Book 8

Magick & Magnolias, Book 9

Mistletoe & Ivy, Book 10

Cakepops, Charms & Do No Harm, Book 11

Wish Upon The Moon, Book 12

THE GYPSY CHRONICLES

Gypsy At Heart, Book 1

Gypsy Spirit, Book 2

DAUGHTERS OF MIDNIGHT SERIES

Midnight Gardens, Book 1

Midnight Masquerade, Book 2

Midnight Prophecy, Book 3

Midnight Star, Book 4

Midnight Secrets, Book 5

Midnight Destiny, Book 6

HEMLOCK HOLLOW TRILOGY

Hemlock Lane, Book 1

Wolfsbane Ridge, Book 2

Nightshade Court, Book 3

HEMLOCK HOLLOW ANTHOLOGY

Bewitched In Hemlock Hollow, Book 1

Beguiled In Hemlock Hollow, Book 2 (Coming 2022)

Beckoned In Hemlock Hollow, Book 3 (Coming 2022)

ACKNOWLEDGMENTS

First and foremost, I want to thank the *Legacy Of Magick* fans. And as always, thanks to my family, friends, beta readers, and editors. Your support and encouragement over the past six years with this series has meant the world.

I finished this book—my twenty-fourth novel and fortieth book over all—a few days after my fortieth wedding anniversary. Yup, forty years. The Hubs and I were married in 1982, and we were eighteen and twenty-one years old at the time. So now we are "officially" an old married couple. As a middle-aged married lady, mother to three, and grandmother to one, it moved me to tears to give Julian and Holly their happy ever after story and to close out the *Legacy Of Magick* series with joy and love.

Love is, after all, the strongest magick I've ever known.

*She belonged to him.
Not because it was something he demanded,
but because it was something she couldn't help.*
JM Storm

Hope is hearing the music of the future. Faith is to dance to it.
Rubem Alves

PROLOGUE

The Drake hunting cabin was tucked cozily into the misty November woods. I hadn't been back to the rustic log cabin in almost a year, but I had always thought that between the surrounding trees and the steep roof lines it was like something straight out of a gothic faery tale. Easing my car around the back, I parked, and with a deep breath I shut off the car and sat in the silence.

I eyeballed the cabin and tried not to let myself get spooked. In the late afternoon light, the cabin and the woods were downright eerie. When a pair of crows called back and forth to one another from the trees at the edge of the clearing, I felt myself startle with a jolt. A sense of déjà vu swept over me, and I suddenly recalled the story of the first Bishop woman who had fallen in love with a Drake man.

Their love story was not a happy one. In fact, it started a family feud that lasted for hundreds of years. It also created a curse...on any Bishop woman and Drake man that fell in love with each other. And that curse seemed to be holding true—at least for me it was.

I shook my head. "Way to stay positive, Holly. Ruminating over the past, a family feud, and an old curse."

With a shaking hand, I pushed my curls out of my face. I climbed out, grabbed my purse, and shut the car door behind me. As I walked across the gravel drive, my sneakers made crunching sounds on the frosty ground. Around me the woods were noisy with the sounds of birds and that pair of crows who I had disturbed at my arrival.

The birds cawed back and forth to one another, and it made me smile. In folklore two crows cawing was an omen of good luck—and I could certainly use that right about now.

I shut my eyes for a moment and tried to ground and center. "My fate is my own." I whispered the words. "My story does not have to end unhappily."

Taking a few moments to steady my nerves, I stayed where I was and absorbed the sounds and calming energy of the surrounding woods. Pulling in a deep breath, I blew away any stress. I opened my eyes and walked forward to the covered porch of the cabin.

One of the crows perched on the edge of the porch roof. He looked beadily down upon me as I climbed up the steps.

"Hello," I said.

The crow cocked his head to one side and waited.

"My grandfather had a crow familiar," I said to the

bird. "Nice to meet you."

The crow cawed loudly at my words and then flew away and into the nearby trees.

Selecting the door key from my key ring, I let myself inside. I reset the locks and went directly to the island in the kitchenette. Sliding my bag across the counter, I stood and took in the one room cabin. Although it was simple, I still found it lovely. The vaulted ceilings and pitch of the roofline made it seem very spacious, and the wood logs in the interior walls gave it a warmth and character.

A leather sofa and sturdy coffee table still faced the brick fireplace. An antique wooden rocking chair remained beside the hearth, and the queen size bed was tucked against a far wall, as it had been before. Seeing that the cabin had been cleaned, I went to check the fridge. I found, with no small amount of relief, that it had been recently stocked with groceries as promised.

After shutting the fridge, I unzipped my jacket and draped it over one of the barstools at the island, recalling the last conversation I'd had with Julian Drake. It had not been a pleasant one. We had argued, and I had accused him of extending his work contract and staying in Charleston on purpose. I was afraid that he'd decided our relationship was simply too much work and far too difficult to maintain.

I considered everything we'd been through. We had managed to keep our relationship a secret for the past four years, and it had not been an easy task. Neither of our families would ever approve of us being together. First: because of the past troubles with the search for the Blood Moon Grimoire. Second: because for a time Julian had been under the awful influence of its dark magick. Thirdly: there was our age difference. He was almost ten years older than me. And last, but not least...because he was my boss.

Although it had been tough keeping a professional façade in place while we worked together in the museum offices five days a week, we had found a way to manage. When we attended the same functions with our families and all their connections, we'd made that work too by simply playing the part of casual work friends whenever our families were together.

Very few people knew that we were lovers, and those that did could be trusted to keep our secret.

We had been talking about going public with our relationship when Julian had been transferred to supervise the expansion of a museum in a city all the way across the country. A huge opportunity for his career, he could not rightfully pass it up. I had even encouraged him to go. We'd been so certain that we could withstand this test as a couple, since it was only a short-term six-month assignment. Surely, we could get through this.

After all, no one would know us in another city, and we could fly or drive to each other if necessary. We plotted out future meetings in a central location that was a half-way point somewhere between St. Louis and

Charleston, in a city where we'd be completely anonymous. It had been a good plan, or so we'd thought. We'd parted, sure of our love for each other and firmly intending to video call, send sexy texts, and to speak on the phone every day. Plans were made to rendezvous with each other at our half-way point city every other weekend too. And well, you know what they say about the road to hell being paved with good intentions...

At first, we *had* seen each other every two weeks. But as the months had dragged on, our reunions had been once a month, and then they were even less. Between his new job and my family obligations, our plans kept getting derailed.

I'd thought as we neared the end of six hellish months apart, we'd finally made it, and then the museum in Charleston extended his contract for *another* six months. We'd argued over it, and now there was more than physical distance between us. There was emotional distance too. Worst of all—there was doubt.

Yet, despite my misery, the world had continued on around me for the past year. The Bishop family tree was growing and branching out quite nicely. My brother Bran had discovered his half-brother, Daniel Stone. Daniel and Candice Jacobs had married in a small but pretty ceremony over the summer. My niece, Belinda, and nephew, Morgan, had turned four and six years old respectively, and Autumn's twins were growing up, deep into their terrible two's. Maggie and Wyatt were expecting their first baby, and Willow, now seven, was over the moon with the idea of becoming a big sister.

But what had really hit me the hardest was when my twin sister, Ivy, and her boyfriend Eric McBriar had gotten engaged. Their wedding was scheduled for mid-January, after the holidays. I was happy for my sister and yet envious that no one questioned her relationship as they would have mine...*if* they'd have known about it.

Determined not to do anything to put a damper on Ivy's wedding plans, I put on a happy face and threw myself into helping with her winter wedding. I was to be a bridesmaid, and the bridal shower was next month.

Everyone around me was so happy, and I'd been alone for most of the past year feeling absolutely miserable. After our last argument, Julian and I had grown farther and farther apart, and I began to worry that he no longer loved me as much as I loved him. For the past months I'd half-expected to get a phone call, or worse, a text message telling me he'd found someone new.

Then when I'd least expected it, Julian called me at the office a week before Thanksgiving. He announced that his Charleston contract was finished a few weeks early and he was coming home. It had taken every ounce of composure I had to answer him and to speak in a professional tone of voice.

"That's good news, Mr. Drake," I said into the phone. "I'll be sure to have your office ready for you, along with a detailed report of the new exhibits in the museum that have been installed in your absence."

"Thank you, Ms. Bishop," he replied smoothly.

He also informed me that he would be sending further instructions about his current projects, and an exhibit that would shortly be sent back to its source museum. I took notes and our phone conversation was nothing but professional. Likewise, there had been nothing in his voice or phrasing that hinted at anything other than a cordial working relationship.

We'd grown far too good at this game over the years.

With my heart pounding in my chest, I wished him a safe trip home, and ended the call. I sat there at my desk and felt my palms sweat. Blowing out a long cleansing breath, I jolted when I heard my cell phone buzz from inside my purse. Fishing it out I saw there had been a text message from Julian.

I got up and went directly into the restroom, closed a stall door in order to ensure privacy, and read the message. The text had included his flight information and a brief note asking me to meet him at the cabin tomorrow afternoon. He wanted to talk and to try and work things out. If I agreed to meet him, he would have it made ready for us.

I took a deep breath and messaged back that I would meet him at the cabin. It was the first communication we'd had without arguing in weeks. Slipping the phone into my pocket, I exited the stall. I walked casually back to my desk and tucked my phone away again, but my hands were shaking so hard that I nearly dropped it.

So here I was, waiting for the man I loved to finally come home and to see if we could find a way to work this out. One thing was for certain—if we were going to continue our relationship, our days of hiding and keeping it a secret had to be over.

While I'd stood there reflecting on the past, night had fallen. It was dark in the cabin, but I didn't want to turn on the lights. Instead, my eyes were drawn to the candles on the mantle and to the kindling and firewood waiting on the hearth. With determination, I squared my shoulders and went to the fireplace. First, I picked up the matches and got a few candles going. Next, I knelt at the hearth to get a fire started. I shook my long curling hair behind my shoulders to keep it out of the way, arranged the kindling, struck a match, and held it for a moment.

"No more secrets," I said and worked an impromptu spell. "If he still loves me, then let our love shine bright for all to see. No more secrets, no more lies, may we be blessed by the moon that sails across the skies."

I held the match to the kindling and the flames caught quickly. Blowing out the match, I patiently fed a larger piece of wood to the kindling. Sitting to be more comfortable, I stayed where I was in my jeans and light sweater before the fire. Before long, there was a nice blaze going.

My eyes fell to the big metal cauldron that was currently used to hold wood. It was easy to imagine it hanging over the fire, bubbling away with a stew or soup. "Wonder what it would be like to cook over an open fire, like they did back in the day," I said to myself.

Sitting before the crackling fire, my mind shifted back to the story of the Colonial era, Patience and James...

The troubles between the Bishop and Drake families had started when Patience Bishop, a wise woman, had fallen in love with a son from a powerful family of magicians. The Drakes had been new to the territory of what would eventually become the state of New Hampshire. Wealthy and powerful, the Drakes had soon become an influential family in their village. According to legend they had three sons and the youngest, James Drake, had been a kind young man.

Knowing their families would never approve of the match, James and Patience had married in secret. Eventually, the marriage was discovered. James abjured the Drake family's style of magicks, and he and his bride settled on Bishop land and built a cabin.

But fate was not so kind to the couple. Shortly after the birth of their first child, influenza ravaged the colony. Patience and her child managed to survive, however, James did not. While the Bishop family had tried to help the other colonists with herbal remedies, there were still many losses.

A week after James had been buried, the Drakes began to spread the rumor that Patience was a Witch—a death sentence back in colonial days. That gossip spread like wildfire. The settlers in the area needed someone to blame for the influenza. So grief and fear turned to suspicion and then eventually to hate. One night the Drake family and a group of colonists came for Patience. Brandishing torches, they surrounded Patience's home and broke down the door, intending to take the child away and to imprison Patience on charges of witchcraft.

But when they broke into her cabin, they found that Patience and her child had vanished. The Bishops accused the Drakes of doing away with her and the baby, while the Drakes in turn accused the Bishops of keeping James' child—a Drake heir—away from his rightful family. The families searched in vain, but no one ever discovered where Patience and her baby had gone…

That had begun a feud between the families, and it had woven itself into an almost three-hundred-year-old curse. Which brought us to today.

Shaking off the old story, I added another log to the fire. "Maybe the curse has lessened over time," I said to myself. "Autumn and Duncan beat the odds, and they are truly happy."

What about Great-Aunt Irene Bishop and her lover, Phillip Drake? My inner voice argued. *After Phillip suddenly died, Aunt Irene went away to have her baby in secret. She gave up her child to keep her safe from evil old Silas Drake.*

"That was over fifty years ago," I said out loud, trying to comfort myself.

Your own mother loved Thomas Drake when she was young, and they couldn't be together either.

"Silas Drake was still alive back then, and besides, if Mom hadn't broken things off with Thomas back in the 80s and eventually gotten together with my Dad ten years later, *I* wouldn't even be here." With a groan, I dropped my head into my hands.

Clearly the stress of the past year had taken its toll.

Because here I sat.

Alone in a cabin.

Arguing out loud with myself.

The tragic tale of Patience Bishop and James Drake, the star-crossed lovers, was simply an old story. *I have enough problems,* I reminded myself. Trying to compare my life to Patience's was bound to cause me only misery. I would make my own fate. With determination, I slid the spark screen shut.

The sound of the cabin's door unlocking startled me out of my thoughts.

The door opened. "Holly?" Julian called my name.

I rose to my feet and met his eyes. At last, I was face to face with Julian Drake for the first time in months.

CHAPTER ONE

By the goddess, I thought. *He still looks amazing.* My eyes swept over him. I saw that his dark brown hair was still cut in the same style, but he'd grown out his scruff into a neat, very close mustache and beard. He was also dressed more casually than I'd ever seen him before.

To my surprise, he wore charcoal jeans and blue trainers that had clearly seen some use. His coat was navy, and I spotted a white Henley shirt underneath. From where he stood by the door, I couldn't make out the colors in his eyes, but I knew by heart which eye had the ring of electric blue against the brown, and which eye had patches of blue against the warm brown.

"Hello, Julian," I said, my voice husky from holding back my emotions.

He shut the door behind him, locked it, and carried his small travel bag to the kitchen island. Placing it onto the surface, he shrugged free from his coat in complete silence.

My hands were shaking. Perhaps it was nerves or fear, I wasn't entirely sure. To cover the reaction, I linked my hands at my waist.

I couldn't read the expression on his face as he dropped his coat to the back of the sofa. Julian strode forward until he was about three feet away from me. He stopped and stared down at me for a long moment.

Finally, he spoke. "I've missed you."

I tilted my head to one side. "Have you?"

I saw the tiniest flicker of emotion in his eyes, and it gave me hope. *Could he be nervous as well?* I wondered.

"I've missed you, every damn day," he said, slowly reaching out. Gently he brushed his fingers through my hair. "Have you missed me?"

I turned my face toward his hand so that his palm was cupping my cheek. "I have missed you too, Julian. Every single second of every day."

Suddenly, I felt his emotions. Usually Julian was carefully shielded, keeping his own empathic abilities tightly contained. He had more control than any other magician I knew. Dropping his shields this way meant one of two things. He was either exhausted from holding all of his emotions back, or he wanted me to feel exactly whatever he was.

He still loves me, I realized. *He loves me every bit as deeply and as desperately as I love him.*

Tears sprang to my eyes in relief. Returning the favor, I dropped *my* energetic shields and let him read my emotions as well. All of my insecurities, all of my longing, and all of my love.

Julian drew in a harsh breath from the force of the emotions crashing into him. However, he didn't waver, and he didn't back away. Instead, he pulled me into his arms.

"I love you," we said at the same time.

Our mouths met with ferocity. This kiss wasn't soft and pretty. It was a desperate dueling of tongues and a clashing of teeth. I groaned when he tangled his hands in my hair and tugged my head back to deepen his kiss. Wrapping my arms around his waist, I hung on. It had been months since we'd been together, and when he drew me down to the leather sofa, I went willingly.

We pulled the clothes from each other in haste. Julian began to kiss his way up my throat. His teeth tested the nape of my neck and in response, I set my teeth into his shoulder. I felt his immediate reaction, and we let go of each other only long enough to strip off the last of our clothes.

Finally, we were naked and fell upon each other again.

"Julian." I hooked one leg around his hips. "Hurry." Reaching out, I guided him to me, and a second later he was pushing his way deep inside. Throwing my head back, I gasped in pleasure.

For a few moments he held perfectly still, and we savored the incredible feeling of unity. Then he dropped his mouth back to mine.

Our kiss went wild as we moved together. It was a frantic pace, and exactly what I wanted after being apart from him for so many months. I tried to hold out for as long as I could, but it had been far too long, and I quickly felt my orgasm building. As I yanked my mouth away to get a full breath, Julian pulled one of my legs up higher. He slung his hips forward and hit a spot deep inside that sent me screaming right over the edge.

Following a few moments later, he collapsed on top of me with a hoarse shout. I lay under him on the couch, held him close, and tried to catch my breath.

He shifted his weight so I could breathe more easily. After a bit of maneuvering, we lay on our sides, spooned together with my back tucked firmly against his chest. Somehow, we managed to stay on the sofa. As our heart rates began to settle we cuddled, warm and cozy in front of the fire.

"I love you," Julian whispered into my ear and then he drew in the scent of my hair. "I dream about your hair. All those long red curls spilling around me..."

"I love you, too." I sighed and reached back to pat his face. "By the way, I like the beard."

"Do you?" He rubbed it over my shoulder, and I couldn't help but giggle.

"You are so beautiful," he murmured, kissing my nape.

"You'll always be prettier than me, Julian," I said.

"And now I want you all over again."

I turned my head to see his expression and it had me

fighting to catch my breath. Julian Drake was a dangerously beautiful man, and I had to shake myself out of the seductive spell he always cast over me and focus on the practicalities.

"We were supposed to *talk*," I reminded him, "so we could work everything out."

"Angel," he said, running his hand over my hip, "I think we did just work it out."

"Julian." I tried to keep a serious tone. "I'm done with sneaking around and hiding how I feel about you."

"I absolutely agree," he said, leaning closer. "No more hiding." He pressed his mouth to mine, and this kiss was soft and sweet.

When the kiss ended, I spoke again. "I love you so much, Julian. I don't care what anyone else says or thinks about us being a couple."

He shifted and began patting around at his coat that was still on the back of the sofa. "I have something for you," he said.

"Oh?"

He pulled something from his pocket and raised up on one elbow. "I've had this for months. Thought over about a hundred different ways to..." He trailed off with a smile. "But I think this is the perfect moment."

I frowned. "Perfect moment?"

"I love you," he said again and handed me a small velvet covered box.

My heart almost stopped in my chest. I looked from the small jeweler's box and back to him, and felt tears begin to gather. "Julian, I..."

"Open it," he said softly.

I pushed the lid open and gasped. There, inside the box, was an engagement ring. The center stone of the ring was a gorgeous oval cut aquamarine. A rectangular cushion of small diamonds was arranged around the blue-green stone in a halo setting. The band was delicate, with more small diamonds marching across the platinum.

"Oh my goddess," I breathed.

"There's a matching wedding band too," he said quietly.

I checked again. A second delicate diamond eternity band snugged against the engagement ring, making the design seamless and elegant.

I raised my eyes to his. "I've never seen such beautiful rings," I managed to say.

He smiled. "Marry me, Angel."

I nodded. "Yes."

Julian pulled the engagement ring from the box and slipped it on my finger. It fit perfectly. "The central stone is three carats," he explained. "It reminded me of you, as it matches the aqua color of your eyes."

I lifted my eyes from the stunning ring to focus back on his gorgeous face. "It's perfect," I said as happy tears rolled down my face.

He kissed me. A brief hard kiss. Then he jumped up, scooped me into his arms and carried me across the cabin towards the bathroom. "I love you. I don't want to wait."

"You don't have to wait." I grinned and tilted my head meaningfully toward the shower. "I could go for another round right now."

"That's not what I meant." He reached in and started the water for the shower. "I *meant*," Julian said, adjusting the water temperature, "that we've been together for four years, and that I don't want to wait to get married."

I blinked. "Meaning what?"

He kissed my nose. "I think we should elope. Tonight."

"Elope?" I sputtered. "*Tonight?*"

He started to chuckle at my reaction.

"Oh," I said. "You're joking."

"No, I'm not," he said, and set two thick towels on the counter. "There's a beautiful bed and breakfast in Hannibal. They specialize in small wedding packages. I have a deposit down. We can leave in an hour if you like."

"You seriously want to elope?" I gaped at him. "Tonight?"

"Sure, why not?" He rummaged in the drawer of the vanity and handed me a hair tie.

"I don't have a bag packed or a dress—" I stopped speaking because he had leaned forward and pressed his lips to mine. Eventually he let me up for air.

"I love you, Holly Bishop," he said. "I am proud to be with you, and I want to marry you right away." He pressed a gentle kiss to my forehead. "We've waited long enough."

At a loss for words, I took the hair tie and bundled my hair up. Julian tugged me into the shower with him and I tried to think our situation over, but that wasn't easy as he had his hands all over me.

As we finished up and began to dry off, I faced a few hard truths. *My brother would be livid,* I realized. Bran would never even approve of my dating, let alone me being engaged to Julian Drake. In fact, my brother would go thermonuclear at the news of an elopement.

Not to mention my twin sister's reaction. Ivy said she had forgiven Julian for what had happened between them in the past. In fact, she'd said several times that she was impressed with how Julian had changed his life...

As I dressed, I thought over all the possible objections the family would have, and my stomach began to churn. "Neither of our families will take the news of us eloping very well," I said. "Besides our friends, Nina and Diego, and my Aunt Faye, no one knows that we're even seeing each other."

"Maggie knows about us, and so do Autumn and Duncan," Julian said.

"They do?" My heart slammed against my ribs. "I had no idea."

"We'll have more support than you think," he said. "But bottom line? I'll be damned if I'll let anyone's opinion change what *we* know is right for the two of us."

"Where would we live?" I wondered. "I don't think we'd be comfortable living in the manor with my family."

"I have two rooms in the mansion that we could use," he pointed out.

"I never even imagined living at the Drake mansion." I pulled a face as I thought over the possibilities. "Nina and Diego took over the cottage on the grounds. Maggie and her family have most of the second floor...and her office and Wyatt's writing studio are on the third. Wouldn't it be too crowded if we moved in? What if your father decides he doesn't want us to live there?"

Julian took my hands in his. "First off, there is plenty of space in that old house. And if for whatever reason we decided not to live there, we'll stay here at the cabin until we can find a home that does suit us." He gave my hands a bolstering squeeze. "I don't care where we live, so long as we are together."

I searched his face silently for several moments. I loved him so much, and as I gazed into his eyes I saw my future. Suddenly, all the nerves smoothed out.

I reached up on my toes and planted a loud smacking kiss on his mouth. "Damn other people's opinions," I said. "I don't want to wait either. I'd love to elope—so long as you let me run back to my house and pack a bag. I'm not getting married to you in a pair of jeans and sneakers."

"I suppose I could give you a half hour to pack..." he said and hugged me tight.

I squeezed him back. "All right, Mister. Let's do this."

We eased back to grin at each other.

"If I let you go," he said, "you get a half hour. Otherwise, I'm coming in after you."

I raised my eyebrows at the warning.

He sent me a simmering look. "I'm not joking, Holly. I'll kick in the door to the manor, march up the stairs—"

I giggled. "You don't even know where my room is."

"Turret room, second floor," he said easily. "I've seen you sitting up there in the window seat of the turret, making wishes upon the moon."

"You have?"

"I have," he admitted. "I'll drive you back to your house, you go pack and then slip out. I'll be waiting there for you."

"What about you?" I asked. "Do you need to pack too?"

He smiled. "My bags are still in my car. No worries."

***

Julian drove me home and parked his car slightly down and across the street from the driveway of the manor. The streetlights flickered out as we approached, leaving the surrounding area dark. I gave him a fast kiss, eased out of the car, and walked across the street to the manor house.

Fortunately, the family was out tonight. Ivy was helping her future in-laws set up at the tree farm for the coming Christmas tree season. Lexie was working second shift, and Bran had gone over to Autumn's house with the kids to make the final plans for Thanksgiving dinner, which was less than a week away.

I let myself in through the kitchen and ran straight up the back stairs to my room.

Quickly, I pulled my largest suitcase from my walk-in closet and grabbed a few dresses, work slacks, and tops. I snatched a warm jacket too. Next, I selected a few pairs of heels and my short dressy boots. While I packed, my eyes scanned the closet rack, giving my handful of formal dresses a critical look. *Would anything in here work for a wedding dress?*

There was the gold and white dress I'd worn to the Drake's masquerade ball a few years ago… That could be an option. I went to pull it. The top was bright gold sequins with cap sleeves and the skirt was short and sassy, made from voluminous white tulle. Then my eyes landed on the pretty, pastel blue skirt I'd bought for Yuletide, and possibly to wear to Ivy's upcoming rehearsal dinner. I'd planned to pair the knee-length tulle skirt with a dressy, soft ivory sweater. I even had new heels and jewelry to go with it. The outfit was soft, romantic, and might be perfect for an elopement.

I checked my phone. I'd spent twelve minutes selecting and packing so far. Unable to decide what to do, I grabbed both outfits and zipped the new shoes in the outside pocket. Carefully, I folded the gold and white dress and the blue tulle skirt on the top of my other clothes. Lastly, I added the sweater.

I raced to my dresser and pulled out bras, panties, stockings, and a short, green night shirt. It wasn't exactly honeymoon-like, but it had spaghetti straps, was silky, and hit me at the knees. With a shrug I rolled it up and tucked it in, zipping all my lingerie inside of an inner suitcase pocket. I grabbed the new jewelry I'd bought to go with the blue tulle skirt and sweater. Choosing a few other pieces from my jewelry box, I zipped them all in a travel case. To finish, I ran to my en-suite bathroom and started grabbing makeup and hair products.

After rechecking everything, I shrugged on my coat, and twenty-five minutes after I'd run up the stairs, I was easing myself back out the rear door. I had left a note to let the family know I'd be out of town for a few days, but back on Thursday for Thanksgiving dinner at Autumn and Duncan's. It was stuck to the fridge with a magnet, where they'd be sure to see it.

As I stood at the back door, I saw that the night had become slightly foggy and more chilly. However, no one was out in our yard, or in Autumn and Duncan's neighboring yard to see me. Taking a moment, I blew out a long breath in an effort to calm myself down, but my stomach was still jumping from excitement.

To stay as quiet as possible, I lifted my suitcase and carried it down to the bottom of the driveway. Julian was right there, standing in the misty shadows, waiting for me. We kissed briefly and he took the suitcase and carried it across the street, sliding it into the backseat of his car.

We eased inside, shut the doors, and he started up his car. He pulled away from the curb and we were off.

I snapped my seatbelt in place and looked over at him with a grin. "Made it. In under thirty minutes."

"Barely," he said. "I was three minutes away from storming the keep."

I started to chuckle.

"I had planned to march up the stairs, toss you over my shoulder, and cart you right out of that house."

"My own dark knight." I patted his knee. "But now that you mention it, that tossing me over your shoulder scenario is kind of hot. Are you trying to turn me on?"

"Yes," he said seriously.

"I already said that I'd marry you," I reminded him.

"Then put your ring back on," he said.

I had taken it off, in case I had bumped into a family member. But now that we were safely away, I reached into my coat pocket and pulled out the ring box. I slipped it on and held my fingers out under Julian's nose. For emphasis, I wiggled my fingers.

He captured my hand and pressed a kiss to my knuckles above the ring. "Don't take it off again."

"I don't plan to," I said. "By the way, we need to get a wedding ring for you too."

"I selected a plain platinum band for myself," he said. "It's in my suitcase."

A laugh bubbled up. "Pretty confident, were you?"

"You know that you love that about me."

"Hmm," I said, rolling my eyes. "Maybe."

"I see I'll have to spend some time convincing you..." He slanted a look my way. "Later."

"You want to convince me right now?" I slid my hand up his thigh.

He groaned. "Behave yourself while I'm driving, or I'll pull this car over."

"Uh-oh." I gave him a sassy smile. "Am I going to get a spanking?"

We stopped at an intersection, and he turned his head to look at me. "After months going without you, I had a lot of time to plot and plan what I wanted to do with you." His voice was low and had an edge of a growl.

Julian had once told me that he was no white knight, and I'd always thought of him more like a dark knight. An anti-hero. He was less of a troubadour on a white horse ready to gently woo his fair maiden with poetry, and much more like the dashing rogue that swooped in and hauled off his woman with steamy kisses and a thorough ravishing. It was one of the things I loved about him.

I shivered just thinking about it. "Have you been holding back on me, Drake?"

He smiled very slowly. "Be assured, Angel, I have a few tricks up my sleeve for the honeymoon."

"Wow," I said, fanning my face with my hand. "I'm going to hold you to that."

"You won't be disappointed," he promised.

We drove north for a few hours, and the mist cleared, revealing all the stars in the sky. I was delighted at the bed and breakfast that Julian had chosen. The old Victorian house boasted views of the Mississippi river, and the owner was waiting to let us in.

She showed us to our room, which was elegantly done in the Victorian style. The adjoining bathroom was decadent. It boasted a huge glass shower and a tub with jets big enough for two. I hid a smile over the tub and went to the double doors, opening them to find a small terrace. The terrace faced the back of the house and was dark and private. I could make out the outlines of a fall garden and a gazebo at the edge of the property.

I slipped off my coat and draped it over a chair as the owner left. There was a bottle of wine resting in an ice bucket and two glasses on a side table, I noticed. Julian rolled the suitcases to one side of the room and went to lock the door. He walked toward the wine where it waited on the table. "Would you like some wine?" he asked me.

"Later," I said. Walking over to him, I pushed the coat from his shoulders.

"No to the wine, then?" he asked deadpan.

"Right now, Julian, all I want is you." I tugged his

shirt free from the waist of his jeans. "Let's try out that tub."

His lips curved. "Far be it from me to argue with the bride."

***

We were married the next afternoon under the pretty gazebo on the grounds of the B&B, overlooking the Mississippi river. The weather was mild, the sky was filled with puffy white clouds, and there were still some leaves clinging to the November trees. I wore the pastel blue tulle skirt and ivory sweater. Julian wore a gray suit and paired it with a light blue shirt, almost as if we had planned it in advance. The officiant's partner was a photographer, and she even took photos for us.

The owner of the bed and breakfast was wonderful. Julian hadn't been exaggerating. They did specialize in small wedding packages. She personally handed me a small hand-tied bouquet of white roses and blue love-in-a-mist flowers. She and her husband witnessed the ceremony and tossed flower petals afterwards, while we shared our first kiss as husband and wife.

We spent the rest of the day in bed and wore each other out. After soaking in the tub later that evening, we loved again and finally climbed back into that big bed to sleep. The next morning, we were starving, and when we came downstairs for breakfast there was an envelope with an email address to look at proof photos from the ceremony. Even viewing them on his phone, I was thrilled to see how wonderful they had turned out. Julian and I went back to our room and decided together which images to order.

The next few days we spent alone. We took long hikes along the river, went on romantic picnics, made love in the big four poster bed in our room, relaxed together in the frothy water of the tub, and simply enjoyed each other. The only other people we saw or spoke to were the owners of the B&B.

It was magickal, and when it was time to check out and return to Williams Ford, a box was waiting for us. Inside was a simple album filled with all of the photos we'd chosen of our intimate wedding.

We arrived back in town on Thanksgiving Day, at noon. Julian parked his car at the curb by Autumn and Duncan's driveway and turned to look at me. "Ready, Angel?"

I pulled my jacket closer around myself and tried not to fidget with the skirt of the dress I wore. "I'm suddenly nervous," I admitted.

"We'll be fine," he insisted. "Your father and stepmother were very happy for us."

That phone call had gone much better than I'd ever hoped. "I'm glad we decided to call Autumn and Duncan, and Nina and Diego, to tell them all yesterday too," I said. "At least now the local gang won't all be caught off guard."

"Full disclosure, Angel," he said, reaching my hand.

"It was Maggie that helped me find the bed and breakfast. She told me they specialized in intimate wedding packages."

I blinked in surprise. "When did you—"

"I called her the week before I came back to Williams Ford. Told her I was going to ask you to marry me, and so she used her contacts and found—"

"The perfect place to elope," I said. "That makes sense. She's an amazing wedding coordinator and event planner. So she knows too."

Julian nodded. "I texted her the day after our ceremony and thanked her for the recommendation. I imagine she told Wyatt the news afterwards."

"That's a half dozen people down." I managed a smile. "Eight if I count my great-aunt Faye and Hal. She was pretty excited for us when we called to tell her this morning."

"Remind me. Where are they living at the moment?" Julian asked as we exited the car.

"Cornwall," I said. "She was serious about us coming over for a visit, you know."

"I'd be open to that. In the spring, maybe?" Julian suggested.

"That would be wonderful," I agreed.

"I'm sure once the family sees how happy we are, they'll support us." He walked around the car and took my hand. "Autumn and Duncan seemed genuinely happy for us yesterday when we spoke to them."

He squeezed my fingers in reassurance and we

walked up the driveway hand-in-hand. We had shown up to dinner a tad before the other guests. Duncan had asked us to arrive early, in fact. Julian gave the storm door a brisk knock, and my stomach promptly tied itself into knots.

Autumn answered the door with her hair bundled on her head and her daughter Erin on her hip. "Here's the bride and groom!"

I smiled and bent forward to hug her.

"Come in. Come in!" She tugged me forward and embraced Julian next.

Erin reached immediately for Julian, and he took the toddler in his arms.

Duncan walked in from the direction of the kitchen with Emma. I barely removed my coat before I got a hug from my cousin's husband and then Emma wanted me to hold her. Together the six of us entered the large, open kitchen. It smelled deliciously of roasting turkey, and I was relieved to see that Autumn and Duncan were both smiling.

"Besides Nina and Diego, does anyone else know?" she asked me.

I cleared my throat. "We called Aunt Faye this morning."

"Maggie and Wyatt know," Julian added.

Duncan raised his eyebrows at his cousin. "You haven't told your father yet?"

"No." Julian shook his head. "We'll tell the rest of the family together, today."

Autumn nodded and went to check the bird in the oven. "What was Nina and Diego's reaction?"

"They were happy for us, and understood why we eloped," Julian said.

Autumn closed the oven door. "I hope you know that Duncan and I support you. I just wished we could have been there to celebrate with you."

"Autumn, I—" My words were cut off when the front door opened and Wyatt, Willow and a heavily pregnant Maggie came in.

"Hey, y'all," Maggie said. "We decided to come early."

"Happy Turkey Day!" Willow shouted.

Wyatt set a large bowl on the counter. "We brought the salad," he said.

"I'll tuck it in the fridge," Duncan said, taking it.

Maggie handed over a covered pie plate. "One pecan pie, as requested," she said.

Autumn gave Maggie a hug and slid the pie on the kitchen counter.

Before I had the chance to say anything, Maggie grabbed me up next in a big hug. Emma, who I was still holding, happily cuddled right in. "Congratulations, Holly." She gave me a quick squeeze, and kissed Julian's cheek. "Blessed be, cousin."

Julian grinned and patted her belly. "Thank you, and you look wonderful."

"Two and a half weeks to go!" Wyatt said proudly.

"I'm as big as a house," she declared. "And Julian,

you look great with a short beard, by the way."

Emma wanted down to chase after Willow, and Erin was soon to follow. The two-and-a half-year-old twins toddled behind Willow and into the living room.

"Let me see that ring!" Maggie said and snatched my hand for a closer inspection.

"Aquamarine?" Autumn asked me and leaned in to look for herself.

"Yes," I said.

"Oh, this is beautiful." Maggie dabbed a few tears from her deep blue eyes.

Nina and Diego arrived with their three-year-old daughter, Isabel, next. There were more congratulatory hugs and kisses, and as soon as I was able, I took my cousin aside. I pulled Autumn into the large pantry off the kitchen. "Thank you for rallying the troops, before the rest of the family gets here."

"Duncan and I have known about you and Julian for a few years now," she said. "I kept your secret. I figured eventually you'd tell us all when you were ready."

"You've kept more than one secret," I murmured, thinking of the reason I'd returned to Williams Ford a few years ago.

Autumn ran her hand over my arm. "I may be a Seer, but I was totally caught off guard when you sprung an elopement on us."

"I'm most worried about how Bran and Julian's father will take the news."

Autumn rolled her eyes. "Probably not well, since

they didn't even know you two were dating."

"And Ivy," I said, starting to panic. "I've blocked her from reading me for years. She's not going to be happy about this...Maybe we shouldn't do this today."

"Oh bullshit," Autumn said. "Everyone is together. This is the best time to announce your elopement. Worst case scenario? There'll be a couple of raised voices."

"I don't want to ruin the family's Thanksgiving dinner," I said as my stomach began to jump.

Maggie pulled open the pantry door. "Well, bless your heart, darlin'," she said. "It's a little too late for that now. Because the rest of the family has arrived."

Suddenly I felt lightheaded from the anxiety. "I think I might pass out." I grabbed for a pantry shelf and hung on.

Maggie waded in belly first and she didn't stop until her baby bump settled against me. "Now you listen to me, Holly Bishop—"

"That'd be Holly Drake, now," Autumn interrupted cheerfully.

Maggie shook her finger. "If I've learned *anything* in the past few years it's that a raised voice is a sign of unwavering affection in the Bishop family."

"Hence, *her* raised voice," Autumn said dryly.

"Everything will be fine," Maggie insisted. "You'll see."

"Where my Witches at?" Ivy's voice traveled clearly.

I stuck my hands in my dress pockets, right before

my sister appeared in the doorway.

"Are we convening the coven in the pantry?" Ivy grinned at her own pun.

"We were debating the proper spices for the stuffing," Maggie fibbed.

"Autumn." Duncan's voice carried to us. "The turkey is done."

"Be right there!" she answered, and she and Maggie both filed out.

Maggie hooked her arm in Ivy's. "How is the set up for the Christmas tree sales going?" she asked, steering my twin sister away from me.

Using the time Maggie had bought me, I turned my back to the room, and quickly tugged my new rings off. I dropped them in my dress pocket and went out to help get the food on the table.

The insanity of eleven adults and six children ranging in ages from seven to two-and-a-half-year-old twins kept everyone busy. At first, I don't think that my brother and sister in law, or my sister and her fiancé even tracked that Julian and I were there together as a couple. After all, we'd both been attending functions with the combined Bishop and Drake families for the past few years.

Julian's father, Thomas, was holding court with all of the children, as per usual. The truth was the kids adored him, and while we bustled around getting food on the tables, Thomas kept the children entertained in the living room.

Finally, we sat down to eat, and Julian and I sat side by side. Diego was to my left and Isabel was on a booster seat between her parents. I felt slightly safer surrounded by Julian and the Vasquez family. Which was, I admitted, an overly dramatic thought. Tucking my hands under the table, I discreetly took my wedding rings out of my pocket. Slowly, as not to draw attention to my actions, I slid them back on.

Julian glanced over. "You took them off?" he whispered, and while his expression was neutral, I *sensed* his disappointment.

"We wanted to tell them all together, right?" I said out of the corner of my mouth. "They are too sparkly to go without notice."

Diego leaned in closer to speak to Julian. "My friend," he said softly. "She's right. You could signal passing planes with those diamonds."

I bit back a laugh at Diego's wry humor, and Julian's lips twitched.

"Before we start to eat..." Duncan's voice rose above the chatter. "There is an announcement to be made." He looked pointedly over to Julian and me, and I reached under the table and gripped Julian's hand—hard—with mine.

CHAPTER TWO

"Thank you, Duncan," Julian said smoothly. "Most of you are probably unaware that Holly and I have been seeing each other for almost four years now..."

"What?" My brother's head whipped around to glare at us. "For four years?" he practically growled.

"*Are you serious?*" Lexie burst out.

"I knew you were seeing someone on the down low," Ivy said to me. "But I never imagined it was Julian."

"Ivy," I said, trying to stay calm.

Julian smiled at my sister. "Nevertheless—"

Ivy cut him off. "You've been keeping secrets from all of us." She glared. "And you lied. To *me*."

"No." I shook my head. "I didn't lie."

"Omission is a lie," Ivy argued.

"Ivy…" I tried again. "I simply kept my private life, private."

"Why?" Ivy asked. "Why him?"

"Because," I said, "we love each other."

"Are you insane?" my sister demanded. "He's your

boss!"

"I'm not insane," I said coolly, "but thank you for so gently inquiring about my mental health."

"Julian is almost ten years older than you are!" Bran snarled. "He's far too old for you to be dating!"

I met my brother's eyes and did not allow myself to flinch. "And *this* sort of reaction is one of the many reasons that we kept our relationship private."

"Be that as it may," Julian continued, as if he hadn't been interrupted, "this past weekend I asked Holly to marry me, and she said yes."

There were several gasps from around the table.

"Julian," Thomas began, "you can't be serious. Think of your position at the museum. This is completely inappropriate."

"Father," Julian said. "I know you are surprised—"

"Surprised?" Thomas snapped back. "Try shocked!"

Julian lifted my left hand to his lips and pressed a kiss right above the rings. "Still, I hope that you can be happy for us."

The stones in the rings blazed under the lights and I watched my sister's eyes grow large. "So you're engaged, Holly?" Ivy wanted to know.

"Actually, Ivy," I said to my twin, "Julian and I are married."

"*Married*?" several people said in unison.

"Yes." Julian nodded. "Holly and I eloped."

There was no response to his announcement at all. In fact, you could have heard a pin drop.

The silence stretched on for several awkward moments. I finally remembered to exhale when I felt Diego give my knee a pat in support from under the table.

"Congratulations," Maggie said brightly, causing several people to jump. "This is wonderful news! I know you two will be very happy together. Thomas, please pass the potatoes."

"Maggie," Thomas said. "This is hardly the time—"

"It's Thanksgiving, and I'm hungry, Thomas." Maggie smiled and rested a hand on her baby bump. "Growing a baby is hard work."

Nina, who was sitting directly across the table from Maggie, picked up the bowl and passed it. "Here you go, Maggie."

"Congratulations, Holly and Julian." Duncan spoke next. "Autumn and I wish you both the best."

"Thank you," Julian and I said in unison.

"I'm hungry!" Erin blurted out.

"Turkey!" Emma added from her booster seat.

"Let's not let the food get cold," Autumn said and began to pass the food around the table.

"Dinner roll?" Diego passed me a basket.

Automatically I took one. "Thank you," I said politely.

"Of course." He nodded. "Nina and I also wish to offer you both our congratulations as well."

"Thank you, my friend," Julian said to Diego.

Nina put some green beans on her daughter Isabel's

plate. "Honestly, it's about time you two made things official. We are beyond thrilled for you."

Lexie zeroed in on that. "So, Nina and Diego knew?"

I focused on my sister-in-law. "That we were a couple? Yes."

"Where did you go for the elopement?" Nina asked me as she served her daughter a slice of turkey, and then took some for herself.

"A pretty Victorian bed and breakfast in Hannibal," I told her.

Diego accepted the platter of turkey from his wife. "That sounds very romantic."

I smiled at him. "It was."

Across the table, Maggie calmly added gravy to her potatoes. "It is a highly rated venue for elopements and smaller, more intimate ceremonies. Julian, did you take advantage of the photography package?"

"Yes, we did." Julian beamed over at Maggie.

"Wait," Bran said. "Maggie knew about this too?"

Maggie smiled down the table at my brother. "Julian hired me to research a private venue for their elopement. I was, after all, only too happy to assist my cousin."

"So it's done, then?" Bran asked.

I met my brother's eyes. "If by that you mean 'are we married?' Then the answer is *yes*."

"Well, holy shit." Lexie blew out a long breath.

Wyatt calmly accepted the gravy boat from his wife.

"I saw the website for the bed and breakfast; it's gorgeous."

"Yes." Julian inclined his head. "We certainly thought so."

Maggie placed some cranberry sauce on Willow's plate. "So, did you get your proofs before you left?"

"The proofs were available the next day," Julian answered her with a smile. "They had our chosen photos ready in a small album for us when we left."

"Perfect," Maggie said.

"That's wonderful." Nina smiled. "Did you bring the album with you?"

"We did," Julian said to Nina. "Holly and I will be happy to show you the photos after we eat."

"I'm looking forward to seeing those," Autumn said from her end of the table.

"Me too," Duncan said kindly, and then began to cut up Emma's food for her.

Thomas regarded Julian. "I assume there is a marriage license to show us as well?" His voice was more than a little grim.

"I'd like to see that paperwork as well," Bran muttered.

"On that, we are in agreement," Thomas said to Bran.

"Father," Julian began.

"I'll speak with you privately after the meal," Thomas said to Julian.

Julian inclined his head. "Of course."

I could feel Ivy's gaze. She'd remained silent for so long that it was unnerving. Finally, I gave in and shifted my attention to my twin sister.

"You really got married?" Ivy asked me quietly.

I gave her a steady look. "Yes, we did."

"Have you told Dad?"

"Yes," I said steadily. "Julian and I called them this morning, to wish Dad and Ruth a happy Thanksgiving and to share our news."

Ivy continued to stare at me like she'd never seen me. "I can't believe you ran off and got married in secret."

"And you know what else I can't believe?" Bran interjected. "That you would upstage your sister's bridal shower and wedding this way."

I snapped my head around at the insult. "I did no such thing!"

"The bridal shower is next week." Ivy arched one brow. "Or had you forgotten while you were busy being selfish?"

"No," I said patiently. "I had not forgotten."

Ivy's eyes narrowed. "I never thought my own sister, my twin, would be so envious that she'd try and take the attention away from my upcoming wedding."

I took a steadying breath. Those particular accusations were the last thing I'd expected. "Ivy, to be fair, your and Erik's wedding is in six weeks—"

"*Fair?*" Ivy asked incredulously. "Couldn't you have waited?" Tears began to gather in her green eyes. "Erik and I have been planning our wedding for over a year, and now all everyone will be talking about is how *you* eloped."

"Ivy—" I began.

"You're my sister. My twin. And I can't even look at you right now." Ivy stood up, tossed down her cloth napkin, and left the table. "Excuse me," she said to Autumn. She paused only long enough to grab her purse and jacket from pegs by the door. Untouched, the screen door swung open, and Ivy marched right out of the house.

A second after she left, the wooden front door slammed smartly behind her all on its own.

Everyone around the table fell silent.

Erik McBriar looked from Julian to me and stood slowly. "I better go after her." He nodded to his hosts. "Excuse me, Duncan and Autumn."

"Of course," Autumn said.

Erik glanced back and met my eyes. "I hope you'll be happy, Holly."

His tone, while polite, did not soften the disapproval that simply radiated off him. I felt it from where I sat, and it was like a sucker punch to the gut. Under the table, I dug my nails into the palm of my hand and tried not to show any other reaction.

Without another word, Erik went after his fiancée. He did, however, open and shut the door gently as he left.

Bran stood up next, but before he could leave Lexie

grabbed his arm. "Sit down, Bran," she said. "I think we've all had enough dramatic exits for one day."

"I want some turkey!" Morgan complained.

"I want pumpkin pie!" Belinda piped in.

"Bran," Lexie said to her husband. "Let's just get through dinner. Okay?"

"By all means," Bran said snidely as he took his seat again. "Let's be civil."

"Can I have pie now?" Belinda wanted to know.

"After dinner," Lexie told her daughter.

"Why is everyone mad?" Morgan asked.

"*That*," Bran said, "is an excellent question. Why don't we ask your Aunt Holly?"

I couldn't help but wince at the vehemence in my brother's tone.

Autumn selected a dinner roll and studied it. "I tell you what, Bran," she said from between her teeth. "You check that nasty attitude right now, otherwise I'm going to throw this dinner roll right at your head."

"I think..." Thomas' voice cut through the bickering. "We can all manage to finish our meal pleasantly, considering there are children at the table."

Wyatt held up a bottle of white wine. "Would anyone like some wine?" he asked the table at large.

"God, yes," I said, and held up my glass.

Every adult at the table, except for Maggie, held up their glass too.

The meal continued, and to say that it was strained was an understatement. Mostly everyone put on a good face for the kids. Once dessert was served, Thomas excused himself and asked Julian to follow him outside so they could speak. I stood up and helped Autumn put her kitchen back to rights. Maggie was firmly told to sit down and put her feet up. She didn't even make a token protest.

Bran went and sat with the children, Autumn scraped the plates, and Nina loaded the dishwasher. Lexie filled the sink with hot water and began washing the larger pots and pans. There was casual clean up conversation, however, Lexie did not make any eye contact or speak directly to me.

Duncan broke down the extra table and folding chairs, and Diego and Wyatt helped him put it all away. Afterward they flipped on the television to watch the football game. Normally after a family meal there were jokes and laughter in the house. This time, everyone was quiet and scrupulously polite. Except for the men watching the game, it seemed as if nothing unusual had happened.

I stood and dried the pots and pans and saw Duncan slip outside with Julian and his father out of my peripheral, to act as a buffer I imagined. Meticulously, I dried everything I was handed and put them all away at Autumn's direction. The Drake men had been outside for about a half hour, but fortunately there had been no raised voices.

Maybe things will be okay... That thought lasted for only a second when I closed a cabinet door and found my brother was up in my face. "A word, Holly."

"All right."

Bran stalked over to the far side of the kitchen and everyone else made themselves scarce.

"I want to know the *real* reason why you eloped," he said.

I crossed my arms. "After seeing the reactions to the news at dinner, you're seriously asking me that?"

"Are you pregnant?" he asked bluntly. "Is that why you ran off?"

I flinched, hard. My brother had no way to know that that particular question would be an especially painful one. "No, Bran," I said, fighting to remain calm. "I am not pregnant."

"Well," he grumbled, "there's something to be thankful for."

I felt my eyes widen in shock. "Excuse me?"

"Have you thought about how the staff at the museum will react to the news that you and Julian have eloped?" He shook his head. "It's going to be ugly, Holly."

"I don't care," I said firmly. "I don't give a damn what anyone says. It's my life—"

"Grow up." Bran cut me off. "You *do* realize that you could lose your position at the museum, or Julian could be fired, for fraternizing with a subordinate."

"There are no anti-fraternization policies for the staff at the museum," I pointed out.

"No, there's not," Bran said. "Nevertheless,

professors, office managers and the top brass are firmly *discouraged* against forming any sort of attachments or having romantic relationships with their aides, teacher's assistants, secretaries, or other employees. It simply isn't done."

"We love each other—"

"Try that argument out with HR department on Monday when you get called into their office. You'll get a 'conflict of interest' lecture at the very least." Bran shook his head. "How long were you working for Julian before he seduced you?"

"By the old gods, Bran." I felt my face go red from embarrassment. "It wasn't like that."

"Then what was it?" he asked. "Did you develop a bad case of hero worship after he rescued you from the attack at the antique store four years ago?"

"Bran—"

He spoke right over me. "And so you decided to give him the ultimate 'thank you' for rescuing you? Is that when all this sneaking around started?"

"Hey!"

"Or was you sleeping with him simply a part of the *hiring process*," he said, making air quotes, "for your position at the museum?"

"I knew you'd be upset," I said, barely managing to keep my voice down. "But I didn't expect you to be so cruel."

"And I can't believe..." His voice was low as he got right up in my face. "That you expected to drop this bombshell on the family and have everyone be happy with the news that you've been screwing your boss and decided to run off together."

His crass words had my temper slipping, and unexpectedly my power lashed out. Bran was knocked back a full two steps away from me.

"You used your magick to strike out at me?" He sounded incredulous.

"You're lucky I didn't physically slap you." I stepped a bit closer to him. "A magickal shove was the least you deserved for speaking to me that way."

"Hey!" Lexie's voice carried to us. "You two need to take it down a few notches. Remember where you are."

I tilted my head and considered my brother, but I didn't move. Bran didn't move either. In a standoff, he glared at me, and I maintained a hard eye contact with him.

A framed picture on the wall beside us began to vibrate. I knew I was losing control, but I don't think I'd ever been so angry with my brother.

"Bran," Lexie said firmly. "That's enough."

From across the room Morgan and Belinda began to bicker.

"Daddy!" Belinda complained to Bran. "Morgan won't share!"

Without another word to me, Bran spun and walked away. He went directly to the living room to sort out his children.

I excused myself and went to use the bathroom on

the main floor. I knew the rest of the family was staring at me, wondering if I would lose control. I refused to let that happen. With great care, I softly shut the door behind myself, and walked over to lean against the sink. I took several deep breaths, trying to calm down, but I could feel my magick straining to be set free.

In fact, the soap dispenser on the bathroom counter began to wobble. Shutting my eyes, I grabbed the front of the sink and tried to center myself. With no small amount of effort, I began to yank my anger *and* my magick back in line.

The scene with Ivy and the words exchanged with Bran had been beyond ugly. Replaying it in my mind had me grimacing. I could only hope that in time everyone would cool off, and we'd all be able to speak calmly. The soap dispenser slowly stopped shaking and I gradually released my death grip on the edge of the sink. After I was sure I had my temper and my powers under control, I exited the bathroom.

Thomas had left, and Julian and Duncan had returned to the house. Duncan had his arm around Julian's shoulder in support, and I was relieved to see that they were speaking easily with one another. Julian gave me a smile, and I went straight to his side and took his hand.

"You okay?" he asked.

"Exchanged a few pleasantries with my brother while you were outside," I whispered.

"I'm sorry for that." Julian squeezed my fingers.

"Don't leave me alone again."

"Never, Angel," he said, pressing a kiss to my hair.

I leaned against Julian's arm for comfort and tried to relearn how to take a full breath, once more. While there'd been little shouting, there had been some nastier moments—like the one between me and Bran. But, I suppose, telling the family could have gone worse. Still, I could think of about a hundred different ways it could have gone better.

Autumn walked in from the kitchen carrying a glass of wine. "All right," she said cheerfully to me and Julian. "Let's see those pictures from your elopement!"

***

The remaining family—with the exception of my brother—had enjoyed seeing the photos. *At least,* I thought to myself, *there are a handful of people legitimately happy for us.*

Nina and Autumn got misty over the photos, and Maggie, bless her, praised my choice of an outfit. In fact, she asked if she could add one of our ceremony photos to her wedding planner website for an intimate wedding and elopement page.

I nodded and said yes. Lexie was polite about the photos, but she used the opportunity to discreetly ask where Julian and I planned to live. I assured her we would not be moving into the Bishop family manor.

Lexie agreed that it would probably be for the best. I

told her I would gather up most of my clothes tomorrow and make arrangements to move out the rest of my things out as soon as possible.

"Good," she said, not even offering a token protest. "I'll have the kids out of the house tomorrow from nine until noon."

I was never so glad to get away from my brother and sister-in-law as I was Thanksgiving night. We drove back to the cabin, and I told myself to not let Bran, Lexie, and Ivy's reactions ruin our happiness. Because I didn't feel one ounce of regret. In fact, I was struck once again at how *lucky* I felt to be married to him.

"I love you, Julian," I said firmly. "I will always choose you, before anyone or anything else. I wanted you to know that."

He reached over and skimmed his hand through my hair, then trailed his fingers slowly down over my shoulder and arm, until he reached my hand. "I love you so much, Angel," he said, entwining his fingers with mine.

"I'm no angel," I reminded him. "In fact, as soon as we get back to the cabin, I'm going to show you exactly how *bad* I can be."

"Is that right?"

"It is," I said. "You'd better be ready, Mr. Drake."

He sent me a look. "Is that a threat, Mrs. Drake, or a promise?"

"It's a warning and a promise," I said.

He lifted our joined hands to his mouth and pressed

a kiss to the back of my hand. "You don't have to prove anything to me, Angel."

No, I thought, *but maybe I need to prove something to myself.*

Bran's remark about Julian seducing me bothered me a lot. His words suggested that I'd needed to be persuaded, and that was simply not the case. It had been mutual attraction between the two of us. Julian had been driving me crazy for weeks and I'd wanted him to the point of madness.

In fact, the first time we'd been together, I'd lost control with Julian, not the other way around. I'd been so desperate to be with him that *I'd* left marks on *him*. Our first time had been intense and had lasted for hours with a variety of positions and multiple orgasms.

Recalling that night made me edgy and achy to be with Julian again. So much that I squirmed a little in the car. The car ride home was going to be long and uncomfortable, being as wound up as I was.

Finally, we reached the cabin and I hurried to open the door.

"We should talk, Angel," Julian said as we walked into the cabin, "and make our plans for the future now that we are back in Williams Ford."

I watched as he removed his coat and hung it on a hook by the door. While I saw his mouth move as he spoke to me, all I could hear was my own blood pounding through my veins. Shrugging off my coat, I let it fall to the floor.

Behind him, the lock on the door flipped over with a loud click. "Julian." I stalked forward and yanked his mouth down to mine by grabbing the scruff of his neck. "Shut up and kiss me."

"Angel." He half laughed, and it slid into a groan when I kissed him passionately. Eventually I let him up for air.

Next, I focused on the buttons of his shirt, and they went flying off to ricochet around the room.

Startled, he jumped. "Well," he said carefully, "I don't think I've ever seen you use your powers this way before..."

I shoved the shirt from his shoulders and began to lick and bite at his chest. Silently, I reached down and unbuckled his belt.

"Holly, I—" His voice died off when I unzipped his slacks, pushed his briefs aside, and helped myself.

"I need you now, Julian," I said.

He hissed out a breath, and I went up on my toes to kiss him again. I tucked my other hand around his waist and drew him across the cabin to the bed. Once we were there, I shoved his slacks down and he stepped out of his shoes. He kicked to free himself from his clothes; as soon as he did I pushed my powers at him, forcing him to lay back on the bed.

"Don't you move," I warned him.

"Wouldn't dream of it," he said.

I reached under the dress to pull my panties off. "Do you want me?" I asked him.

"Angel, *yes*." He breathed the nickname and it caused me to shiver.

I couldn't wait any longer. Yanking my dress off, I tossed it to the floor and climbed up to range myself over him. Deliberately, I slid down, taking him deep inside of me.

Reaching for his hands, I gripped them tightly and rode him hard. He asked me to slow down, to make it last longer and I ignored him. I wanted him to be completely under *my* spell, and I didn't stop until he shouted in completion.

Afterwards, I dropped a brief hard kiss on his lips. "You are mine, Julian," I said. "You belong to me, and don't you ever forget it."

"Believe me." He sighed happily. "I won't."

I eased off and shifted over to cuddle beside him. Julian tucked an arm around me and pulled me even closer to his side. As he pressed kisses over my hair, I felt how tired he was. He'd put on a good front with our families, but he was exhausted.

Get some sleep. I pushed the thought at him and watched as his eyes drooped lower. "Rest now, my love," I whispered to him and smiled as he fell deeply asleep.

Sitting back up, I peeled off my bra and reached for the blanket folded over the foot of the bed. I pulled it over the both of us and lay beside him again and tried to get some rest. *Too bad my healing and empathic linking abilities don't work on myself,* I thought.

I lay awake for hours going over everything that had happened with the families today. With a sigh, I finally reminded myself that Julian and I truly loved each other, we were married, and were happy and safe in our cabin tucked deep in the woods.

For now, that was enough.

***

The next morning, Julian and I decided that we would stay at the cabin for the foreseeable future. It was, in reality, not unlike a big studio apartment. Driving to and from work took longer, but the cabin was secluded and private, and I found that I was more comfortable with the idea of being farther away from the rest of the town and our families.

We took the long holiday weekend for ourselves. It was almost an extension of our honeymoon trip. Monday at the museum—and all the conjecture from the staff—would be here soon enough, and so we took the time to settle into our new life.

We went over to the manor on Friday morning and gathered up my clothes and personal items. Ivy was at the tree farm taking photos, and Bran was suspiciously absent. Lexie was, as she'd told me she'd be, out with the kids, and so there were no issues. It did, however, feel like a sort of punishment that no one was home.

I sucked it up and told myself it was better than having a big family drama over me moving out. Julian and I loaded up his car and stopped at a grocery store on the way back to the cabin. We managed to squeeze the groceries in and spent the rest of the day unpacking and setting up the cabin as a home, not merely a weekend retreat.

Saturday morning Julian took me out to brunch. Afterward we swung by a tree lot to pick out a small tree, a wreath, and greenery for Yuletide. Normally I would have suggested the McBriar's tree farm, but I wasn't up for running into Erik or Ivy. Erik would be busy managing the tree farm, and Ivy would be taking holiday photos at the *Mistletoe Mercantile* store on the property. Best to avoid them both and let things calm down.

The tree lot we found was on the outskirts of town and run by the local Scouts. Purchasing the tree and greenery from them supported the troop. Julian and I laughed as we tied the four-foot tree to the rack of his car, and then we detoured to another store to get some ribbon and boxes of multi-colored strands of lights. Instead of buying glass ornaments, I asked Julian to take me to the grocery store again to purchase some natural items to decorate the tree and the cabin with.

Once we returned to the cabin, I sliced up several oranges and put them in the oven on low heat to dry out. It would take several hours, and so we used that time to string lights on the front porch of the cabin, hang a wreath on the door, and tuck that fresh greenery we'd purchased around the cabin.

By the time dusk fell on Saturday, the tree was trimmed with slices of dried oranges and small bundles of cinnamon sticks. Along with pinecones I'd found in the woods, they were tied to the branches with string. The mantle above the fireplace was layered with fresh pine, pomegranates, more pinecones, and sprigs of variegated holly. I threaded some red, battery-operated rice lights through the mantle greenery and clicked them on. It was truly lovely.

"Would you like some more wine?" Julian asked me as we sat side by side on the couch, stringing popcorn and cranberries for our first tree.

"Sure," I said and knotted the end of the long strand I had made. Then I got up and went over to the tree to drape the popcorn garland over the branches.

Julian topped off our glasses. "I've never made a cranberry garland for a tree before."

I threw a look at him from over my shoulder. "I'll bet not. I've seen the trees at the Drake mansion. They're very glitz and glam. Don't you hire a professional decorator for the holidays to 'deck the halls' as it were?"

Julian threaded more berries. "We used to, before Duncan and Autumn got married. Now with Maggie, Wyatt and Willow living at the mansion, it's more of a family affair."

His words hit me hard. "So, you're missing the tree trimming this year because we eloped."

Searching my face with his eyes, he replied, "I'd

much rather be here with you, celebrating our marriage and trimming our first Yule tree together."

I smiled. He'd said exactly the right thing. "I have to admit, I really like how old fashioned the handmade ornaments all look. Plus, we can hang the fruit, popcorn, and berries outside after Yule for the birds."

Julian rose to his feet and together we draped the final strand of cranberries on our tree.

"There," I said. "I think that's got it."

Mission complete, Julian and I quickly tidied all of our tree trimming supplies away.

"What do you want to do with the extra orange slices?" he asked.

"Leave them on the counter," I said. "I'll tuck them in the front door wreath tomorrow."

I picked up our wine and waited for him to turn off the other lights and finally plug in the tree to see how it looked. The tree lights came on and I started to grin. Our tree was absolutely enchanting with its simple handmade and natural ornaments. Besides the tree, the only other light in the room was from the mantel and the flames in the fireplace.

Julian moved to stand beside me. "It looks very old-fashioned and absolutely wonderful," he said.

"It's rustic and romantic." I handed his wine glass to him. "Here's to our first Yuletide together as husband and wife."

We sipped our wine and then Julian took the glass out of my hand. "You know what I've always wanted to do?" he asked, setting the glasses aside.

"What?" I asked suspiciously. There was a look in his eye that I knew very well.

"I always wanted to make love by a Yule tree..." He tossed a few throw pillows from the couch to the rug. "In front of the fire with my wife."

"What a coincidence," I said. "I've always wanted to be made love to in front of the fire, next to the Yule tree, by my husband."

"I love you," he said as he reached for me.

I smiled as he drew me down to the rug. "And I love you, Julian."

***

I'd pretty much avoided thinking about it all weekend, but Monday morning arrived whether I liked it or not. Choosing my outfit with care, I wore a pretty green sweater and dark slacks with my low-heeled boots. Julian chose one of his dark suits and added a deep green tie to his white shirt. We'd spoken about it before hand and had decided to drive in separate cars to work as he had meetings that would keep him at the museum for a few hours after my shift ended.

I followed behind him and parked next to him. We walked across the lot together with his hand tucked firmly around my waist.

"Aw, hell," I said suddenly. "I never thought about how we are going to formally address each other from here out."

His brows raised. "Meaning?"

I blew a stray curl out of my face. "It's ridiculous for me to refer to you as Mr. Drake at the office."

"Now that you mention it, I can't call you Ms. Bishop anymore either."

I sent him a look. "That's *Mrs. Drake* to you, mister."

"True." He nodded. "I suppose we will simply continue to address each other using our first names, as we typically did."

"Or I can start calling you 'stud-muffin.' That sounds *very* professional, don't you think?" I batted my eyes at him and made my voice all breathy. "You have a call on line one, *stud-muffin*."

His lips twitched, but he managed to keep his composure. "Only if I get to call you, *Kitten*."

"Don't you dare," I said, fighting against laughter.

He reached for the doors. "Ready, Mrs. Drake?"

I gave him a wink. "As I'll ever be."

CHAPTER THREE

We walked to our offices, and I counted no less than four jaws dropping and two double-takes. There were audible gasps, and the whispering began instantly.

My shoulders were tight as I sat at my desk as usual. Julian went to his office and left the adjourning door slightly open—as he typically did whenever he was in.

Taking a moment for myself, I grounded my energy and then booted up my computer. I went through all of the interoffice emails and communications that I'd missed in the past few days while we'd been on our honeymoon. Dutifully, I slogged my way through it all.

About a half hour before lunch, I was finally caught up and so I took out the folder I'd set aside the week prior. After double checking the contents, I stood to take the paperwork in to Julian, so we'd be ready for our afternoon meeting. We were scheduled to meet with the collection specialists, and to review the exhibits that had been added or removed during his absence.

I knocked on the door jam as I typically did, "I have

the paperwork you requested for our meeting with the —"

"Julian." Margaret from Human Resources walked right in, rudely shouldering her way past me.

Julian glanced up from his paperwork. "Margaret. How lovely to see you." His tone of voice conveyed that it was anything but.

"We need to talk," she said, sending me a significant look. I watched as her eyes slid down to look at my left hand. "Preferably alone," she added.

"Of course." He folded his hands on the desk. "If you will excuse us, Holly?"

"Certainly." I backed out of his office, closing the door behind me.

I returned to my desk and slid the folder in my top drawer. *Here we go,* I thought.

Margaret launched into a top-volume speech that began with, "What were you thinking?" She seemed to catch herself and quickly lowered her voice.

With a sigh, I shook my head. If I concentrated, I could just make out what they were saying; but it didn't take a psychic to figure out what their conversation was about. It sounded like they were going to be in a conference for a while, so I left them to it.

Julian and I had planned to go to lunch together, but clearly that wouldn't be possible now. So I sent him a quick text telling him I was going to the café in the museum to get a cup of soup and a sandwich.

The café was busy and there weren't any tables free.

However, the weather was mild, and I thought maybe I could sit outside and eat my lunch on a bench in the sunshine. After paying, I stood in line waiting for my order and felt several sets of eyes on me. Tuning in to the strongest vibrations, I picked up on the conversation of a pair of assistants to the director, and a docent from the museum.

"Oh my god," one of the women said. "It *is* true! He married her!"

"Did you see her rings?"

I slid my eyes over to the trio who sat with their heads together at a nearby table.

"Kind of hard to miss those rocks," came a third voice.

"Guess she decided to sleep her way into a promotion..."

Bitch, I thought.

"Honey," one of the women said, "I don't imagine *sleeping* had anything to do with it." Some very snide laughter followed that comment.

"I bet she's pregnant," one of the other women said, causing me to flinch.

"Probably," the third of the trio replied. "The only way she'd get a gorgeous, successful man like that to marry someone like her is if she trapped him."

The malicious energy emanating from the trio had my stomach clenching. I focused on my own psychic shields and pulled my aura in closer to my body, making the protective barrier tighter, closer, and more dense.

As they continued to stage whisper back and forth, I had to fight the urge to make their coffees boil over...but I didn't give in to the temptation. I held myself together and focused on maintaining my composure.

But truthfully, I wasn't composed. I was insulted, hurt, and the comment about me being pregnant was like a knife to the heart. Finally, my order was called, and I picked up my to-go bag and headed for the door with relief.

I managed about ten minutes of peace and had only begun to calm down before my cousin Autumn showed up.

"May I join you?" She smiled over at me.

"Of course." I patted the bench in an invitation.

She sat beside me. "How are you holding up, Blondie?"

When I'd been younger my hair had been more of a strawberry-blonde color. Now it was red. Still, I chuckled at the old nickname. "You haven't called me that in a long time."

She adjusted her glasses. "Like I've always said, calling you 'Strawberry-Blondie' is ridiculous."

I raised my eyebrows. "No more ridiculous than calling a redhead, *Blondie*."

"I am allowed to have a few quirks," Autumn said and pulled a sandwich from a brown paper bag. "Besides, I figured you could use a smile today."

"I definitely could."

"It's too pretty of a fall day to sit inside." Autumn unwrapped her sandwich. "I like to get out of the museum at lunch if I can."

"Margaret from HR came storming into Julian's office a while ago," I said softly.

"Figures." Autumn rolled her eyes. "I never liked her."

"Be honest," I said to my cousin. "There's really nothing they can do to boot me out of my job now that Julian and I are a public couple, right?"

"As there isn't a non-fraternization policy in place, they can't do a thing." Autumn took a bite of her meatloaf sandwich. "Plus, you're married. That sort of takes it up several notches from casual dating."

I sighed. "To be clear, Julian and I never *casually* dated."

"Holly," Autumn began, "they may not be able to do anything against you professionally, but the gossip that is going around at the museum is—"

"Ugly," I finished for her. "I overheard some women in the café betting I was pregnant and had trapped Julian into marrying me."

Autumn covered my hand with hers. "I'm sorry. That must have hurt."

"Well, it wasn't pleasant." I blew out a long breath. "And yet, I maintained control and did *not* make their cups of coffee explode all over their table." I slanted a look over to my cousin. "I wanted to, though."

"Those obnoxious bitches," Autumn said. "No one better be stupid enough to say anything snide like that in front of me."

"Especially as you are the Archivist." I nodded. "You're at the top of the pecking order around here."

"Julian's position is lateral to mine," Autumn pointed out. "As the outreach coordinator, and head of development operations, he may take a hit to his reputation over the news of your elopement, but otherwise I think it will be all right."

I truly hoped it would be that simple. But I knew in my heart it wouldn't be. Julian was in charge of the museum's marketing, public relations, promotions and advertising for special exhibits. He was very active in the broader community beyond the university too. There probably would be a fall out of some kind.

I smiled gratefully as Autumn switched the subject to our cousin Maggie.

"I'm telling you," she said, "that baby has dropped. There's no way Maggie will make it another two weeks. I'm betting the little guy will show up in the next few days."

"You think so?"

"First of December," Autumn predicted.

Comforted by the happier subject, I sat in the late November sunshine with my cousin and tried to relax. The gossip over my elopement with Julian would surely fizzle out soon. I only had to ride it out.

***

Autumn's prediction for our cousin Maggie was right on the money. Maggie and Wyatt's first child, a boy, was born on the morning of December the first. Phillip Drake Hastings weighed in at eight pounds even and had a head full of dark hair.

Julian and I went to visit the proud parents and big sister the weekend after the new family had come home to the Drake mansion. Willow was in awe of her baby brother, and Maggie was doing very well. Wyatt was changing diapers like a pro and joked that his career of writing murder mystery novels had not prepared him for some of the more gruesome aspects of diaper duty.

Thomas, Julian's father, was very much in his element as the proud honorary grandfather. In fact, he was so enamored of baby Phillip that he smiled and was pleasant to Julian and me when we arrived. We didn't stay long and after our visit we popped into the stone cottage on the estate to visit with Diego, Nina and Isabel.

The cottage that once belonged to Maggie and Willow when they first arrived in Williams Ford suited the Vasquez family. It gave the family their privacy and Nina was able to quickly walk to the mansion as the household manager and chef. Diego still had a short commute to the local garage where he worked as a mechanic.

Nina and I sat on the sofa while Isabel colored in a

coloring book on the sturdy coffee table. Isabel handed me a crayon and I started coloring with her.

"Maggie asked me to bring her bridal shower gift to Ivy tomorrow," she said. "Since the baby showed up a week and a half early, she won't make the shower."

"Blue!" Isabel said.

I smiled and tapped on the fat crayon she was using. "Yes, that's blue."

Isabel pointed to my long curls. "Red!"

"Yes," I said. "My hair is red."

Nina gave me a gentle elbow nudge. "Are you ready for the bridal shower tomorrow?"

I tucked a wayward curl behind my ear. "I was supposed to be co-hosting the shower with Autumn and Lexie, but since Thanksgiving I haven't heard much from my family—with the exception of Autumn."

"I'm sorry that your family didn't take the news of the elopement well."

I shrugged. "I'll take silence over the innuendo and gossip at the museum."

"Is it bad?" Nina wanted to know.

I slid my eyes over to where Diego and Julian were chatting in the kitchen. "It's worse for me than Julian."

"How so?"

"Apparently the news of our being a secret couple, that then eloped, has given him a sort of *street cred* with the men I guess you could say. When it comes to the women at work, he's seen as sexy and romantic, and even more desirable now."

Isabel grabbed the coloring book, called Julian's name, and went racing over to him to show him the page she'd been coloring.

"That's ridiculous!" Nina hissed. "So, because you're younger, he's seen as a macho stud, and that makes you, what?"

I lowered my voice. "I'm seen as an opportunist who either slept her way into her job, or worse, a slut who trapped him into a quickie marriage."

Nina shook her head. "Academia can be very prudish, can't they?"

"Yes," I agreed. "Basically, there's a whole lot of slut shaming going on at the museum. Sometimes I overhear things, but other times, the insults are right to my face."

Nina scowled. "What does Julian have to say about all of that?"

"I'm sure he's aware there is rude gossip, but I haven't told him about the direct comments I've received. He has enough going on."

"Holly." Nina frowned at me. "You shouldn't let this sort of thing continue. Speak to HR."

"It was the head of the HR department herself who has been the worst offender." I sighed. "I figured out pretty quickly that she must have been harboring a crush on Julian for a while. Finding out we were married did not sit well with her. I think she figures if she puts enough pressure on me, I'll quit."

"You're kidding."

"No." I shook my head. "The first time Julian stepped out of the building she called me into her office and gave me a lecture about decorum and what sort of professional behavior the museum staff strives for. Which does not include any sort of romantic escapades in the office..."

"Escapades?" Nina's eyes grew large. "She did not."

I smirked. "You should have seen Margaret's face when I told her that we would make every effort *not* to tear each other's clothes off and go at it on top of Julian's desk like a couple of wild animals during business hours."

Nina burst out laughing.

"Probably not the most professional comeback to her lecture," I admitted. "But I could only take so much."

"Take so much, what?" Julian asked, dropping beside Nina on the sofa.

"Nothing," I said with a smile.

Isabel then ran over and threw herself on Julian's lap. That effectively ended the conversation.

***

The day of the bridal shower was clear and chilly. I arrived early at the manor house and helped Autumn and Lexie decorate and set up all the food. Bran had taken the kids over to Autumn's next door, and he and Duncan would be riding herd on all the kids. The groom-to-be was also expected to be hanging out at

Autumn and Duncan's place.

Candice Jacobs-Stone and her husband Daniel delivered the desserts for the shower: cupcakes all done in burgundy, black and white, the colors of Ivy's winter wedding theme. I stayed in the background while Daniel set the cupcake stand on the dining room table. He dropped a kiss on his wife's head and announced to the room that he was escaping to safety before the bridal shower started.

"Oh, sure," Candice teased him. "Run away next door with the men and hide at Autumn and Duncan's."

Daniel sent her a look. "I promised Bran I'd help keep an eye on all of the kids."

Lexie rolled her eyes. "Oh bullshit. We know you're going to be watching football with your brother, Duncan, Erik and his dad."

"Maybe..." Daniel grinned at his sister-in-law. "We talked about ordering pizza too."

"I suggest not letting Morgan and Belinda have any soda unless you want them to turn into maniacs," Lexie said firmly.

"Yeah, yeah." Daniel laughed and let himself out.

Candice began to unbox the cupcakes and arrange them on the stand. I went to offer my help and as soon as she saw me, she started to grin. "Holly!" Candice grabbed me up in a fierce hug. "What's this I hear about you eloping?"

"Hello, Candice," I hugged her back. "Yes, Julian and I were married the weekend before Thanksgiving."

"Let me see those rings!" She pulled back to inspect my hand. "They're gorgeous." Her eyes lifted to mine. "And you look happier than I've seen you in a long time."

"Thank you," I said. "That means a lot."

"Daniel called it you know, at Maggie's wedding," she said as we filled the cupcakes stand.

"Called what?" I asked as I placed cupcakes on the tiers.

"That Ivy wouldn't be the next Bishop bride," Candice said. "In fact, he said that Ivy wouldn't be the next one to be married, and then he mentioned *you*."

I felt a chill run down my spine.

"I mean *I* wasn't a Bishop bride," Candice said. "I married Daniel this past summer, and although he's Bran's—your adopted brother's—biological half brother..." She shook her head and her short platinum blonde curls bounced.

"Genetically, Bran and I are first cousins," I pointed out, sliding another cupcake into place. "Bran's father gave up custody to his sister and—my mother Gwen—adopted Bran when he was a toddler."

"Right. Bran and Daniel are connected by their biological *mother's* family, the Sutherlands." Candice pressed a hand to her temple. "Good grief. I'm giving myself a headache."

I laughed. "It gets confusing all the ways we are connected. But I get what you're saying."

"Anyway," she said. "I wanted to wish you well and

offer my congratulations."

I smiled. "Thank you, Candice."

Violet Bell, florist extraordinaire, came bustling in the back door bringing her bridal shower gift, as well as a centerpiece of seasonal flowers for the table. Autumn took the flowers, and after Violet hung up her coat, she walked directly over to me.

"Holly," she began, "I wanted to offer my congratulations on your marriage."

I inclined my head. "Thank you, Violet."

"How are things going for you at the museum now that you're back?"

A bit startled by her question, I frowned.

Before I could respond she continued, "Matthew has heard some disturbing rumors all the way to the English department."

I narrowed my eyes. "How very exciting for him."

"Holly." Violet's voice was low. "I didn't mean it that way. I know how up tight and prissy some of the academics at the university can be. I only wondered if you were okay."

"Why wouldn't I be?"

"Well..." Violet brushed her purple tipped hair away from her face. "The news of your elopement was pretty shocking," she said. "You're so young and I worried that perhaps you were pressured into this, or got caught up in the moment and—"

"Now I'm going to have to stop you right there," I said firmly. "Julian and I were a couple for four *years* before we decided to elope."

"Four years?" she asked. "I had no idea you'd been seeing each other."

As Violet spoke, Autumn, Lexie, and Candice gathered in to listen to our conversation.

"Is everything okay?" Autumn asked me.

I smiled at the group, and it wasn't particularly friendly. "Violet wanted me to know there's been some gossip at the university."

"The talk is horrible, Holly," Violet insisted. "I was only worried for you, and your reputation."

"*My* reputation?" I crossed my arms over my chest. "You know, Violet, I could be catty and point out that you and Matthew got back together in a matter of weeks, after he moved back to town a few years ago."

"Oh, snap." Candice's eyes danced as she pressed a hand to her mouth. "Claws are out."

"In fact," I continued, "you moved in with him and his daughter less than a month after your reunion. I didn't hear anyone question you or your reputation about *that*."

Violet tipped her head to one side. "Touché."

Pointedly, I glanced at the clock over her shoulder. "If you'll excuse me, the bride-to-be is going to arrive shortly. I want to make sure everything is perfect for her. This is Ivy's day. Let's keep the focus on her, shall we?"

Lexie stepped forward. "I agree."

"As do I," Violet said. "But ladies, you should surely

be aware that I'm not the only guest who will be asking questions about Holly eloping with Julian Drake."

I focused my attention on Lexie. "I can leave the bridal shower before it starts if you think that my attending will create a problem."

"Don't you dare leave!" Lexie said. "If you're not here it will only make for more talk."

On cue there was a knock on the manor's front door. It opened a second later. "Hello!" a cheerful voice called out.

"I'll go greet the guests and take their coats," Lexie said and went to the foyer.

I nudged Autumn forward. "Go show the guests where they can sit. I'll stay in the kitchen and serve the punch."

Ivy had arrived with a large group of guests. Our friend Cypress Rousseau and Ginny Chandler, Erik's sister, came first—both of whom were also bridesmaids in the wedding. Gracie and Gabby Chandler, Erik's nieces and the flower girls, came in next. They arrived with Diane McBriar and Greta Larson, Erik's mother and grandmother. Behind them Nina Vasquez slipped in. She blew a kiss to Ivy and went to add her and Maggie's gifts to the pile of presents.

Nina politely greeted Autumn and Lexie but kept her eyes on my face the entire time. Without another word, she walked directly to me and attached herself to my side.

"I'm right here," she whispered.

"I'm okay, Nina."

She patted my hand. "You're looking more than a little pale, my friend."

I forced myself to smile and pretended like nothing was amiss.

During the bridal shower, I tried to stay in the background as much as possible. Violet's mother, Cora, had a kind smile for me, but she didn't speak to me unless it was to answer if she'd like a piece of cake. Candice's mother, Carol, gave me a hug and offered her support silently. Erik's mother largely ignored me, but to be fair, she was distracted by her future daughter-in-law and young Gabby and Gracie who were overly excited to be included in the bridal shower.

Once the shower was over, Erik and his father Ezra came back to the manor to see the gifts. I went directly into clean-up mode. It was a good distraction, and more importantly it kept me out of sight. When Duncan and Bran returned with the children, I saw my opportunity for a discreet exit, and so I slipped out the back of the manor house through the potting room.

I don't think I took a full breath again until I'd been on the road for a good fifteen minutes, driving back to our cabin.

***

The holidays arrived, and on the morning of the winter solstice Julian and I exchanged gifts. My choices for him were a new sturdy outdoor coat, heavy flannel shirts, and thick leather work gloves for his outdoor chores around the cabin. I also gave him a snow shovel with a big red bow tied to the handle.

In turn, he gifted me with some new pots and pans— we didn't have any decent ones at the cabin— and a stand mixer. I was thrilled to get them. Next, I opened a pair of flannel pajamas in red and black buffalo check. He even got himself a pair of matching pajama bottoms, and I laughed over the silly pajamas until I cried. My last present was a pair of aquamarine and diamond earrings in a similar style to my wedding rings. I threw myself into his arms for a thank you kiss, and we ended up making love in the discarded wrapping paper next to the tree and by the fireplace.

The next few days we spent puttering around the cabin. Julian impressed the hell out of me by cutting up a fallen tree with a chainsaw and chopping up the logs into a stack of wood for the fireplace. I had no idea he even knew how to use a chainsaw or an axe—or any of the other tools stored in the shed behind the cabin. Pointing out that the work gloves would protect his hands, I joked that no one in the office would ever know he moonlighted as a lumberjack.

Over the next few days, we made cocoa, baked cookies, watched romantic holiday movies, and I put all the new kitchen tools to work and cooked elaborate meals. It was magickal, and I reveled in our time alone.

Soon, the family all needed to be faced again. Now

that so many of our relatives had their own families, we had started the tradition of getting together at the Drake mansion for a combined Bishop and Drake formal gathering and gift exchange on the evening of the twenty-fifth. Nina and Diego were also included in the family celebration, and I knew I could sit with them at least since Autumn and Duncan would be chasing down Emma and Erin, and Maggie had an infant and Willow to contend with.

It would be loud and insane, so I psyched myself up and put on a happy face. Bran's disapproval and Lexie's cold shoulder wouldn't ruin the holidays for me. I had no idea what to expect from my sister and her fiancé. Knowing Ivy, she'd simply ignore me, or if she was feeling particularly peevish, she might jinx me.

I decided to wear a silver sequined and beaded dress and paired it with glittery rhinestone heels. Carefully, I pulled on my last pair of panty hose. I'd meant to purchase more after the elopement, but I'd forgotten.

I sat on the edge of our bed and strapped on my sparkly heels. Standing up, I tightened the back of one of the aquamarine earrings, and then I smoothed down the beaded skirt. "What do you think?" I asked Julian.

He was stepping out from the bathroom, where he'd been tying his tie in the bathroom mirror. At the sight of me, he stopped and stared in silence.

"Is this dress okay to wear to the holiday party?" I asked when he didn't respond. "The skirt hits mid-thigh but still it's pretty short. I need to be careful and remember to squat down, and not bend over in it."

"If you bend over in that dress in front of me, we'll never get out of here tonight." He sounded dead serious.

I raised my eyebrows. "Meaning what?"

"Meaning I'll lay you face down over the nearest convenient surface I can find, flip that pretty skirt up and—"

"My goodness," was all I could think to say.

"I'll be gentle," he said.

"And if I didn't want you to be gentle?"

His answer had me sucking in my breath. As Julian went on to describe in exquisite detail exactly what he'd do, all I could manage was to stand there and gawk at him.

I blew out a shaky breath. "Do me a favor and don't talk to me like that again unless you mean business." My knees were quivering, and my throat had gone dry.

He smiled. "Oh, I mean business, Angel."

I gulped. "Perhaps I should have said, unless you mean business *and* we have the time to explore all those options." Keeping my eyes on him, I went to get my wool dress coat.

"Nervous?" he asked.

I slipped the coat on. "Of seeing the family again? I'd say anxious is a better word."

Silently, he walked—or perhaps stalked would be a better description—slowly toward me.

I held up a hand, palm out. "Julian, we need to leave

right now, or we'll be late to the family gathering. There's a backseat full of gifts for the children, and despite the family issues, I'd still like to see them."

"I'd rather stay home, alone with you," he said.

"How about a compromise?" I suggested. "We'll leave early, come back here, and then I'll show you what I have on under this dress."

He raised a single brow.

I buttoned up my blue winter coat. "I'll give you a hint. It's not much of anything..." Pausing, I pulled the gloves out of my pockets. "And because I love you, I'll let you rip my last pair of pantyhose right off me," I said as I fluttered my eyelashes at him. "Suddenly I find that I'm in the mood for a good ravishing this evening."

I heard him draw in a harsh breath. "Angel, do *me* a favor. Don't talk that way to me again unless *you* mean business."

I grinned at him as he took his charcoal wool coat and slipped it on over his suit. Standing next to the door, I waited silently for him. Then together we walked down the steps and went to the car to drive to the family event.

The evening went fairly well. Fortunately, the children were wound up and running everywhere which provided a good distraction. Despite all the noise, Maggie sat serenely in a big comfy chair holding baby Phillip while Willow, Morgan, Belinda, Isabel and the twins tore through their presents. You could always count on the children to keep everyone entertained.

Thomas, to my surprise, made an effort to be welcoming. He actually spoke to me a few times, asking how we were settling into the cabin and if we needed anything. It was a start, and I was happy for Julian that his father was trying.

Served buffet style, the food was excellent, and for the most part everyone was civil during dinner. Julian and I sat with Nina and Diego and Ivy made no move to speak directly to me. In fact, she stayed as far away from Julian and me as possible. Bran and Lexie did the same. Autumn and Duncan, and Maggie and Wyatt were their usual selves, and that helped me feel a bit more relaxed.

When Maggie took baby Phillip upstairs to change him, I followed along. We had a nice chat alone, and I admired the nursery. It was lovely and done in shades of pale blue, mint green, and tan with a forest and deer theme. While she changed the baby we talked and I discovered that she was still managing to run her wedding planning business, even while on maternity leave.

The only current wedding she had in the works was Ivy's fortunately, but after listening to her remark about a few spring and summer brides who kept messaging her, I volunteered to give her a hand slogging through her correspondence if she ever needed extra help.

"I might take you up on that," Maggie said while changing the baby's diaper. "One of my spring brides blew up my phone with texts on Christmas eve. She was so worried about her florist."

I narrowed my eyes. "A *spring* bride blew up your phone?"

"Yup." Maggie nodded. "Her wedding is in April, bless her heart."

I passed the baby wipes to Maggie. "Why would an April bride bug you now, during the holidays *and* while you are on maternity leave?"

"Because darlin'," Maggie drawled, "some brides never consider that there is anything else in the world beyond their wedding day."

"Besides Ivy's wedding in three weeks, you're clear until March, right?" I asked.

"Yes, ma'am." Maggie tossed the dirty diaper in the pail. "Will you keep an eye on the baby for a minute?"

"Sure," I said.

Maggie went to wash her hands in the adjoining bathroom, and I immediately scooped up the baby from the changing table to give him a smooch on the cheek. The baby made a half smile and so I snuck another kiss.

"He smells so good," I said, as Maggie walked back into the nursery.

"He smells good, *now*," Maggie joked.

"Seriously Maggie," I said, tucking the baby in the crook of my arm. "If you need a hand with paperwork or returning calls, I would be glad to help you."

"Don't tease me," Maggie joked as we went back downstairs to rejoin the family. "I'd hire you in a hot second."

We returned to the chaos of the family, and as soon as I walked in the room, Wyatt took his son and announced he needed to teach baby Phillip the finer points of poker.

Later while the annual card game was happening, the children were playing with their new toys, and the women sat and talked of babies and the upcoming wedding, Julian slipped an arm around my waist. "Ready to go?" he asked.

"I absolutely am," I said, "but we should probably say goodbye to your father first."

Julian took my hand and we walked to Thomas to say our goodbyes. Quietly, we gathered up our gifts and slipped out. As we drove, I admired all of the lights decorating the houses in my old neighborhood and was content to listen to holiday music on the radio, enjoying the ride home.

"Are you all right, Angel?" Julian asked.

I smiled. "I'm simply enjoying the quiet. After it being only the two of us for the past month, I had sort of forgotten how *loud* the families are when everyone is together."

Julian reached for my hand. "Did Ivy or Bran speak to you at all tonight?"

"Nope," I said. "They and their partners pretty much avoided me."

Julian lifted my hand to his lips. "Well, your sister's wedding is in three weeks. Perhaps things will settle down by the big day."

"Let's hope so."

We went home to our cabin, and I carried in the gifts we'd received from the family. Maggie and Wyatt had given me a sweater, and Nina and Diego had given us a huge, red and black checked fleece lined blanket. Autumn and Duncan had given us a tool set, which would come in very handy living at the cabin, but the rest were gift cards to home improvement stores. I suppose everyone had decided that was the easiest thing...either that or they hadn't cared enough to do any more.

I set the gifts on the counter and slipped my coat off to hang on a peg by the front door. Julian went immediately to build a fire, and I decided to pour us each a glass of wine. Then I switched on the holiday playlist and soft instrumental holiday carols began to play. The music was relaxing, mostly guitar and harp with a sort of Celtic flair.

I pulled out a few cookies, arranged them on a plate, and nibbled on one. Sitting on a barstool at the kitchen island, I looked over our home. The lights on the rustic tree shone, the greenery on the mantle was fragrant, and the fire was crackling to life in the hearth. I thought about unstrapping my glittery heels, but decided I was feeling too lazy. Instead, I swung a foot back and forth in time with the music.

Julian slid the spark screen shut, brushed off his hands, and joined me at the kitchen island. He dropped a kiss on my hair and accepted the wine I held out.

"Alone at last," he said and helped himself to a cookie.

I felt the tension slip away from my shoulders and I sighed happily. "I'm glad to be home," I said, smiling over at him. "Tonight was fun seeing all of the kids, but it was tense because of Bran and Ivy."

"Perhaps I can help to relieve all that tension."

I raised my brows. "Oh yeah?"

Julian took a sip of wine, set his glass down and drew me to my feet. "Dance with me."

"Love to," I said.

We swayed back and forth to the holiday music. I rested my head against his shoulder and began to smile when I felt his hand roam down from my waist and settle on my butt. Slowly, his hand drifted down to the edge of my skirt. His fingers danced softly up and underneath, and his touch left me quivering.

"Do you happen to remember what we talked about before leaving tonight?" His voice was low and husky.

"I do," I said, shifting slightly to allow him more access. "Feel free to help your—" I stopped speaking when his fingers roamed. "Yourself," I managed to say.

"Oh, I will," he said.

CHAPTER FOUR

Unexpectedly, Julian spun and danced us a few steps closer until we were standing beside the couch. He reached down, hooked his hand behind one of my knees, and raised my leg up bringing my ankle behind his hips. Clutching at his shoulders, I ended up perched on the back of the couch while he stood close.

He swooped in and kissed me passionately. His tongue pushed its way into my mouth, and I hung on, trusting him to keep us steady. While we kissed, I felt him reach up and run his fingers over the crotch of my pantyhose.

He lifted his mouth from mine. "I believe you told me it was fine to rip these..." He yanked and I heard the pantyhose tear. "...right off of you."

"Feel free." I shivered as he shredded them.

He tugged my lace panties aside next, and I groaned with pleasure when he slid one finger deep inside me.

"Holly," he whispered and began to cruise kisses and little bites down the side of my throat.

"Julian." I gasped his name when he added a second finger. Gently, he stretched me and slid his fingers even deeper. Overcome, I began to shake in his embrace, on the verge of coming.

"You're so wet," he whispered, and to my surprise, he gently withdrew. Slowly he lowered my leg so that both of my feet were back on the floor.

"Why did you stop?" I panted. "Don't you dare stop!"

"I believe a good ravishing was requested?"

His tone of voice had me shivering. "Yes, please," I said.

His eyes shimmered in shades of blue and brown. "Do you trust me?"

Overwhelmed with my desire for him, I could only nod.

In one quick move Julian spun me around so that my front was pressed against the back of the couch. He tangled his fingers in my hair and gently pushed me forward so that my hips were up and I was bent over the back of the sofa. I braced myself with my hands on the seat cushions, and my toes barely touched the floor.

The skirt of my dress and my slip was pushed up and aside. With a growl, he made short work of the lace panties by tearing them right off me.

I managed to look at him from over my shoulder. My mouth went dry when he began to unbuckle and unzip. "Don't you move," he said.

"Yes, Julian." I deliberately used a soft and

submissive tone and watched as a wild look slid across his face. He was holding on to control just barely, and seeing him on the verge, I squirmed.

A second later he was once again testing my readiness with his fingers. His other hand was anchored tightly in my hair, firmly holding me in place. I felt him bump against my entrance and I tilted my hips higher trying to urge him on.

In one move, he thrust deep inside my core.

"Yes!" I shouted. It was an incredible sensation at this angle.

Slowly, Julian began to move. I squirmed again and he tightened his grip. With one of his hands in my hair and the other holding tight on my waist, he rolled his hips. I felt him bump against my cervix, and in answer I clamped down all my feminine muscles tight around him.

Draped over the leather sofa as I was, Julian was in complete control of our love making. He could do anything he wanted, and I absolutely loved it.

The tempo began to speed up. As the power of his thrusts increased, the couch began to scoot across the floor. The hand holding onto my waist slid down and around. I screamed when I felt his fingers began to tease and rub over my most sensitive area.

"Oh god," I managed.

"I told you what I planned to do with you when we came home." He ground the words out and all I could do was pant and enjoy the rough ride. The orgasm built and built and when it finally peaked, it was devastating. I shouted my way through it and Julian held me firmly in place. Only after I'd reached completion did he allow himself to find release.

Eventually he collapsed on top of me. Once my eyes uncrossed, I lifted my head to discover the couch had traveled several feet across the room. The area rug was also all bunched up and pinned between the table and the hearth. I snorted out a laugh upon seeing it.

"What?" he asked.

"Good thing the coffee table and rug was between the couch and the hearth," I managed to say.

"Hmm?" His reply was lazy and sounded very satisfied.

"Otherwise, I think we would have scooted right into the fireplace."

Julian lifted his head, saw where we were, and began to chuckle.

He pressed a kiss to my ear and nipped it. "You made me crazy, wondering what was under that dress all night long."

Julian withdrew and pulled me upright. The room spun once but he steadied me. There we stood, me still in my dress and heels and what was left of my pantyhose, him still mostly dressed with his slacks undone and briefs shoved out of the way. He gave me a moment to get my bearings, and we started to grin at each other. Our grins turned to chuckles, and that became helpless laughter.

"Julian," I managed to say as I staggered again, "*that* was one hell of a ravishment."

Together, we made our way across the room and headed for the shower. He started the water and I managed to get my shoes off. I tossed them across the room, and while he undressed, I pulled the dress off and over my head. Suddenly cold in only a short satin slip and my bra, I stood there shivering.

Julian moved behind me. He dropped a kiss on my shoulder and nudged the slip straps off my shoulders. The slip slid down and puddled around my feet. Julian unhooked my bra next, and his fingers skimmed over my breasts as the bra fell to the floor.

"You neglected those," I told him.

"I'll make it up to you," he said, nudging me into the shower.

Normally I would have bundled my curly hair out of the way, but tonight I was simply too spent to bother. He pulled me into his arms, and we stood beneath the warm spray of the shower and kissed.

The kiss was tender in contrast to our earlier love making. We lingered in the shower, I scrubbed his back and then he washed mine. Of course, his hands were everywhere else too, and I braced myself against the tile wall as he kissed his way down my spine and found that I wanted him all over again. Before I knew it, I was lowering myself over his lap on the narrow shower bench.

I settled over him with my back pressed firmly to his

chest. I leaned my head back, and Julian's mouth latched on to the nape of my neck. His hands covered my breasts as we made love again. By contrast, the second round was slow and gentle, and by the time we were finished with each other all the hot water had run out.

We collapsed into bed around midnight, and before I fell asleep I heard him say, "Get some sleep, Angel."

"Thanks for the ravishing," I said around a tired yawn.

"You are most welcome." Julian pulled me closer. "I love you."

"Love you too," I said and fell asleep.

***

The winter holidays were over far too quickly for my taste. When we went back to work in January, I had hoped that talk about our elopement would settle down, but instead the gossip only grew worse. With the exception of Autumn and her executive assistant, Olivia, most of my fellow employees were so busy throwing shade that I wondered how anything else was getting accomplished at the museum at all.

Julian told me to ignore the whispers and felt sure the gossip would subside soon. I managed to get through the first few weeks by keeping my head down, eating lunch at my desk and avoiding the rest of the museum staff as much as possible.

As an empath, it was excruciating to have so much negativity and bad energy thrown my way. To counteract it I built up my energetic shields, carried protective crystals in my pockets, and kept to myself. Keeping physical distance from the rest of the museum office staff was the best way to avoid all of the hurtful barbs that were being slung my way whenever I dared to venture out of my office. Or was foolish enough to go to the café or eat in the lunchroom alone…

The day before Ivy's rehearsal dinner, Julian was out of the office for a meeting, and I was once again eating lunch at my desk. I popped the top of a lemon-lime soda and began to unwrap my roast beef sandwich. Unexpectedly, the smell of the meat hit me hard.

Has the roast beef gone bad? Tentatively, I sniffed the lunch meat again, and my stomach lurched. I guess that it had. My stomach rumbled in protest, and so I shoved the sandwich back in the paper bag.

Screw it, I decided. I would go get some soup at the café. Rising to my feet, I slung my purse over my shoulder, picked up my soda, and tossed my lunch bag in a hall garbage can on my way out.

I found there was vegetable soup on the menu today, and so I ordered that with some crackers and claimed a two-top table to sit at in the corner.

The soup smelled wonderful. Relieved that my stomach had seemed to have settled, I took a swig of my soda and ripped open the final package of crackers. I had one half-way to my mouth when someone stopped in front of my table.

"Soup and crackers, eh?"

I glanced up and saw it was Margret, head of HR.

"Hello, Margaret," I said, trying to be polite.

"You certainly have been wolfing down the crackers." Her smile was nasty and full of spite. "Morning sickness hitting you hard, I suppose?"

I flinched.

There was movement in my peripheral, and Autumn's assistant, Olivia, plopped herself in the chair right next to me. "Hey, Holly." She smiled broadly. "Thanks for saving me a seat."

Olivia was in her late fifties, full figured, and her brown hair was liberally streaked with silver. She had a penchant for wearing loud and very colorful sweaters to work. Today her sweater was royal blue and white. It featured snowmen.

"Hi, Olivia." I smiled gratefully at the woman.

Olivia spared Margaret a glance. "Don't let us keep you, Margaret."

With a huff, Margaret flounced over to the order pick up line.

Olivia picked up a french fry and considered it. "Never could stand her, or the beige wardrobe, *or* that woman's boney ass."

I bit back a snort of laughter. "I never noticed it before, Olivia, but now that you mention it...she does wear a lot of neutrals."

"Is she still giving you a hard time?" Olivia wanted

to know.

"Yes."

"What a bitch," Olivia grumbled.

"No argument there," I said, watching as Margaret carried her food tray to a nearby table.

Olivia took a bite of her club sandwich. "You should report her."

"Sort of hard to do that when she's the head of human resources."

Olivia passed me a french fry. "Then hex her."

I accepted the french fry. "Despite the gossip in town, the Bishops don't—as a rule—hex people."

"Oh, trust me sweetie, I know that." Olivia gave me an elbow nudge. "But I live in hope. It would certainly liven things up around here."

Despite myself I started to laugh.

Olivia grinned. "Did Autumn ever tell you that I knew your great aunt Irene?"

"No," I said. "I didn't know that."

Olivia ate another fry. "Irene Bishop was an amazing woman. She worked miracles for my sister. We both adored her. Plenty of other folks in Williams Ford swore that Irene Bishop trafficked in dark magick. But I can tell you for a fact, that she did not."

"I'd love to hear that story," I told Olivia.

"How much time do you have left on lunch break?" Olivia gave me an exaggerated eyebrow wiggle. "Wouldn't want your new husband to be miffed if you came back to work late."

I chuckled. "He's out of the office for the rest of the afternoon, and it's fine."

"Perfect." Olivia smiled and told me about her sister Jane and how Irene had helped her some thirty years prior. Turns out that Jane's daughter and I had something in common: we shared the same middle name. Both of our mothers had named us after Irene Bishop.

It was a fascinating tale, and yet another connection. After lunch, Olivia walked me back to my office and we parted ways with a hug. Automatically, I worked my way through emails and hit the buttons to print out a file. Leaning back in my chair, I took a break and considered everything I'd learned today.

Like me, Irene Bishop also fell in love with a Drake man. Sadly, their relationship had ended in tragedy when Phillip unexpectedly died. I sighed thinking about it. Still, Irene had gone on with her life alone, despite being ostracized by her own family.

Back when Autumn had bought Irene's house and begun work renovating it, Irene's ghost had frightened off every contractor my cousin had hired, until she hired Duncan Quinn. It was during the renovation that Autumn and Duncan had reconnected.

Irene had continued to haunt her old house until Autumn and Duncan discovered the truth about Irene and Phillip Drake's secret child, Patricia. Patricia's existence had been hidden from both the Bishops and the Drakes for more than fifty years. Their daughter had been adopted by close friends of Irene's. Irene had known her child and eventually Patricia had given birth to a daughter of her own—Maggie.

This made Maggie a cousin to Julian through the Drake side of the family and also a cousin to me from the Bishop side. Recently Maggie had named her son after her paternal grandfather, Phillip Drake, and when you stopped and thought about it, it was fascinating how things seemed to run in a circle.

I stood up to fetch the documents from the printer and the room spun. Making a grab for the edge of my desk, I laughed at myself. Thinking about the family tree and trying to keep all the convoluted family connections straight was enough to make anyone dizzy.

***

Ivy and Erik's Friday rehearsal dinner and the Saturday ceremony and reception were all to be held at the McBriar family wedding barn. My father and stepmother, Ruth, had arrived from Iowa, and Aunt Faye and her new husband, Professor Hal Meyer, also returned to town for the wedding.

While I cherished my father and stepmother, I had never been more grateful to see my elegant, high maintenance great aunt as I was that night. Faye adored Julian. She had since the night several years before when he had saved both her and Autumn's life during the final battle over the Blood Moon Grimoire.

"Julian! Holly!" Aunt Faye called our names and rushed forward. She enfolded Julian and then me into big, fierce hugs. She gave me a smacking kiss on the cheek too and loudly congratulated us on our wedding, while the rest of the group stared.

Aunt Faye remarked that secret elopements for the Bishop women were suddenly *en vogue*. After all she and Hal had eloped while they'd been off touring the world. Faye looped her arm through mine and stuck to my side like glue; that is until we had to run through the ceremony.

I dutifully took my place with the other attendants and paid attention during the rehearsal. As soon as the ceremony rehearsal was finished, the food was served, and Faye and Hal sat right beside Julian and me for the entire meal. It was almost as if she was daring anyone to do or say anything about it.

"Well." Aunt Faye arched a brow as we moved down the buffet line. "Barbeque and potato salad served on disposable plates for a wedding rehearsal?" Faye lifted a buffalo plaid print paper napkin. "Isn't this...charming, in a down home sort of way?"

"Burgundy and black are Ivy and Erik's colors for the wedding," I said as I helped myself to the potato salad. "I believe that the buffalo plaid was supposed to be a nod to Erik's family farm."

"How...rustic," Faye said, and I fought hard not to smile as she scowled at the plastic forks and knives.

Maggie happened to be within earshot of my aunt's

comment, and she stopped. "They are keeping it casual because the wedding dinner is also here tomorrow. Less clean up tonight and I assure you, Faye, there will be no paper or plastic anywhere in sight tomorrow."

"I love the idea of barbeque," Hal said affably.

"It's spicy!" The caterer smiled at Hal.

"Good!" Hal grinned at the news. "Exactly the way I like it."

"Magnolia." Aunt Faye stopped Maggie before she could walk away.

"Yes, ma'am?" Maggie's voice was just this side of polite. Perhaps it was Faye's use of her full name.

"I wanted to say congratulations on the birth of your son."

Maggie blinked in surprise. "Why thank you."

"You named him Phillip, did you not?"

"Yes." Maggie nodded. "After his grandfather."

"That's lovely." Faye smiled. "Perhaps tomorrow after the ceremony, you will show me some photos of the baby?"

Maggie's entire face softened. She knew this was Faye's attempt at healing the tension between them. "I think that can be arranged."

"Excellent." Faye gave her the slightest of smiles. "Now I won't keep you any longer. I know that you're busy."

I discovered my mouth was hanging open and I shut it. Aunt Faye and Maggie had never particularly gotten along. It was good to see my great-aunt trying to make things easier between them.

We moved down the line and walked back to our table. Faye chatted up Julian while we ate, and afterwards Hal offered to get us all fresh drinks. I asked for ginger ale. The barbeque was not sitting well on my stomach at all.

I sipped on the ginger ale, but the wedding barn suddenly felt very overheated, and my stomach was starting to bother me. Excusing myself from the table, I went to the barn door and slipped outside to get some cold air on my face.

Maggie was only a few seconds behind me. "Everything okay?" she asked.

"Don't think the spicy barbeque is agreeing with me." I managed a smile. "Or it's probably nerves from all the nastiness at work and stress from being around the family."

Maggie rubbed a hand over my shoulders. "Having second thoughts about staying at the museum?"

"Only every day," I admitted.

"I was entirely serious about having you come to work for me, you know."

I did a double take. "Are we talking full time or part time?"

"Full time," Maggie said. "The baby is almost seven weeks old, and though I gave myself a few months off, those spring weddings are getting closer. *Magnolia Bridal and Events* is growing by leaps and bounds and I need another set of hands. I would have to hire someone soon, and you already have plenty of office experience and people skills."

"My degree is in art history, not business," I began.

"Which means you have a good eye, and I know you have taste. I can train you in everything else." Maggie then named a salary that had my eyes widening.

"Seriously?" It was far more than I earned at the museum.

Maggie smiled. "Very serious. You'd rarely have a free Saturday."

"Don't you typically take off Monday and Tuesday?"

Maggie grinned. "That's right."

"That could work for me." I smiled. "I'll speak to Julian about it tonight and have an answer for you after Ivy's wedding."

***

The next morning, I woke, felt my stomach pitch, and ran straight for the bathroom. I hung over the toilet for a while, sweating and shivering, convinced I was about to be sick, but never actually threw up. Slowly it passed, and I climbed to my feet, splashed some water on my face, and brushed my teeth, hoping the mint toothpaste would help.

I studied my reflection and saw that I was paler than usual. "Shit," I said, frowning over how my freckles stood out starkly against the pallor of my skin.

"Angel?" Julian hovered in the doorway. "Are you

all right?"

I leaned against the sink. "That barbeque did a number on my stomach."

"Why don't you come back to bed and lie down for a while?"

"Can't." I shook my head. "I have to report to the wedding barn in two hours for hair and makeup. "I don't know why Ivy insisted on me having my hair done. My curly hair is hopeless."

"Your hair is wild and beautiful," Julian said. "*You* are beautiful."

"I feel anything but beautiful this morning." I made a face at myself in the mirror. "Damn it! Look at the circles under my eyes. It looks like I was out partying all night long."

"I know last night was difficult for you," Julian said, moving up behind me. "There's been a lot of stress between the museum and your sister's wedding."

"Maggie's job offer is sounding better all of the time."

Julian slipped his arms around me. "I'd miss you at the office. I like having you there with me, but I know you've been taking a lot of grief from Margaret and other staff."

Our eyes met in the mirror. "I didn't know that you were aware of how bad it's gotten."

"While no one is foolish enough to have said anything derogatory within my hearing, the mood at the offices has become spiteful and mean. I know you've been spending a lot of energy shielding against it." He sighed and kissed the top of my head. "If you want to work with Maggie, I have no objections. I only want you to be happy."

I rested against his chest. "I really love you." I stayed there for a moment taking comfort from him and then I straightened. "It's an hour drive to the farm. Like it or not, I need to get moving."

"I'll make you a cup of tea," Julian offered. "It should help your stomach."

"That sounds nice." Pulling my nightgown over my head, I marched into the shower.

Julian dropped me off right on time at the wedding barn on the McBriar's property. There'd been a light snow overnight and the temperatures were hovering in the low thirties. The fresh snow made everything a bit more festive, and I smiled to see it.

After being a bridesmaid at Autumn's wedding, I knew the drill. I reported for duty and resigned myself to a day of *hurry up and wait*. I had wisely showed up in comfy clothes: leggings, sneakers and a jacket I could zip off and on—as not to mess up my hair or makeup. I hung up my attendant's dress, chatted with the other bridesmaids—Cypress Rousseau and Ginny, Erik's sister—and waited my turn for hair and makeup.

The McBriar's had recently converted the loft above the barn into a bridal area, and I sat at a table with Ivy, Ginny, and Cypress while the flower girls had their hair done by the two stylists. There was a platter of fruit, cheese, and crackers available for the bridal party, and I nibbled on a couple of grapes.

"Problem with the cheese tray?" Ivy asked me.

"No. Of course not." I smiled and took a sip from my bottle of water.

Ginny leaned forward. "We need to get Mom up here to have her hair done."

Diane was currently running around in sneakers below, helping Maggie and the wedding barn team put the finishing touches on the ceremony and reception space. Apparently, Ivy had asked for a last-minute change to the setup.

The bride was happy, but she seemed intent on micro-managing the team who were trying to set up below. Maggie distracted her by sending up a bottle of champagne, and I decided to pour the bubbly. Ivy was content, for the moment, to sip her wine and watch the flower girls have their hair done.

Curious if there was a real problem below, I slipped back downstairs to check out the progress. I sat on the loft stairs, where I could see everything but stay well out of the way.

Watching Maggie at work was an education. She was dressed neatly and professionally in dark slacks, a white top, and a burgundy blazer. Maggie moved like lightning in a pair of low-heeled shoes and seemed to be everywhere at once, somehow managing to exude a sort of calm energy in the eye of the storm. The guest tables were already dressed in black cloth and the vintage wooden chairs popped against the dark linen. At the center of each table were fresh flowers and LED candles. Above the tables, party lights sparkled as they hung in swoops from the rafters of the barn.

As I watched, a few round tables were lifted and moved into a different position. Once a table was in its new place the chairs were moved and tucked into place again.

In contrast to the guest tables, the table for the wedding party was long, narrow, and left plain. The black chargers and plates contrasted nicely against the old worn wooden grain. Down the center of the farm table stood old silver candelabras and other candle holders holding long black tapers. Short, squatty black glass vases in a variety of shapes held fresh flowers. From here I could make out deep red roses, white anemones, maroon pincushion flowers, and burgundy carnations. They were combined with trailing wine-red amaranth and the silvery-green foliage of seeded eucalyptus

Maggie stopped at the base of the stairs. "What do you think?" she asked.

"Only Ivy could find a way to combine a gothic theme with a rustic barn venue and make it look this good."

"Truth," Maggie agreed, tucking a tendril of her dark hair back into a neat bun at the nape of her neck. "And if she pops down here again with any more changes, I'm going to hog-tie her to a chair and keep her upstairs until the ceremony."

"I've been thinking about that job offer," I said quickly, while I had her.

"Oh?"

"I'm going to turn in my two weeks notice on Monday at the museum."

Maggie grinned. "I can't wait to start to work with you."

I smiled in return. "I'm looking forward to it as well."

"Maggie!" Diane called across the floor. "The caterers have arrived."

"Okay!" Maggie called back to Erik's mother. "You should go upstairs and get your hair and makeup done, Diane. We've got this under control."

Diane blew out a long breath. "Are you sure?"

"Yes. Absolutely." She gave Diane the thumb's up. "Gotta go," she said to me and was off.

The caterer began to load in, and I could smell the food from where I sat. Immediately, my stomach began to turn. "I will *never* eat barbeque again," I muttered to myself.

Diane started up the stairs and I stood to make way for her. She passed me with a broad smile, and I saw that the bartender was also setting up across the space. I went over and got a lemon-lime soda. I was walking back when I spotted Ginny on the steps. She was waving me over, so I plastered a smile on my face and went to go get my hair done.

Carrying my drink back up the stairs, I sat in a chair while the hairdresser did what she could with my explosion of curls. She settled for twisting the front back and away from my face, leaving the rest to fall in long corkscrew curls down my back. It wasn't tamed, but it would work.

I shifted to go sit in the makeup artist's chair next.

"Oh my goodness," she said. "What beautiful freckles."

"I know I'm too pale." I smirked at her. "Do the best you can."

She bent down until she was looking me square in the eyes. "Nonsense, your skin tone is amazing. I can hide the circles under your eyes."

Beside me Cypress laughed. "Partied too hard last night, girlfriend?"

"No," I said to Cypress. "I'm afraid the spicy barbeque didn't sit well on my stomach."

Ivy's head snapped up. "Are you going to complain about the rehearsal dinner food like Aunt Faye did?" Her tone was offended and angry.

"No." I made myself smile and lied through my teeth. "It was wonderful." I slanted my eyes over toward Cypress. Meeting her eyes, I silently asked for her to intercede.

"Ivy," Cypress began, "do you remember that night in our senior year at college when we went on the pub crawl? We had fiery buffalo wings and it was so spicy that I threw them up all over the front steps of Crowley

Hall?"

The bride burst out laughing and I shut my eyes in relief that Ivy had been distracted. While the makeup artist started working on my face, I kept my eyes closed and stayed silent.

Once she was finished with me, I thanked her and went to sit as far away from the bride as I could manage. It was an awful thing to be a bridesmaid to your twin sister and know that if you even moved the wrong way, she would jump down your throat.

Diane, the mother of the groom, was currently working wonders keeping Ivy busy and distracted. In order to appear as if I were happy to be there, I sat and talked to Erik's young nieces. For a while things were cheerful and calmer in the bridal area.

Finally, it was time to get dressed. I helped Ginny with her daughters, and Gracie and Gabby were adorable in their flower girl dresses. The dresses were deep burgundy with short sleeves, and burgundy and black paisley sashes tied around their waists that matched the patterns of the ties and vests of the groomsmen's black suits.

It came as no surprise to anyone that Ivy had chosen black bridesmaid dresses. Made from a black chiffon, they had a V-neck with fluttery sleeves that fell to the elbows and were finished with high-low skirts.

Ivy's bridal gown was truly stunning and unique. It was floor length with a traditional white shimmering full tulle skirt, but the bodice of the dress was made of black embroidered lace and a black bead applique. The black lace ended at the waist and created a bold statement with its V-neck, snug bodice, and midnight-hued long lace sleeves.

My sister kept her long bob simple with casual waves and one side secured back from her face with a sparkly white beaded and jeweled comb.

Violet arrived and handed out the bouquets. The bride's was all deep wine-colored roses, which she fretted over. When Ivy began to question Violet on whether or not she thought her rose bouquet was big enough or needed longer lace streamers, Diane stepped in and distracted her again.

The last thing I'd ever expected my sister to be on her wedding day was a Bridezilla, but she was skating the edge pretty closely. Honestly, I thought the flowers were amazing. Violet had, as usual, done an incredible job. The flowers for the attendants' bouquets and the flower girls' white baskets were a mixture of the dramatic flowers from the tables: white anemones, burgundy carnations, maroon pincushion flowers, deep red amaranth, and black seeded eucalyptus.

The photographer arrived and it was time for first looks and the group wedding party photos. I saw as we began to line up that Julian had arrived. He stood at the back of the barn chatting with Maggie. I smiled and meant it when I saw him. Wearing a tailored black suit with a white shirt and a dark tie, I was struck once again with how incredibly handsome he was.

Once the group photos were finished, I went directly to him and lifted my mouth for a kiss. Afterward, he pulled me close.

"You have no idea," I whispered in his ear, "how *glad* I am that we eloped."

He eased back to look at me. "I wondered if you would regret not having a big fancy wedding after today."

I mock-shuddered. "Gods, *no*. Our wedding day was absolutely perfect," I said, rising up on my toes to kiss him again.

From across the room the bride was asking for a change to something. Apparently, Ivy wanted the food setup rearranged and the caterer was scrambling to make adjustments. Erik's mother, Diane, our stepmother, Ruth, and the groom were all trying to talk her out of it. Ivy's voice was uncharacteristically sharp and carried clearly to where we stood.

Julian spoke softly. "Your twin seems to have gone Bridezilla."

"I know, right?" I whispered back, as Ivy called the caterer over to her and Erik.

"Lesson number one," Maggie said so only we could hear. "Know when it's time to wrangle the bride and soothe or distract her before she ruins all of her own plans."

I bit back a smile. "Go get her, boss."

Maggie took a deep breath and was headed straight toward the bride and a very upset looking caterer.

The photographer was suddenly in front of Julian and I. "Hi," she said. "You two must be the newlyweds I've been hearing so much about."

I opened my mouth to speak, and the photographer barreled right over whatever I would have said. "I was wondering if I could get a quick shot of you two outside." She wiggled her eyebrows. "In the snow. If you're game."

"Angel?" Julian asked me.

Nervously, I eyed the bride and groom who were deep in a conversation with Diane, Maggie, and the caterer.

"It'll be quick. I promise." The photographer smiled and nudged us right out the barn doors. "Bring your flowers," she said to me. "Trust me, the bride is busy at the moment. She'll never notice we slipped out."

The photographer was a cheerful steamroller, and I figured in her line of work that personality trait probably came in very handy. I couldn't help but smile as she pointed where she wanted us to stand. She shifted us so that the fields of Christmas trees were in the background, and to my surprise she didn't pose us in the traditional type of attendant and spouse pose. In fact, she told us to ignore that she was there and just kiss each other. "Be spontaneous," she said.

Julian nodded soberly at her directions. "Spontaneous you say?" He paused to straighten his cuffs and then to smooth down his dark tie. "Well, if you insist."

Before I knew what he was about, he shifted from standing and dipped me backwards. Julian planted a quick hard kiss on my mouth. When he lifted his mouth from mine, he gave me such an open and happy smile that I began to laugh in delight.

"Perfect!" the photographer called out.

I hooked my arms around his neck, flowers and all, and kissed him again.

"That's got it!"

Julian and I stepped apart and we went back inside to warm up. To our surprise, the photographer showed us a few of the images she'd captured.

There was one that I loved right away. My hair was flying at that moment Julian had dipped me backwards and we'd both been laughing. The snowy trees were out of focus behind us, and the black of my dress, deep red of the bridesmaid's bouquet, and his dark suit popped against the snow.

"We're going to want a few copies of this one," Julian said.

"Of course," she said. "I'd love to photograph the two of you, anytime." The photographer passed him her card. "If you'll excuse me, I need to go track down the groom's family for some more photos."

CHAPTER FIVE

Once we were back inside the wedding barn, I saw that Maggie had done her magick and Ivy was momentarily content. The ceremony itself was less than an hour away now, and Maggie rounded up all of us to stay upstairs in the bridal suite until the service began. Our hair and makeup were touched back up and the photographer circled around, getting more candid shots.

Finally, it was time for the ceremony to start. I took my place standing between Cypress and Ginny and watched as my twin was escorted down the aisle by our father. Everything was lovely, and despite all that had happened, I was very happy for Ivy and Erik.

The reception was a joyful blur. I avoided the beef and had some pasta and a green salad instead. It seemed to sit easier than the food from the night before. After the obligatory toasts and the bridal party dance, I was able to go and sit with Julian, Aunt Faye and Hal at one of the guest tables. Faye wanted to know how we were settling into newlywed life at the cabin. We had an incredibly fun evening.

Julian and I danced several times, which was the best part of the night as far as I was concerned. We were able to spend some time with my parents as well, and my father seemed to like Julian very much.

At one point I found Maggie and Wyatt sitting together with Faye and Hal. They were showing my great-aunt and her new husband photos of their baby son. And to my surprise, Willow was sitting beside Faye while she told Faye and Hal all about what it was like to be a big sister. Faye listened intently and I watched as she ran a hand gently over Willow's long hair. It made me a little choked up. At least one part of the family was making steps toward a reconciliation.

Finally, the party wound down, and I promised my father and stepmother we would come up to Iowa for a long weekend in the spring. We parted with hugs, and I went to gather up all my things and Julian took them out to the car.

Maggie was on hand to make sure the cards and gifts were secured, the crew was clearing and cleaning, and we didn't argue when she told us to head home. I stifled back a yawn as we walked to our car and fell asleep on the drive back to our cabin.

My full intention when I went to work on Monday was to turn in my two weeks' notice at noon. I had emailed my resignation letter to myself and printed it off at work. Julian was working at the museum proper today; he and the curator were on hand for the installation of an exhibit that was on loan. Even Autumn, as the archivist, was present. This exhibit was a huge deal, and an honor for the museum. I expected him back in the office later in the afternoon.

Julian had asked me to wait to turn in my resignation until he would be there. He seemed worried that I'd be upset or nervous. I tried to explain to him that I was looking forward to it and excited about working with Maggie. But still, he was concerned.

Even though I had promised him that I would wait, when lunch came I made up my mind to handle this on my own. I was a strong woman; I did not need to hide behind my husband. With that thought in mind, I squared my shoulders, picked up my resignation letter, and headed straight to the HR department for a talk with Margaret.

I had barely made it down the hall before I practically ran into her.

"Margaret," I said. "I was literally on my way to your office."

Her eyebrows went way up. "Yes?"

Behind Margaret I saw a woman wearing a bright purple sweater stop on her way to the water cooler. It was Olivia. There was no missing her silvered hair or the colorful top. She had folded her arms over her chest and was standing her ground, shamelessly eavesdropping on the conversation.

I handed Margaret the letter. "I have already spoken to Julian, but I'm officially turning in my two weeks' notice."

Margaret scanned my resignation letter for the briefest of moments. "Good," she said. "Saves me the trouble of finding a reason to fire you. We don't want your kind here."

"Excuse me?" My face flushed with anger and embarrassment. I hadn't expected her to be so blatant. Especially not where anyone could overhear her.

"Margaret!" Olivia's voice was shocked as she began to walk forward. "That comment was completely uncalled for."

"Stay out of this!" Margaret glared at Olivia. "Unless you want to find yourself written up for insubordination."

Olivia laughed at the threat. "I'd like to see you try."

"Leave Olivia alone," I said to Margaret, as the water cooler directly across from her began to loudly bubble and gurgle.

Margaret flashed me a thin smile. "Your resignation is accepted and effective immediately, Ms. Bishop."

"That's *Mrs. Drake*, to you," I snapped back. My temper was slipping, and in response the overhead lights began to flicker.

"For now." Margaret looked down her nose at me. "I'm sure he'll see you for the whore you truly are soon enough; and that will be that."

Her hateful words had me seeing red. The lights above us blew out in direct response to my temper. I clenched my fists, trying to hold back my magick, but I could feel it *and* the shields I'd always been so careful to keep in place at the museum slipping out of my control as electricity continued to surge throughout the offices.

"This is awesome!" Olivia yelled excitedly.

Aw shit, I thought, and tried valiantly to hold on, but now a breeze began to ripple inside of the building. It came whistling along the hall pushing my hair back from my face. All around us people were exclaiming over the power surging and going off and on.

A fellow worker came to their doorway, glancing from Margaret and back to me. "What on earth is happening?" she asked.

"Go clear out your desk," Margret said to me over the ruckus. "I'll have security escort you from the building."

The gurgling inside the water cooler had become so violent it appeared to be boiling. Olivia squinted over at it and wisely backed away.

My chin went up. "A security escort won't be necessary, Margaret."

"Oh, I think it is. In fact, I'll oversee your departure myself." And then Margaret made a huge mistake. She grabbed ahold of my arm in an attempt to steer me down the hall. "You," she said, "are nothing but an opportunistic slut."

My magick lashed furiously outwards, knocking the woman back and away from me. At the same time, the big plastic tank that held the drinking water exploded all over the hall. Margaret was standing right in the line of fire and was completely drenched.

She screamed even as the whole building went dark. The wind I'd called died as suddenly as it had appeared, and for a moment everything was silent.

Then the emergency lights clicked on, and there Margret stood, soaking wet in her beige dress. It was as if she'd jumped in a swimming pool.

"You did that!" she shrieked. "I know you did!"

Everyone came rushing to the hall to see what had happened. I tried not to smile. Tragically, I failed.

"*Witch*," she hissed. "I've always hated you!"

I stood there three feet away from her and yet was completely dry. I moved a tad closer to the dripping wet woman and had the satisfaction of seeing her flinch back. "Julian never even noticed you, Margaret," I said quietly, "and *that's* what you really hate."

"Security!" Margaret screamed.

***

Bad news? I was not allowed to retrieve my personal items. Olivia offered to go and fetch my purse and coat while Margaret screeched hysterically about calling the police and several other folks were talking about calling maintenance to hopefully restore the power.

It was chaos. Everyone was speaking at once. People were complaining that the computer systems were most likely fried due to the odd power surges...and I was, in fact, escorted by the security team none-too-gently from the offices of the Williams Ford University Museum.

Good news? It could have been worse.

No one had been hurt, and at least they didn't call the police. I mean, how bad would it have sucked if Lexie would have been the responding officer?

I did call Maggie on my cell phone while I drove back to the cabin and informed her that I could start working for her as early as tomorrow. Simply telling her there'd been a change in plans, I left out the part about letting my magick loose and causing havoc in the museum office.

Not that she would have been upset with me about that. I once watched Maggie pin Julian to the ceiling and leave him hanging there, when he had purposefully goaded her into losing control of her powers.

Maggie was pleased at the news that I would be available earlier and asked me to come to the Drake mansion, where she kept her office, the very next day. We'd get started the next morning at nine. I could hear the baby fussing in the background and so we said our goodbyes.

At the first stoplight I fired off a text to my husband. It simply said: *Change of plans. My two weeks' notice was waived. I'll explain when you get home tonight.*

I knew he probably wouldn't see the text for a few hours. Still, I hoped the message would keep him from being annoyed with me for *not* waiting for him to be there when I turned in my notice to HR. Feeling happy to be away from the non-stop drama at the museum offices, I cranked up the radio and sang along as I drove home.

Once I got to our cabin, I changed clothes. I tossed on an old pair of black yoga pants and a pink sweatshirt, bundled my hair up and out of the way, and decided to put together a stew for supper. Maybe I'd even make some cornbread; I definitely wanted a big glass of wine.

By the time Julian arrived home that evening, I had the counter set with bowls and plates. The stew was keeping warm on the stove, a pan of cornbread was baking in the oven, and more than half of the bottle of wine was gone.

"Hey, handsome!" I jumped up from the couch and the room tilted. Making a grab for the couch, I overcompensated and stumbled a bit. "Damn it," I swore at the wine that sloshed over the rim of my glass and hit the rug. "Oh well, it's white wine. It won't stain." Then I gave him my best 'come hither' look. "Come over here and kiss me, Julian."

"Holly." Julian tipped his head to one side. "Have you been drinking?"

"Jus' a couple glasses of wine..." I said, gesturing with the glass.

Now he started to smile. "Angel, you're spilling the wine."

I frowned. "I am?"

"You are." He walked over and nipped the wine

glass from my hand. "I would ask what you did with the rest of your day, but I can see the answer for myself."

"I made chicken stew and cornbread." Leaning forward, I tried to kiss him. I almost got him on the mouth.

He turned his head and kissed me to rectify the near miss. "It smells wonderful."

"Mmmm..." I nuzzled his neck. "So do you."

"We should talk about today," he began. "I heard about the water cooler incident."

I couldn't help but laugh. "Is *that* what they're calling it?"

"Olivia, Autumn's executive assistant, filled me in. She claims to have seen the whole thing."

"Yeah. She was right there."

"You have a fan," Julian said.

"It's mutual," I said. "With the exception of Autumn, Olivia has been the only other person who's been kind to me at the office in the past few months."

"I knew Margret was a problem," Julian said, loosening his tie. "I never imagined she'd take things as far as she did."

"She has a thing for you," I told him.

A distinct red flush appeared over my husband's face. "That would explain her increasingly combative behavior since you and I were married." He tossed back what was left in my wine glass. "I had no idea."

"Margaret's been taking her frustrations out on me on a daily basis for a while. She's the one behind all the gossip. You know that, right?"

"I know it now. Thanks to Olivia." He sighed. "You should have told me how truly bad it was at the office for you."

"I would have sounded like a whiner," I pointed out. "Hey, was the power back on when you arrived?"

"When we walked in, everyone was running around and talking about how there'd been an unexplained series of power surges in the building...at precisely the same time you and Margaret had your altercation."

I shrugged. "How mysterious."

He took my chin with his fingers. "Holly, we both know the price for losing control of our magick. There's a reason I wanted to be with you when you spoke to Margaret."

"*Pfft.*" I tossed my head. "That beige bitch is lucky I didn't set her on fire."

Julian almost laughed but caught himself and turned it into a cough. "Holly." He tried to give me a stern look.

"No one got hurt, Julian," I argued, taking my wine glass back.

"The power surges took out the entire computer system for a few hours."

I poured myself another glass of wine. "They have backup hard drives for the most important systems."

"That's true," he said. "However, Margaret was hysterical by the time I came back to the office."

"She probably," I said, hiccupping, "needs to get

laid."

Julian burst out laughing

I pointed a finger at him. "So long as you're not the one doing the honors..."

He was wiping his eyes now he was laughing so hard.

"What?" I frowned at him.

"I've never seen you like this."

"You know what?" I set the wine glass down. "I think...I am sloshed."

He grinned. "I have to agree."

The buzzer sounded from the stove, and I jumped. "Cornbread's done!" I rushed to the stove to take the pan from the oven.

"I'm going to change," Julian said.

"Okay." Realizing I *was* tipsy, I pulled the cornbread out and set it with exaggerated care on a folded towel on the counter. I placed the butter next to the cornbread and set out a jar of honey. A few minutes later, Julian was back in gray sweats and a pull over.

I eyeballed him as he approached. "You know, I used to think you were sexiest in one of your tailored suits...but I have to say, those sweatpants just sort of *do it* for me."

"I'm happy to hear it." He smiled when I ran my hands over his butt.

I gave his backside a friendly squeeze. "Julian..."

"Why don't we get some food into you?" Julian eased out of my reach and gently steered me to a barstool.

"It's fine," I said. "Let me serve up the stew."

"No. I've got it." He shooed me away and began to dish up the chicken and vegetables into the waiting bowls.

We ate at the kitchen island, and I told him how excited I was to start working with Maggie in the morning. He listened with a smile and gave me his full attention. After supper, we cleaned up the kitchen together and he poured me a glass of water, took me by the elbow, and steered me to the couch.

As soon as he sat down, I set the glass aside, threw a leg over his lap and straddled him. "Pucker up, pal." Leaning forward, I planted one on him.

"Holly," he said, as I shifted to run kisses down the side of his throat. "We should talk more about what happened at the museum today."

"Talking is overrated." I nipped his ear. "I'm trying to seduce you, Julian. Pay attention."

"Oh, I am." His voice was serious and dry, even as his hands slid under my sweatshirt. "Believe me."

"Take me to bed, Julian." I ran my tongue along the side of his jaw. "Or take me right here."

"Angel," he groaned.

"I'm all keyed up from the magick."

"I noticed," he said dryly.

"Are you complaining?" I asked.

"Not at all," he said.

Julian scooted forward on the couch, wrapped me in

his arms and stood. I curled myself around him tightly, and our kiss was hot, deep, and urgent. A few steps later he lowered me to sit on the side of the bed.

I pulled my sweatshirt over my head, tossed it aside, and reached out to yank his sweats down his thighs.

"Let me," I said. Leaning forward, I guided him to my mouth and helped myself. He sunk his hands in my hair as I pleasured him.

His voice was ragged when he told me to stop. I ignored his plea and he pulled away from my grasp. Julian pushed me backwards on the mattress and I laughed when my shoulders bounced against the bed.

Silently, he reached for the waistband of my yoga pants. He pulled them and my panties free from my legs with a few firm tugs. I reached out for him, expecting that he would cover me, but instead he dropped down and buried his face between my legs.

I clutched the back of his head and held on as he kissed and licked at my most sensitive area. He growled against me, and it reminded me of the first time we were together. The orgasm hit me hard, and I lay there shaking and gasping for breath. Eventually he began to kiss his way back up my body.

It seemed like he spent forever on my breasts, kissing and suckling. Drawing him closer, I tipped my pelvis up in welcome, and he slid inside.

Julian sunk his hands in my hair and kissed me. Our kiss went on and on and his tongue began to keep time with his deliberate strokes. Slowly the tempo increased, and I began to shake as I felt a second orgasm begin to build. I dug my nails into his shoulders, clamped myself around him, and then it hit. I yanked my mouth away from his to scream in pleasure.

I held him close as our breathing began to even out and our hearts settled. "I love you," I whispered into his hair.

Shifting his weight onto his arms, he smiled down at me. "I love you."

I moved beneath him. He was still deep inside of me and hard. "Didn't you?" I asked.

"Angel." A playful smirk danced across his face. "I'm not finished with you yet."

"Ooh, are you gonna go all dark knight on me?" I smiled even as he took one of my hands and pressed it over my head until my fingertips touched the edge of the wooden headboard.

"And if I did?" His voice was deep, rumbly and made me shiver.

"You'd probably make me come again."

"You may want to hang on to something," he said, with a gleam in his eye.

It was all the warning I got, because Julian slammed his hips forward and I let out a happy shout in response.

"Oh, gods!" I managed to say as he yanked my legs up higher and hammered away.

The headboard began to thump against the wall of the cabin and my breath whooshed out in time with each of his deep thrusts. It was insane, it was rough, and it was absolutely amazing.

Julian reached completion with something that sounded like a battle cry, and he collapsed beside me. I lay there shaking, spent, and happily exhausted. He pulled me close to his side, I shut my eyes, yawned once, and was out.

I woke several hours later, naked and freezing cold. The palest of light was coming through the windows of the cabin. Checking the bedside clock, I saw it was six o'clock in the morning. Julian was snoring lightly and sleeping flat on his back. With a grin, I sat up and pulled a blanket from the foot of the bed up and over the both of us. I tried to go back to sleep but nature called, and I couldn't ignore a full bladder forever. Letting out a sigh, I rolled out of bed and staggered over to the bathroom.

When I finished, I was startled to see a tinge of pink on the toilet paper. I patted myself again and saw a bit more color, but considering how we'd gone after each other, I wasn't too surprised. The night before had left me a sticky mess, though. As I considered my reflection, I saw a few love marks on my throat and breasts. I ran a finger over one and discovered that my breasts were very tender.

Well, I reminded myself, he'd spent a lot of time on them last night. With a shrug, I turned the water on and got in the shower. The hot water sorted out my aches and pains and made me feel much better. I finished my shower and wrapped myself up in a big bath towel.

Then I patted my curly hair dry, put some leave-in conditioner on, and worked it through my hair. Once that was finished, I decided to make a big breakfast for the two of us. Something with lots of protein. We'd certainly earned it.

I drove into Williams Ford a few hours later happy yet wondering why in the hell the bacon and eggs we'd had for breakfast had left such a bad taste in my mouth. Without taking my eyes off the road, I patted around in my purse, found the inner zipper and pulled it open. Reaching my hand in, I quickly felt the roll of antacid I kept there and pulled it out. I popped a couple of tablets and chewed them up, hoping the mint would get rid of the bitter taste.

I was eager and looking forward to beginning working with *Magnolia Bridal and Events*. Maggie's business was booming, and I was excited to become a part of it.

***

The first week working with Maggie was an eye-opener. I took reams of notes, studied several different files filled with exquisitely detailed information on the spring weddings she was coordinating, and tried to memorize as much as I could. It wore me out to the point that I would head home in the evening, get through supper and go directly to bed.

By week two, I suppose all my hard work paid off,

because I was given a work cell phone and a stack of *Magnolia Bridal and Events* business cards with my name and work cell number on it. I also graduated from answering correspondence and placing follow-up calls and confirming dates with vendors to meeting with a bride and groom for a taste testing at *Charming Cakepops*.

I arrived at Candice's pretty bakery fifteen minutes early with a folder in hand. As I walked in, I gave a wave to Candice, who was working the front counter, and took a table by the window. Slipping my wool coat off, I draped it over the back of my chair and took a seat.

The bakery was all done in shades of pink and white. Overhead a hot pink chandelier shone down, and the scent of vanilla and chocolate hung in the air. My stomach made an unhappy growling noise. Considering my waistband was feeling uncomfortably tight today, I'd undone the top button of my slacks in the car. I tucked the fabric behind the zipper and was glad my pale green sweater was loose and in the tunic style—clearly all the holiday food and homemade cookies had gotten me.

Smoothing the tunic sweater over my lap, I went over the client information one more time. Bride: Lena. Groom: Kaleb. Their May wedding colors were pale yellow and navy blue. Yellow was the bride's favorite color, and that was reflected in the pastel yellow chiffon bridesmaids' dresses and the yellow roses and gerbera daisies the bride had requested for her bridal flowers.

"Hello, wedding consultant apprentice." Candice walked over. "Would you like something to drink? Tea, coffee or a soft drink?"

"Hi ya, Candice." I smiled. "Lemon lime soda, if you have it."

Candice detoured and plucked a bottle from a clear glass refrigerator. "Here you go."

I accepted the bottle, twisted the cap off, and sipped at it. "Thank you."

"I have the taste testing ready to go. Just as soon as the bride and groom get here, I'll bring everything out."

"Excellent." I tapped the papers together and slipped them back in my folder.

"Lena is leaning toward either vanilla or lemon for her cupcakes. However, the groom loves chocolate; and we want him to be happy as well."

"Absolutely." I nervously brushed a hand over the sleeve of my sweater.

"Candice?" George, Candice's handsome cake decorator popped his head out from the kitchen. "You have a phone call."

"Be right there!" Candice excused herself and went to take the call, and George came out to say hello.

"If it isn't my favorite red-head." He gave my hair a friendly tug. "How's the new job treating you?"

"George." I smiled up at him. "I love my new job and honestly, you get better looking every time I see you."

"Lies." He plopped down in the chair next to me. "Lie a little more."

"George, you are without a doubt one of the only men I know who could wear a bright pink apron and still look hot." I smiled and meant it. "How are you?"

"Well, you know me..." he said, settling his baker's hat over his dark hair. "I'm up to my elbows in buttercream and Swiss meringue. Meanwhile, the love of my life is looking for a second job, *again*. Managing the university theatre group doesn't pay Vincent nearly enough."

I perked up. I knew Vincent. He was quiet and somewhat broody, but he had done amazing things organizing the theater group. "Does Vincent have any administrative experience?" I asked.

George narrowed his eyes. "You'd be surprised. He spends more time doing paperwork, taking phone calls, and accounting than you could possibly imagine."

I drummed my fingers on the countertop. "How are his computer skills?"

"Terrific," George said.

"I happen to know of someone at the University who is looking for an executive assistant. It's a Monday through Friday job. Occasionally he might have to work an evening or two on a weekend, for bigger fundraisers and so forth."

"Really? Who is it?"

"Julian."

George blinked. "You're kidding."

"I'm very serious. Julian is going to need a full-time replacement now that I've left. He's got a temp for the time being, but he's not happy with them. I can pass along Julian's work number if you like. Tell Vincent to call him and to set up an interview."

George whipped his phone from his apron pocket. "I will. Give me that number, Red."

I gave him Julian's direct number at the museum and sent Julian a quick text on my personal phone to let him know to expect a call from Vincent.

"This is great!" George reached for my hand and gave it a squeeze. "Thanks for the tip, Holly."

"Of course," I said. The door to the bakery opened and I saw that my clients had arrived.

George stood immediately and greeted the couple. Lena and Kaleb joined me, and George slipped in the back. Candice came out a few moments later with a tray loaded with bottles of water, samples of cakes, fillings, and icing flavors.

We spent a pleasant half hour on the tasting, and the bride chose lemon cupcakes with a blueberry jam filling. The cupcakes were going to be topped with piped vanilla buttercream and a fresh blueberry. I expected the groom to push for chocolate, but once he tasted the blueberry filling with the lemon cake, he was sold. Lena asked me for my opinion, so I tried a sample as well. It was wonderful. At that first bite, my stomach growled loudly, and Candice chuckled, got up, and brought me a cupcake to eat to hold me over.

I'll have a salad for dinner, I decided, *and start a diet tomorrow.*

I made my notes and got a copy of their order from Candice. After, George came out with a small box filled with complimentary cakepops for the couple to take home. Then I handed the bride my new business card and was thrilled when she thanked me for my help.

The happy couple left, and I waved goodbye to Candice and George and headed for my car to return to the Drake mansion to fill Maggie in on how the taste testing had gone. I parked my car in the garage behind the mansion and started across the brick courtyard to the rear of the mansion. Slipping once on a patch of ice, I caught myself and slowed my pace down, making my way carefully through the melting snow.

The late January temperatures were above freezing today, and the sun was trying to peep through the clouds, but still, it felt like it was a million miles to walk through all the slush, ice, and snow. I heard my personal cell phone ring, and I dug it out while trying to juggle the folder and my purse, which seemed determined to slide off my shoulder.

Finally, I grabbed it. "Hello?"

"Holly Bishop?"

"It's Holly Drake, now," I said. "I'm recently married."

"Oh, well congratulations! This is Tracey from Dr. Anderson's office."

"Yes?" I frowned wondering why my gynecologist's

office would be calling me.

"We've had an issue with our computer system, and while it is now fixed, I'm sorry to inform you that you are several weeks behind for your next Depo shot."

I stopped dead in my tracks. "What?"

"You'll need to come in right away and get your birth control shot."

"Of course," I said. "Do you have any time today or tomorrow?"

"Let me check," the nurse said, as she tapped away at her computer. "You'll need to have a pregnancy test first, of course, just to be on the safe side."

It was as though her voice was far, far away. I shook my head and managed to croak out a single word. "*What*?"

"When was your last period?" she asked.

"Umm...I... Well, I'm not entirely sure." Stunned, I staggered over to the edge of a walled garden to sit down before I fell over. I sat right in the snow and didn't even care.

"Holly?"

I tried to think. "My periods are very light and irregular on the Depo shot," I said, and my voice sounded desperate to my own ears.

"That's normal," she said. "Are you having any pregnancy symptoms?"

My purse and the folder hit the ground with a splat. *Oh gods,* I thought as my breath began to hitch. *The tiredness, the weight gain. The nausea.* "I...I'm not sure.

Maybe."

"Holly." The nurse's voice was soft and kind. "I think you need to come in, right away."

"Okay." It took everything I had not to start bawling.

"Can you be here in an hour?" she asked.

I glanced at my phone and noted the time. The office was only a twenty-minute drive away. "I think I can."

"Perfect," she said. "Be sure to bring your photo ID and proof of insurance with you."

"Thank you," I said and disconnected the call.

I sat on the edge of the stone wall, in the snow, and stared blankly at the courtyard. Tears rolled down my face and my mind raced with all the horrible possibilities.

Pregnant? I couldn't be. Not after everyone assumed that's why we eloped. What would people say? Julian and I haven't even talked about having kids...and what if I miscarried again? There was that pink on the toilet paper the other morning. What if things were already going wrong? I couldn't tell Julian, only to get his hopes up and then disappoint him that way...

"But...I can't *not* tell him either." I whispered the words and began to sob.

I jumped almost a foot straight into the air when Diego appeared in my peripheral vision.

"Holly? What's wrong?" he asked, rushing toward me.

"Diego?" Confused at his sudden appearance, I tried to focus on him.

Diego reached down and took hold of my arms. "What has happened?"

"I can't go through this," I cried. "Not again."

"Go through what?"

Suddenly, the smell of motor oil from his mechanic's uniform hit me. I yanked my head away, and promptly threw up the soda, the cake samples, and the cupcake I'd eaten right into the snow.

Forty-five minutes later, I sat in the waiting room of the gynecologist's office with Diego. He'd had to change his clothes since I'd gotten him a bit when I'd thrown up. To his credit, he hadn't so much as flinched at my getting sick. In his quiet, no-nonsense way, he discreetly took me straight to the cottage, made me sit down, and called Julian.

Diego had given me some peppermint gum to get the sour taste from my mouth. Handing me some tissues, he'd told me to mop up my face and then personally drove me to the gynecologist's office. Julian was going to meet us there, so I could still make the appointment on time.

Of course, the doctor was running behind, and now I sat stiff, silent, and stressed out with my friend. I was trying not to panic, but I was absolutely terrified. "Thank you for coming with me," I whispered to him.

Diego slipped an arm around my shoulders and gave me a gentle squeeze. "I'd never drop you off to go in alone."

I tried to smile but more tears began to roll.

"It's going to be fine, Holly," he said. "Take this one step at a time."

I wiped my eyes with a tissue. "Sorry I babbled to you in the car on the ride over." *Babbled was a gentle euphemism,* I thought. *Truthfully, I was semi-hysterical.*

I had fallen apart all over him, and now Diego knew about my previous miscarriage. Cringing from embarrassment, I tried to apologize. "I'm very sorry, Diego, that I threw up on you and carried on that way."

He patted my shoulder. "I'm tough. I can take it. Nina threw up every morning for two months straight when she carried Isabel."

"Don't," I shuddered. "I can't even go there right now."

"Were you this sick the last time?" he asked very quietly.

"No. Not like this," I whispered.

"That's a good sign that there's lots of baby hormones doing their thing in there."

"Do you truly think so?"

"Have a little faith, *Mija.*"

Julian rushed into the lobby, spotted us, and walked quickly over.

Diego stood. "They're running behind."

Julian nodded. "Thank you for bringing her in, and for waiting with her."

"Of course. It's what family does for one another." Diego smiled. "I'm going to give you two some privacy now. Nina doesn't know that I brought her in. I'll keep it that way. Call me later and let me know how it goes."

"We will," Julian said as Diego walked away.

Julian sat beside me and put his arm around my shoulders. "Are you all right, Angel?"

"No," I managed to say before more tears began to fall. "I'm terrified."

"Holly Drake?" A nurse called my name.

I stood quickly. Julian reached for my hand, and we went in together.

CHAPTER SIX

The pregnancy test was positive. Fortunately, I was sitting down when they gave us the news because I would have probably fallen over otherwise. As it was, I recoiled so hard that the nurse and Julian reached out to steady me at the same time.

I sat mutely as the nurse launched into a cheerful speech of congratulations, followed by the offer to do an immediate standard baby ultrasound so they could ascertain how far along I was. Looking to Julian, I was unsure of what to do next, half thrilled and half terrified at the prospect of actually seeing *something*.

The last time I'd been pregnant, I'd never made it to having an ultrasound. And that thought kept circling in my mind as we were ushered into the ultrasound room and waited for the tech. I laid there on my back with my pants unbuttoned and my underwear pushed down to my hips while she squirted some cold goo across my abdomen. She chatted away while cheerfully explaining the procedure.

"Okay..." She smiled at me. "Here we go." The monitor was rotated towards her and away from us as she worked. She narrowed her eyes at the screen and I saw her nod when she shifted the transducer to a different section of my belly. Then her entire expression changed. Shifting the transducer back again to the original spot, she quickly turned off the monitor.

"What's wrong?" I asked.

She patted my leg. "Sit tight for a moment, Holly. I'd like the doctor to come in." Then she left the room in haste.

"Oh no." I started to shake in fear.

"Angel." Julian rose from the chair he'd been sitting in and leaned over so we were face to face. "Breathe. Don't jump to conclusions."

"It must be bad," I whispered. "Did you see her face?"

"Hello, Mr. and Mrs. Drake." Dr. Anderson strolled right in and was all smiles. My obstetrician was an attractive woman in her mid-fifties. "The ultrasound tech noticed something surprising, and she'd like me to take a look."

"It's not a viable pregnancy," I blurted out. "I miscarried again, didn't I?"

"Holly," Dr. Anderson said, "I'm going to need you to try and stay calm."

Julian hitched his chair closer to my side, sat again, and we held onto each other's hands for dear life.

The tech went right to work and was looking intently

at the screen. Soon the doctor joined her and they both studied the monitor, which was still twisted away from us.

I clamped onto Julian's fingers. "I'm so sorry," I said to him and began to cry in earnest.

"Hey." My doctor patted my leg. "There's definitely a baby on board, we simply want to take a closer look and see everything that's going on in there."

"There's a live baby?" I asked through my tears.

Beside me, Julian released the breath he'd been holding.

"There sure is," the doctor said as the tech continued with the ultrasound. "We're currently taking some measurements. I'll show you both in a moment."

Julian pressed a kiss to my hand as I clutched his.

"Breathe, Holly." Dr. Anderson winked at us both. "Nice deep breaths. You're both going to want to start practicing that." I gave a watery laugh and Julian passed me a nearby box of tissues.

"Okay." My doctor rotated the screen towards us. "Look here," she said, pointing to the screen. "This baby is measuring at eight weeks and five days. You can see the leg and arm buds. There's the head, and see how it's moving around?"

"Oh my goddess," I said through fresh tears.

"Then..." The ultrasound tech moved the transducer. "We have a *second* baby."

"*What?*" Julian and I exclaimed simultaneously.

Doctor Anderson chuckled. "We're calling this one

Baby B, and like its twin, it is measuring the same gestational age, and we can also see the head, arm and leg buds."

"Twins," Julian said as a huge grin spread across his face. "Are you sure?"

"Well, I keep looking for another," the tech said cheekily. "But I'm only seeing two so far."

"Correct me if I'm wrong," the doctor said smoothly. "You are a fraternal twin yourself, aren't you, Holly?"

"Yes, I am." All I could was stare as the tech moved the transducer again and both babies appeared on the monitor at the same time. While I heard the tech say she was taking pictures for us, I wasn't paying attention to her words. I was transfixed at the image of two tiny babies inside of me. They were both wriggling around, and I started crying all over again when they turned up the volume so we could hear the heartbeats.

The tech asked Julian if he'd like to record this on his cell phone and my suave, smooth husband dropped his phone in his haste to take it out of his jacket pocket. But he was able to get the video. They took a ton of measurements and pictures, and Julian had quite a few photos on his phone of Baby A and Baby B too.

"When can we find out gender?" Julian asked.

"Around the twentieth week mark," Doctor Anderson replied. "If Holly wants to."

"Do you want to find out the gender?" Julian asked me.

"Yes," I said, trying to stay positive for his sake.

Please let me stay pregnant, I thought desperately. But after seeing those babies, I was terrified on a whole new level that I'd lose them.

Once they were done with the ultrasound, they printed out a roll of photos for us, and the doctor asked us to come in her office for a chat.

We made a follow up appointment for later in the week. I was encouraged to begin prenatal vitamins and given a stack of paperwork to read and forms to fill out. Julian took all the paperwork and promised to take care of it. I asked the doctor lots of questions, especially since I'd miscarried before. By the time we left, the office was empty. It seemed we'd been the last patients of the day.

I rolled up all of the ultrasound photos and put them in my purse. Julian took my hand and we walked together to his car. Neither of us spoke; I think we were both shocked.

As I sat in the car for a moment, I stared blindly out the windshield.

"Angel." Julian's voice had me jumping. "Put your seatbelt on."

"Oh." I fumbled for the seatbelt. "Sorry."

I managed to buckle up, and when I lifted my eyes Julian had leaned across and was close to my face. "You're terrified," he said. It was a statement not a question.

"As in...there's no spit in my mouth," I admitted.

"We will get through this pregnancy together, one

day at a time."

I blew out a long breath.

"I know you are scared, but you heard what Dr. Anderson told us. The babies look good, their heartbeats are strong, and you are healthy."

"I barely made it to seven weeks when I miscarried before."

"That was five years ago," Julian said, and dropped a soft kiss on my mouth. "And besides, the babies will be nine weeks along in just two more days."

I tried to slow my breathing down. "That's true."

"I figured we conceived on our honeymoon," Julian said thoughtfully. "Or right afterward, maybe around Thanksgiving."

Mutely, I nodded. Dr. Anderson had also said a due date of mid to late August. My heart skipped a beat. I couldn't even let myself think that far ahead.

"I can't wait to call Diego and Nina," he said and started the car.

I placed a restraining hand on his arm. "Julian, I don't want to tell anyone for a while."

"Why?" He frowned.

"Most women wait until they are in the second trimester to make any announcements." I waited a beat before I added, "Most miscarriages occur in the first trimester, Julian. I still have to get through the next four weeks without anything going wrong."

"Not *I*," he said. "We. *We* will get through the next four weeks. And all the weeks after that. Together,

Angel."

I managed to work up a smile for him.

"This pregnancy was certainly a surprise for the both of us," he said.

"That's putting it mildly."

"But I believe that everything happens for a reason."

I let my head fall back against the headrest. He reached for my hand, and held it for the drive back to the cabin.

Julian did speak to Diego. He simply told him that we were pregnant, but nothing about the twins. Diego completely understood that we wouldn't be making any announcements until the second trimester. He promised to keep the news to himself and wished us well.

I was sitting on the couch at the cabin when Julian finished the conversation. "Diego says that you should try and rest."

"He is simply one of the best men I've ever known," I said. "Diego didn't even flinch when I threw up on him out in the courtyard."

Julian chuckled at that.

"He listened to me fall apart when he drove me to the doctor's," I said, "and he stayed totally calm and cool. We're so blessed to have him as a friend."

"Yes, we are," Julian agreed.

"I swear, if things work out, I want him to be a godparent."

Julian grinned. "Nina too. I'd like to return the honor they gave to me."

I yawned and closed my eyes. "That's right. You're Isabel's godfather."

He sat beside me and put an arm around my shoulders. "They named her after me too. Her middle name is Julianna."

I laid my head on his shoulder. "Hopefully, we'll be able to have a discussion about names in a few more months."

Julian pressed a kiss against my hair. "Have a little faith, Angel."

My eyes began to droop. "That's what Diego told me in the waiting room." I rested my hands over my abdomen. "Only he called me *Mija*."

"It's an endearment," Julian said. "Something you'd call a close female friend, or even a daughter."

"I thought so." I left my hands over my belly, and it eased my anxiety a bit.

Julian stood and scooped me up from the couch. "I'm taking you to bed, Angel."

I smiled. "I'm not really up for a romp at the moment, Julian."

He dropped a kiss on my nose. "To rest. I'm going to tuck you in and as soon as you're settled, I'm going to start on that mountain of paperwork from the doctor's office."

***

The next morning, I got up slowly. I felt light-headed

and queasy, but I desperately needed to pee. Afterward, I patted myself and checked the toilet paper for any blood. There was none. I blew out a relieved breath and jolted when I saw Julian standing in the doorway.

"Everything okay?" he asked gently.

"No spotting," I said and went to wash my hands and then to brush my teeth.

He nodded. "How are you feeling this morning?"

I spit toothpaste in the sink. "Kind of dizzy and while I'm hungry, my stomach is not acting too sure about food at the moment."

"How about a cup of tea?" Julian suggested. "Dr. Anderson said decaffeinated black tea or peppermint tea was fine." He held my fuzzy robe out for me, and I bundled myself into it.

"I think I have some peppermint tea in the cupboard. Let's try that."

Julian escorted me to the kitchen island, and I sat on a barstool. In a few minutes he had hot water in a mug and handed me the box of tea. I dunked in the tea bag and swung my foot back and forth. My stomach growled, so I hopped up to make myself a piece of toast.

"Sit down, Angel. I can get whatever you need."

I ignored that and opened the cupboard. "I'm not an invalid. I can manage to drop some bread into the toaster."

"I want you to promise me that you won't overdo it," he said. "No heavy lifting or climbing on ladders."

I rolled my eyes. "And here I was going to rearrange all the furniture in the cabin and take up mountain climbing."

He gave me a doleful stare.

I grabbed the toast when it popped up and bit in. "Does this mean I can't go skiing on my lunch break?"

He crossed his arms over his chest.

"I can compromise. The giant slalom would be fun." I slanted a look over at him. "Or snowboarding. I bet I could do a Frontside 360."

"That smart mouth is going to get you into trouble one of these days."

I sighed. "Julian I am already extremely anxious about all of this. Trust me. I won't do *anything* to risk this pregnancy."

"I know that," he said, rubbing his hand across my shoulders. "The anxiety is radiating off of you. Try and relax. The stress isn't good for you or the babies."

He was right about that, and so I didn't bother to argue. "I'll try to work on the stress." My stomach growled loudly. "Hey, do we have any of that instant oatmeal left?"

He opened a cabinet to check. "We do. Sit down with your toast and I'll make it for you."

I sat none too graciously. "You know you can't continue to wait on me hand and foot for the next thirty weeks or so."

"Watch me," he said, straight faced.

I sipped my tea and let loose a very loud sigh.

He ignored that. "Today, I'll drive you into town and drop you off at the mansion."

I did a double take. "I am perfectly capable of driving myself to work."

"You said you felt dizzy earlier," he pointed out. "I would feel better if I drove you in to work with Maggie today."

I dropped my head into my hands.

"I'll pick you up at four."

"There's no need to hover." I scowled. "You don't normally leave the museum until five."

"That's all about to change." He shrugged. "Get used to my hovering, Angel."

Since the oatmeal seemed okay on my stomach, I went to get dressed for the day only to encounter another surprise. All of my other dress slacks were also uncomfortably tight at the waist. While I didn't have a "bump," my waist was definitely bigger.

"I can't believe it," I said to him.

"What?" he asked and sat on the edge of our bed.

"I can't do the top button on any of my dress pants."

"Really?" He grinned at the news.

I scowled at him. "How will we keep the pregnancy private if I'm already showing?"

Julian reached out and pulled me close. He seemed as thrilled about the discovery, as I was concerned. "You're almost nine weeks pregnant with twins." He settled me on his lap. "I'm not surprised your waistband is tight. I read an article last night online about twin pregnancy weight gain as opposed to singletons."

"You did?"

Julian pressed a kiss to my hair. "Remember, the doctor told us that gaining a pound per week in the first trimester was not only typical but encouraged for good fetal development."

I made sure that when I spoke my voice was calm. "Julian let's not get ahead of ourselves. Anything can happen."

"Do I need to repeat myself?" he said. "Have some faith, Angel."

I shut my eyes at his gentle rebuke. "I'm trying."

He reached over for a kiss, and it was soft and comforting. I relaxed against him, and we sat like that together for a while.

I ended up wearing a pair of leggings and another tunic style sweater to work. Once I arrived at the mansion, I took a good grip on the elaborately carved wooden handrail before starting up the stairs toward the third floor. My stomach gave one hard flip thinking of how I'd been jogging up and down those stairs for the past two weeks. Images of falling filled my brain, forcing me to stop and breathe my way through the anxiety attack.

On gaining the third floor, I made every attempt to appear to be casually strolling down the hall. I could hear Maggie's voice as I approached the rooms that she made into a home office. Taking a second, I put a smile on my face and walked in with a wave for my boss.

Maggie was holding baby Phillip in one arm while he snoozed and speaking into the phone at the same time. She tucked the phone under her ear and waved at me as she finished her conversation. "Absolutely," she said, "I have it added to my calendar that either myself or my associate will accompany your daughter and her bridesmaids in two weeks while they choose their attendants' dresses."

I went and hung up my coat and placed my lunch in the mini fridge across the room. After tucking my purse in my desk drawer, I sat down at my desk and booted up my computer. When it was ready, I pulled up the file with the bridal schedule and waited to add the appointment for the fitting, as soon as Maggie had finished.

Maggie ended her call. "Good morning," she said cheerfully.

I smiled. "I have the calendar open. Which bridal party is going to be choosing their dresses?"

"The Emily Smythe and Ron Jonas wedding," Maggie said.

I turned back around to enter in the information. "Found it," I said.

"There's three bridesmaids and one maid of honor," Maggie added.

I glanced back. "Four in total? Didn't there used to be two bridesmaids?"

Maggie nodded her head in agreement. "And heaven help us, the bride also keeps changing her mind on the colors of the dresses."

"I thought Emily was leaning towards purple?"

"True," Maggie said. "However, she can't decide what shade of purple. This is going to be a *long* seven months until August."

I flinched at her words and the unintended double entendre. Hard enough that I knocked over the cup holding the pens and pencils on my desk. "Oops," I said and began to straighten it all up.

"I may have you take point on their August wedding," Maggie was saying. "That gives you plenty of time to ease your way into the whole process."

I gulped even as my stomach churned. If things worked out, I'd be very pregnant with twins in August. There'd be no way I could be in charge of that wedding. Twins typically came early, even I knew that. A bead of nervous sweat rolled down my back.

"I'm going to go lay Phillip down in his portacrib." She stood with the sleepy baby in her arms. "Be right back."

Maggie went into an adjoining room to lay the baby down for a nap, and guilt all but smothered me. I'd started a new job not knowing I was pregnant. While I had to fight the urge to confide in my cousin, I simply could not bring myself to do it.

***

February arrived and with it came snow showers and

extreme cold. I had my first OB visit, and my doctor was pleased with my progress. For the next two weeks nausea was my constant companion, not to mention the fatigue. I started going to bed as soon as dinner was over and found that if I slept propped up, I didn't feel quite so bad. Julian ordered one of those bed lounge pillows with the arms for me, and that made me more comfortable.

I did my best to learn everything about *Magnolia Bridal and Events* as possible. Julian ended up hiring Vincent to be his new executive assistant, and he was pleased with how things were working with him in the office. Margaret was now staying away from Julian altogether, which I was happy to hear, and Julian informed me that Vincent was learning the ropes quickly. I was sure that with Vincent already knowing so many people at the university, it made it easier for him to adapt to a new office.

I ended up dropping by the museum offices one afternoon to pick up Julian for lunch and waved at Vincent, who was working away at his computer. Seeing that he had a human skull on his desk and was using it as a paperweight, I drew up short.

It was fake—a prop from the theater's production of *Hamlet*—I was told. But Vincent swore it was his lucky charm. "Keeps the hag from HR away from me," he said, completely straight faced.

"Ah," I said. "You've met Margaret."

Vincent straightened his horn-rimmed glasses. "The

beige banshee."

"By the goddess." I pressed my fingers to my lips, trying to squelch down a snicker.

"I hope I haven't offended you," Vincent said. He tried to look repentant but didn't quite pull it off.

"Honestly, Vincent?" I said. "That comment only makes me like you better."

Julian came out from his office, and Vincent waved us off. "Get out of here you two."

The days ticked by. It was a strange sort of limbo to be in. Every day I half-expected something to go wrong, but so far it hadn't. My nausea was better some days, and worse others. The fatigue was tough to deal with and my breasts were swollen and very tender.

Julian researched some pregnancy hacks and discovered a trick where women took a stretchy ponytail holder, threaded it through the buttonhole on their slacks, and looped it over the button. By leaving the zipper partially undone, the new stretchy waistband would give you some extra room, still allowing you to wear your slacks until true maternity pants were needed. It worked pretty well, too. To cover it all up, I ordered some more tunic style tops and long sweaters to wear to work. I ordered up a cup size in bras too and paid extra to get everything shipped to me as quickly as possible.

I still had lots of anxiety about something going horribly wrong. It also worried me that Julian would be upset that I was usually too tired to make love. Even though I felt rough, I missed the intimacy, and that confused the hell out of me.

Really, I just missed us. I missed the spontaneity of diving after each other and going at it, any time and anywhere we wanted. It was doubtful there was any place in the cabin that we hadn't "christened," so to speak.

But Julian never complained. Instead, he tried to make me as comfortable as possible, with flannel sheets, soft fuzzy blankets on our bed, and simply holding me at night. Through it all Julian was wonderful, but he also never made any advances. He was attentive and thoughtful, but there was nothing sexual about it at all. It annoyed the hell out of me, even though I wasn't up for romance. I told myself—I sincerely hoped, anyway—that all my mixed emotions were probably from the raging hormones.

Julian began reading pregnancy and baby books and I purposefully avoided them. At least I tried to. But I was curious, and one evening before he came home from the museum, I made the mistake of looking at the chapter on multiples and what to expect during a twin pregnancy.

If I wasn't afraid before, I was absolutely terrified now. There were so many things that could go wrong with multiples—especially if they shared the same amniotic sac. Reading that chapter brought on a shaking, heart pounding, sweating, panic attack. It got so bad that I ended up racing to the bathroom and throwing up. Afterward, I hung over the toilet and cried.

Julian found me sitting on the bathroom floor and I could see by his expression that I'd truly frightened him. Once he realized I'd only been sick, and that nothing else was wrong, he helped me clean up and then we sat together on the couch and had a long talk.

He reminded me that the doctor had told us the twins each had their own amniotic sac. In fact, he pulled out the ultrasound photos and pointed out to me the two separate babies and sacs. He rattled off more information and it had me goggling at him.

"How in the hell do you remember all of that?"

"Angel, the tech told us, *and* the doctor went over it all again in her office. Don't you remember?"

"No," I admitted. "I don't think I heard most of what they said. My brain sort of shut down, and fear took over. I don't remember too much about the appointment at all. It's mostly a blur."

"You could have reviewed the ultrasound photos."

I shook my head. "I haven't looked at them. Not since the first day."

"Why?" he asked.

"Because it will only hurt more if I lose them," I said, starting to cry again. "I don't want to disappoint you by not being able to carry the babies to term. You'd hate me if anything happened."

"No, I would not," he said firmly.

"Well, *I'd* hate me," I cried. "What about Maggie? I don't want to let her down. She hired me to help with her business, and what if I can't do everything she needs me to do? Carry things, or haul boxes... What if they put me on bed rest? What if—"

"Angel." He gave a quiet sigh.

His sigh totally pissed me off. In a flash I was boiling angry. "We haven't even made love since we found out about the pregnancy. You don't want me anymore, do you?"

"I want you more than you could possibly imagine."

"And I'm supposed to know that how? The doctor said there were no restriction on us having sex."

"I thought you didn't remember what the doctor said?"

"I managed to remember *that*." I poked his shoulder. "I would think as long as we don't swing from the chandelier, we'd be okay."

"Damn," he said mildly, "there goes my plans for Valentine's Day."

I glared. "Are you making fun of me?"

"No." He took my hands and pressed a kiss to the back of each. "I only wanted to let you rest. You've been exhausted or nauseous around the clock. I was trying to be considerate."

I shut my eyes. He was being so kind, and I was acting like a lunatic. "I'm sorry. I'm so moody. It's like being on a rollercoaster." Covering my face with my hands, I began to cry all over again.

Julian pulled me into his arms and held on. "You need to talk to someone about your fears—your doctor or a therapist."

I only cried harder because he was right. I needed help. The constant swing of emotions was brutal, and the fear was eating me alive. "I can't talk to my family, for so many reasons..." I hiccupped as the words spilled out of me. "Only you and Autumn know that I miscarried years ago when I was still in college..."

"Autumn had a rough start when she was pregnant with Erin and Emma. She *will* understand."

I managed a watery smile. "I hope so. I can't imagine what Ivy will say. Or Bran. Especially considering that he asked if the reason we eloped was because I got pregnant."

"When did that happen?" Julian demanded.

"On Thanksgiving."

"You never told me."

"I meant to but there was all that gossip and venom at the office. All those people whispering that I'd trapped you into marriage, or insinuating I had morning sickness..." I sat straight up. "Well, shit. The joke's on me. I probably was pregnant. Only we didn't know it yet."

"Angel, we didn't conceive until *after* we were married," Julian pointed out.

I wiped my eyes. "I doubt anyone would believe us. Everyone will think I'm much farther along because of the twins. Oh gods, what will your father say? He wasn't thrilled with us eloping—"

My stomach cramped and I jumped up and raced for

the bathroom. I made it with seconds to spare and had a lovely round of dry heaves. There was nothing left to come up.

Julian was right there sitting on the floor beside me. Once the heaving stopped, he stroked my hair away from my face. "All of this stress is making you sick."

"I can't even argue with that," I said, leaning back against him. We sat there on the bathroom floor, Julian behind me and holding me upright. I rested my head against his shoulder and tried to breathe normally.

"Let me call Dr. Anderson and see what she recommends," he said, rubbing my back.

"Okay," I said and burrowed closer for comfort.

Once I was sure I was done heaving, Julian scooped me up and carried me to bed. He called the doctor and I dozed off while he spoke to her. Eventually he came to bed himself, and I turned to him wanting to make love, but instead he held me tenderly and told me to rest.

He held me all night and his presence was truly comforting. Eventually he fell asleep, and I lay there and agonized about why he didn't seem to want to make love anymore.

Then again, could I really blame him? Between the heaving, the crying, and the mood swings I was a hot mess. But still, we normally had sex all of the time: wild sex, crazy sex, intense heart pounding sex. Would that type of intensity even be possible anymore now that I was pregnant with twins? If the pregnancy was successful, would it only push us further apart?

Another nasty thought intruded, and it made my heart thud hard against my ribs. *What if sex was all we had between us?*

If that was gone, what would be left?

***

Two days later, I was sitting in the waiting room at the office of a therapist.

Nervous and somewhat embarrassed to be there, my stomach roiled, and I pulled a bag of mini pretzels from my purse and began to nibble on one. I somehow managed to keep myself from bursting into tears in the waiting room, but it wasn't easy.

Julian signed us in at the receptionist's desk and took a seat beside me.

"So," I said quietly as he sat, "did you sacrifice a chicken or something to get an appointment this quickly?"

He jolted and turned a laugh into a cough. "Angel," he began.

"I was wondering," I said around a pretzel, "if poppets and pins were involved."

"Holly—"

"It's going to be tough to work with a therapist if they're under an enchantment, Julian."

He covered my hand with his. "I understand you are using humor to cope with the stress—"

"It's either that or I start the ever-delightful hormone

induced sobbing again." I eyeballed a water cooler across the waiting room. "Maybe I could blow that up instead."

Julian raised an eyebrow at my snark. He was on the verge of saying something in response, but they called out our name and we went back to see the therapist together.

I hadn't expected it to help, but getting all of my fears and worries off my chest, dumping it all on the table, and getting it out in the open made me feel substantially better.

The therapist assured me that any anxiety and fear that I had about my pregnancy was *okay* and *normal*. She told me to give myself some grace and to enjoy each day that I was pregnant. Yes, anyone would be a tad nervous about carrying twins, but I couldn't let that worry take over my entire life or rob me of enjoying the experience.

After the session, I tried to take her advice to heart and threw myself into working with Maggie, managing to hide how rotten I felt. I did begin to get some very interesting side-eye from Nina whenever I saw her at the mansion. She didn't ask me anything outright, but she did tell me that whenever I was ready to talk, she would be available to listen.

Maggie, bless her, was so busy training me for *Magnolia Bridal and Events* that she didn't seem to notice anything different. Well, that, and she was still sleep deprived from baby Phillip.

Thomas, Julian's father, watched me closely, which was unnerving since I saw him almost every day. Typically, it was when I was either sitting behind my desk, or arriving or leaving, and was wearing my winter coat. It was excellent camouflage. I was usually granted a polite smile and nod in acknowledgment, with an occasional reminder to 'drive safe' as I left for the day.

It wasn't hard to lay low with my family. I hadn't seen or heard from Ivy since her wedding day, Bran and Lexie still weren't speaking to me, and while Autumn texted me often, I understood that she and Duncan were busy with their girls and their lives.

Two more weeks passed, and I was beginning my second trimester. By some miracle I'd made it to the thirteen weeks mark. I was still nauseous, but not as much as I had been. I'd learned to nibble on crackers or pretzels throughout the day. It helped and it seemed my stomach was less upset if I kept something in it.

I was definitely starting to show. All of the sudden my belly had "popped," which delighted Julian. I did my best to conceal it and had graduated to mostly wearing a size bigger in leggings and very loose or flowing tops and tunic sweaters.

The afternoon before my second ultrasound, a pretty snow began to fall. It was soft and puffy and stuck to the roads right away. I guessed Julian hadn't realized the snow was coming in so soon, otherwise he would have blown up my phone and told me not to drive. Regardless, I slowed down on my drive home, taking my time, but was relieved when I pulled down the long gravel drive to the cabin. I drove around to the back and parked the car.

Almost as if it had waited, the snow began dumping in earnest now that I was home. Cotton-ball sized snowflakes were falling thick and fast. Relieved that I could soon put my feet up, I climbed out, taking my things with me.

I pushed my knit hat down over my head, shut the car door, and stopped to appreciate the pretty snowfall. Tipping my face up to the sky, I laughed at the huge snowflakes that landed on my face. "Gorgeous," I breathed.

I hoped it wouldn't snow too much and make the roads tricky tomorrow. The last thing I needed was more stress before my OB appointment. Now that I was in the second trimester, I was looking forward to speaking to the doctor about what to expect next. I had started to feel tiny flutters. It was probably wishful thinking, but maybe it was the babies. I wasn't sure when that started.

After freaking myself out once before, I refused to read the baby books, or search online, or to put one of those pregnancy apps on my phone because it only added to my anxiety. I *had,* however, managed to start looking at our ultrasound pictures from four weeks ago. The therapist had encouraged me to, and it was comforting.

I felt another flutter, like butterfly wings on the

inside, and it made me wonder about the twins. Were they both boys, both girls, or one of each?

As I glanced over at the surrounding trees, I thought about how I truly loved it here, deep in the woods. Far enough away from town that we had our privacy, it was so quiet that I could hear the snow hitting the roof of the cabin and the ground. I began to walk toward the cabin when movement within the trees had me pausing. I froze in shock as a miracle stepped daintily into the clearing on the far side of the cabin.

"A white hind," I gasped.

I stood transfixed as a white doe began to graze on the winter grass at the edge of our yard. She was close enough that I saw she was, in fact, a piebald whitetail deer.

She was almost entirely white with only a small patch of brown on her side. The doe's eyes were dark and very intelligent as she regarded me from across the clearing.

Seeing a white deer was a rare and magickal thing. A white doe or stag—traditionally called a hind or a hart — were symbols of hope, inspiration, and miracles. This sighting was a blessing from the oldest of the gods. Slowly, I bowed my head in respect to the beautiful gift I'd been given.

After a moment, I lifted my eyes expecting the doe to be gone. But she remained, nibbling on a few tufts of grass. I stayed where I was, watching as she continued to graze, and the snow fell all around me.

And for the first time since I'd found out I was pregnant, I felt hope.

Hope, I thought as I felt another flutter. If one of the babies was a girl, I'd definitely use that for a middle name.

CHAPTER SEVEN

By the time Julian came home, the white hind was gone, except for the hoof prints left behind in the snow. The next afternoon rolled around, and Julian left the museum a bit early to pick me up from the mansion. While I was still nervous, it wasn't as severe as the last two visits.

The checkup went well, and the ultrasound was more enjoyable instead of stressful this time. The babies' heartbeats were strong, and the tech measured each baby, telling us they were basically the same size. They were fraternal twins and were moving around a *lot,* but the ultrasound tech managed to get pictures of Baby A's and Baby B's profile.

Julian blew his sophisticated, composed image and fumbled his phone again. When it bounced noisily off the floor, I saw that his hands were shaking from excitement. It made me only love him more. Eventually, he was able to make another recording on his cell phone, and the tech printed out a bunch of photos for us, saying that everything looked perfect. She even gave me a hug as we left. We would see her again in four to five weeks, when we should be able to determine gender.

When I had spoken to Dr. Anderson at my appointment, I asked about whether or not it was safe for us to have sex. She said yes, and advised that since my belly had popped, that we try different positions so that I would be more comfortable. She followed that up with the caveat that if I noticed any spotting or had cramping after sex, to let her know immediately. She also asked how my therapy was going, and I admitted that I still had some rough days, but for the most part, I was doing better.

Julian and I left the doctor's office hand in hand, bundled up against the blustery wind. March might have been around the corner, but the breeze was bitterly cold.

Julian gave my gloved fingers a squeeze. "You have the most beautiful smile."

I turned my head to look at him. "I don't think I've stopped smiling since we saw the babies on the ultrasound."

"I know." He grinned. "Me either."

We walked to the car and climbed in. While we waited for the car to warm up, we studied all of our new photos. "They're beautiful," I said, "and I bet they're both girls."

"Probably," Julian agreed. "Also, I think Baby B has

your nose."

That made me chuckle. "We can't tell who they look like at this stage. I was just thrilled to see them moving around so much. No wonder I've been feeling flutters."

"I can't wait to feel them kick," he said.

"I think that won't be too far off." I took a deep breath before I continued. "Hey, Julian?"

"Yes, Angel?"

I glanced up from the ultrasound photos and met his eyes. "It's time to tell the family."

His whole face lit up. "I'd like to start with my father."

"Agreed. Can we arrange to have Maggie and Wyatt and Nina and Diego there and tell them all at the same time?"

He reached over and planted a kiss on me. "Yes. Let's make it tonight."

"Okay," I said. "Here's hoping Maggie won't be upset when I tell her I won't be able to take point for the August wedding on the schedule."

Julian patted my hand reassuringly. "She'll be thrilled for us. You'll see."

"Nina's going to be pissed that Diego has known about this for a month and never said anything."

"Well," Julian said. "He didn't know *all* of it."

I couldn't help but laugh. "True."

"I'm going to need to send a few texts." He pulled his phone out and began to fire off messages. While he did, my stomach growled, loudly.

He raised a single eyebrow at the sound. "Hungry, Angel?"

"Starving," I said as he finished up sending a group text. "I want a cheeseburger and sweet potato fries."

"I can make that happen," he said and began to back out of the parking space.

We stopped for an early supper at the diner where Nina and Diego used to work.

"I'd like to tell Autumn and Duncan tonight too," I told him after we had ordered. "Maybe we can go over to their house after we tell all the inmates at the mansion?"

"*Inmates*? Don't let my father hear you say that." He laughed. "I have a clever idea for how we can segue into telling Duncan and Autumn about the twins."

"What's that?"

"I'll tell Duncan I need his advice on expanding the cabin."

"That's a sneaky way to start the conversation. I love it."

"But practical," he pointed out as our food arrived. "We are going to have to expand if we want to stay at the cabin after the twins arrive."

"I hadn't thought that far ahead," I admitted, "but you're right."

"Do you want to stay at the cabin or look for a different house?" he asked.

I didn't even have to think about it. "I want to stay at the cabin. I love it there."

"So do I," he agreed.

While we ate, we talked over some ideas for expanding the cabin. Julian wondered about adding a two-story addition. Which would—in theory—give us a primary suite and an office on the top floor, with two more bedrooms and another bathroom on the main floor.

"With the bed out of the main space, the great room would feel much bigger," I said, dunking my fries in a honey mustard dipping sauce.

"We could push the island farther out and into the main room," he said, "making the kitchen larger while we're at it."

We kicked around some plans for the expansion, but soon realized we would truly need Duncan's expertise and advice. It would be a big project. While we talked, I devoured all of the sweet potato fries, and most of the cheeseburger.

I hadn't eaten so much in weeks, and I sat back with a satisfied sigh. "The kids were starving," I said, folding my hands over my bump.

From across the booth, Julian's eyes flashed to mine.

"What?" I asked, concerned at the intensity in his gaze.

"You have no idea what it does to me, hearing you speak about the twins with so much hope and happiness in your voice."

"Oh yeah?" I leaned across the booth and took his hand. "I suddenly remember what we did right after the last time we ate at this diner."

A slow smile spread across his face. "It was the first time I took you to the cabin."

I entwined my fingers with his. "Do we have enough time to take a 'detour'..." I wiggled my eyebrows. "... before we go see you father?"

Julian glanced at his watch. "Unfortunately, no."

"Well, let's get this show on the road." I began to scoot out from the booth.

Julian was waiting for me and helped me put my coat back on.

He even tried to button it up.

"It won't button anymore." I laughed.

He stopped at the second button. "It's too tight at the waist."

"Yeah," I said. "I've been leaving it unbuttoned."

He gave my belly a pat. "We'll have to see about getting you a larger coat."

I jumped in surprise at him patting my belly in public. It was so sweet that it made me want to cry.

He simply tucked my hand in the crook of his arm. "I love you," he said.

I squeezed his arm. "You'd better."

When we arrived at the Drake mansion everyone was gathered in the family room. It was a gorgeous room, huge, with a trio of leather sofas and more club chairs all arranged in a way that encouraged conversation. As we entered, Willow was chasing Isabel around the furniture and Diego was sitting in a chair and discussing classic cars with Thomas. Nina was sitting with her feet up on a hassock and sipping a glass of wine, while Wyatt was feeding the baby a bottle and Maggie was valiantly trying to get the girls to settle down.

"Hello," Julian said.

"Good evening," Thomas said.

"Hi!" Isabel made a beeline for her godfather.

Julian scooped her up and she threw her arms around his neck. In response, he gave her a noisy kiss on the cheek, making her giggle. He set her down and she was off in a second.

"Hey, ya'll," Maggie said. "What's up?"

It took everything I had not to fidget or to pull at the hem of my tunic sweater.

"Come in, have a seat." Thomas gestured to the room, and Julian and I went and sat on one of the sofas together. I immediately reached for Julian's hand.

The only person I was comfortably able to make eye contact with was Diego. He gave me the slightest of nods and an encouraging smile. Out of my peripheral, I saw Nina narrow her eyes in suspicion.

"Holly and I have some news," Julian began.

"What sort of news?" Thomas' eyebrows rose as the room collectively held its breath.

My heart began to beat harder in my chest. Thomas had not taken the news of our marriage well at all. How he would react to the news that he was about to become a grandfather was anybody's guess. While he adored children, I knew that he still didn't approve of me.

Julian smiled. "Last month Holly and I were given a big surprise."

"That's an understatement," I muttered, and Julian gave my hand an encouraging squeeze.

"Are you being transferred?" Thomas asked his son. "Are you going back to the museum in Charleston?"

"No," Julian said, "but we wanted to tell you all together, that Holly and I are expecting this summer." Julian met his father's eyes. "You're going to be a grandfather."

"What?" Thomas' jaw dropped. I could practically watch him do the mental math, as he tried to figure out if we'd conceived before or after our elopement.

Wyatt, Maggie, Diego and Nina all jumped to their feet excitedly. There was a babble of voices, and I was pulled to my feet by Maggie and given a big hug.

"Not sure how this will affect the weddings I'm scheduled to help with," I said.

"Oh hush, you!" She was bouncing in excitement. "We'll work it out."

Wyatt gave me a one-armed hug as he still held Phillip. "Congratulations."

Nina was next. "I knew it! I *knew* something was up with you!" She gave me a full hug, and our mid sections pressed together. She pulled back and glanced down at my belly. "Whoa! How far along are you?"

"Thirteen weeks and four days."

Nina blinked. "That's a very specific number."

Diego nudged Nina aside for a hug of his own. "Are you feeling better now, *Mija*?" he asked me.

"You knew?" Nina smacked her husband on the arm.

"I was on hand last month to drive Holly to the doctor. She was in the courtyard and not feeling well. So, I drove her in and waited with her until Julian arrived."

"I threw up on him," I said to Nina. "It was the smell of the motor oil on his uniform that got me."

Nina shuddered. "Oh, that smell always made me horribly sick when I carried Isabel."

"I remember all too well how you were with Isabel." Diego smiled at Nina.

She rolled her eyes at him. "I can't believe you kept it a secret from me!"

Diego shrugged. "It wasn't my news to tell."

"Don't worry, Nina," I said, so only she would hear. "He doesn't know *everything*."

"What do you mean?" she asked.

"Why did you wait so long to make the announcement?" Thomas' voice cut through the room.

I answered before Julian could. "Many women wait until the second trimester to announce a pregnancy."

Thomas' eyes went straight to my belly. "You seem to be showing quite a bit."

"There's a reason for that," Julian said, trying not to smile. "Angel, why don't you get the ultrasound photos?"

I reached back for my purse and pulled out the roll

of pictures and silently handed them to Julian.

"Reason?" Thomas' scowled. "Is Holly farther along than you thought?"

"No," Julian said, holding up the pictures. "She's bigger, because we are having twins."

Pandemonium broke loose.

It ends up that it's harder than you'd think trying to show your family ultrasound pictures when they're all losing their minds. There was so much jumping up and down, tears and laughter that Willow and Isabel joined in, even though they weren't sure what was actually happening.

Thomas stood very still in the center of it all while Julian showed him the photos, pointing out Baby A and Baby B.

His father had seemed completely composed, until I saw that his hands were shaking. "We have a video on Julian's phone of today's ultrasound, Thomas," I said, "if you'd like to see it."

Thomas smiled at my words, reached out, and carefully pulled me into his arms. "Congratulations." His voice was thick with emotion as he patted my back.

I risked it and gave Julian's father a little hug. "Congratulations to you, *Grandpa*."

He chuckled at the title and let go to embrace Julian next. "Do you know the genders yet?" he asked him.

"That's next month," Julian said. "For now, the babies are measuring at thirteen weeks and four days, and they are fraternal twins."

"So they could be one of each," Thomas said.

"Maybe." I shrugged. "But it seems that fraternal twin girls do run hard in the family."

"Right." Thomas took me by the arm and steered me straight to the couch. "You should sit down."

"Well, I—" I began, only to be spoken over.

"Wyatt?" Thomas asked. "Perhaps you could fetch Holly some water."

"Sure thing." Wyatt grinned and moved to the bar.

Thomas slid the hassock over and lifted my ankles. "Put your feet up, dear."

Wyatt handed me a short bottle of water. "Here you go. It's important to stay hydrated."

"Thanks," I said. "I'm—"

"When is your next doctor's appointment, Holly?" Thomas asked me.

"In about four weeks."

He took the bottle from me, twisted off the top and handed it back. "Does your obstetrician specialize in multiples? If not, I can make some calls and find a specialist—"

"Father," Julian cut him off. "We have the same obstetrician that Autumn and Duncan used. Dr. Anderson."

"Good." Thomas nodded. "I'm familiar with her. Brenna Anderson is a lovely woman, and an excellent physician."

"Watch out," Maggie said to me in a stage whisper. "Or he'll be maneuvering to come with you to the next ultrasound and bombard the tech and the doctor with questions."

"I enjoyed going to the ultrasound appointment with Maggie and Wyatt, when they were expecting baby Phillip," Thomas said innocently.

I blanched at that thought. "You're joking, right?" I never expected Thomas would want to go a doctor's appointment with us.

"It's important for the expectant parents to have support," Thomas said to the room. Then he smiled and focused on me. "Drink your water."

"Yes, sir," I said automatically and took a swig. I glanced over at Julian. He stood there grinning. I was relieved that his family had taken the news so well. Besides Autumn and Duncan, I couldn't even imagine how my family would react.

Julian had pulled out his phone to cue up the video of the most recent ultrasound. "If our doctor's office allows grandparents at an ultrasound appointment," he began, "and *if* Holly is comfortable with it, I have no objections, Father."

Thomas looked directly at me.

"Well..." I said, trying to be diplomatic. "We have another six months to go, and there'll be lots of ultrasounds to check on the babies' progress..."

"Excellent," Thomas said, "it's all settled." He rubbed his hands together. "Now show me that ultrasound video."

***

By the time we arrived at Autumn's, their girls were already in bed. Duncan and Autumn were thrilled at our news. While Duncan and Julian began plotting ideas for expanding the cabin, Autumn steered me over to the couch and we went over all of the ultrasound photos together, again. It was comforting having another twin mom to speak to about a twin pregnancy. My cousin immediately offered to let us borrow their infant car seats. As Emma and Erin were going to be three in a few months, they had graduated to bigger ones.

"We can talk about that more later," I said. "When I hit the third trimester."

"I've got their infant car seats all wrapped up in big plastic bags in the basement," she said. "Whenever you're ready, we'll bring them over and Duncan can install them." Autumn reached for my hand. "How are you doing?"

I blew out a shaky breath. "After four weeks, it's finally started to sink in."

"Gods, how I remember the shock of finding out we had two on board." Autumn shook her head. "I thought Duncan was going to pass out."

I told her about the day we'd found out we were expecting and everything that had happened at our scan, including my terror that it hadn't been viable and the heart pounding wait only to be informed that we had not one, but two.

"Oh, Holly." Autumn teared up. "I'm sorry that you had such a scary start to what should have been a beautiful time." She gave me a supportive hug.

"I feel much more secure in this pregnancy hitting the thirteen weeks mark," I said.

"I remember feeling relieved when I hit the second trimester with the girls. Everyone hovered over me and..." She stopped speaking and pulled back to meet my eyes. "By the goddess. Thomas is going to be a handful."

I chuckled. "He's already maneuvering to go along to an ultrasound in the future."

Autumn burst out laughing. "Blame Maggie. She should never have let him come along to one of hers while she was expecting baby Phillip."

Julian called me over to show me a rough sketch he'd done of a two-story expansion to the cabin.

"Will we be able to live there during the renovation?" I asked Duncan.

"Probably not," Duncan said. "It'll be too chaotic—"

"Not to mention dusty and messy," Autumn added.

"Oh. I hadn't considered that. Where would we live during the renovations?" I asked Julian.

Julian shrugged. "We can rent a house or an apartment temporarily."

"For how long?" I asked.

"Three or four months," Duncan said, studying the drawing.

My heart sank. I didn't want to give up our sanctuary

in the country. But, if I wanted to live there long term, and goddess willing, raise my children there...I would need to temporarily relocate.

Autumn tossed an arm around my shoulder. "You know...There's a brick house right down the street that's available for lease. College students typically rent it out, but it's vacant currently."

Julian's head snapped up. "Do you have the address?"

Autumn grinned. "I can do you one better. It's only a short walk. Four doors down. We can pop over and you can get a look."

Before I could blink, Autumn and Julian had tossed their coats on and were out the door. I found myself left behind with Duncan. I had wanted to go along, but that had been firmly vetoed as the sidewalks had yet to be shoveled. Seems they were all worried about me slipping and falling.

The door shut and I crossed my arms over my chest. "You know," I said to Duncan, "out of all of us, the person most likely to slip and fall in the snow isn't me—"

"It's Autumn," Duncan agreed with a good-humored grin. "Julian will keep an eye on her."

I tried not to pout. "I suppose it would be nice living in the old neighborhood for a few months."

"You could walk to the Drake mansion to work if you liked," Duncan said amiably. "It's a few blocks away. And bonus: this neighborhood is very pretty in the spring. With all of the old dogwoods and saucer magnolias blooming..."

"I remember," I said. "At least you, Autumn, and the girls would be close by."

Duncan hooked his thumb toward the Bishop manor that was right next door. "So would Bran, Lexie and the kids."

"That's not particularly a selling point to me at the moment," I said.

Duncan frowned. "Are you going to tell them that you're expecting?"

"Not now." I shook my head.

Duncan settled back in his chair. "I'd assumed you'd be going over to tell them next."

I swiped a long curl from my face. "You assumed incorrectly."

"Why wouldn't you share the news with them?" Duncan was genuinely confused.

"I have my reasons," I said.

"Okay," he said, but his blue eyes were disapproving.

"Duncan," I said, "I've had zero contact from my brother, Lexie or even with Ivy since her wedding back in January."

"I'm sorry. I didn't realize that," he said. "Are they still upset about the elopement?"

Taking a breath and working to stay dispassionate, I shared the conversation I'd had with Bran on Thanksgiving Day.

After I'd finished, Duncan's eyes went wide. "Damn, that's harsh."

"I certainly thought so," I said wryly.

"Bran honestly said that to you?"

My breath huffed out. "I have no reason to lie to you, Duncan."

"I know that you wouldn't lie, that was more of a rhetorical—*are you kidding me?*—sort of shocked response." He rubbed his hands over his face. "I can see why you would be hesitant to share the news with him and Lexie."

I rose to my feet. "Excuse me for a moment." I headed for the downstairs bathroom as I needed to pee, *again*. It was aggravating, but as long as I was there I admired the pretty bathroom Duncan had built.

The slick white subway tile and vintage looking black and white hexagon floor tile was offset by hot pink painted walls. My cousin had worked to have the new bathroom blend in with the 1920's style of her home. The newer wall color was all Autumn. She loved bright colors.

After taking care of business, I dried my hands on the pink hand towels and reminded myself that at least I didn't have to wonder if Duncan would be up to the renovation. He was a talented contractor. I also wondered how long after Julian and I left it would take for Autumn to call Bran and tell him the news.

My pregnancy wasn't a secret any longer. I was past the point where I could easily hide it, nor did I want to.

If my brother and sister could not be happy for us, then that was Bran and Ivy's loss. I didn't need the negativity in my life. I had my babies to focus on and protect.

Perhaps living in the old neighborhood wasn't such a good idea after all... Maybe we should look for an apartment or a rental closer to the cabin. *I'll grab my phone,* I thought, *and get online and see what else is available.*

I exited the bathroom as Julian and Autumn returned. It only took one look at Julian's face to know that he was very excited about the rental property. In fact, he already had his phone out and pulled up to the realtor's webpage. He eagerly showed me the photos of the interior and I stayed quiet and let him talk about his plans.

After he'd kindly acquiesced to my request to keep the pregnancy a secret for the past month, this was the least I could do.

***

The next morning Julian and I sat side by side on the couch at our cabin and called my father and stepmother and told them the news. They were very excited, and Ruth announced she'd get started on making quilts for the babies right away. We called Aunt Faye and Hal next, and my great-aunt was over the moon.

"Looks like we won't be making a trip to Cornwall

this spring after all," I said. "Sorry about that."

I answered their questions about the due date and what we knew so far. Faye quickly got down to practicalities.

"I know you love your cabin in the woods," she said. "But dear, you're going to need a bigger space."

"You must be psychic," I said, making her laugh, and explained that Duncan was drawing up plans for an expansion.

I switched it over to speakerphone, and Julian told her about the rental he was looking into.

"How did your brother and sister take the news?" Aunt Faye asked.

"I haven't told them yet," I said.

"Do you plan to?" she asked, bluntly.

"I suppose I'll have to." I blew out a breath. "You know they won't be happy for us."

"Would you like me to have a word with them?" she asked kindly.

"No, that's all right," I said quickly.

"My dear," Faye began, "I have always been your and Julian's staunchest ally."

"Yes, you have," Julian agreed.

"Let me have a few words with Bran and Ivy," she said. "Perhaps I can smooth things over. You are family. It's not right that they aren't supporting you in this."

I felt a big weight slide off my shoulders. "Are you sure?" I asked.

"Holly, I deeply regret that I never made amends

with my sister, Irene, while she was alive. I'll be damned if I'll stand by and watch another member of my family feel they must keep what should be the happiest of news, a secret."

A few tears spilled over. "Thank you, Aunt Faye," I said. "I *would* appreciate it if you spoke to them."

"Of course. You know that Hal and I love the both of you, my darlings."

"We love you too, Faye," Julian said.

"Well then." She sounded very satisfied. "I'll close up this conversation and remind you that if one of those babies is a girl, that *Faye* is both a lovely and magickal middle name."

Julian chuckled. "I will add it to our list of possible names."

"See that you do," she said. "I'll speak to you soon, and congratulations again."

We ended the call. "You know," I said to Julian, "she's probably calling Bran right now."

Julian raised a single eyebrow. "And she's going to enjoy the hell out of giving him a piece of her mind."

I brushed my hair back. "If anyone can get through to my brother and sister it's probably Faye. She once chewed my ass after my mother died. Told me I was acting like a snot, and she was right. Dare I mention, the day she came up with a plan to sneak into the Drake mansion?"

Julian's eyes danced with laughter. "What?"

"Oh yeah," I said. "Her plan was to snoop around

and search for the missing Bishop family brooch." I rolled my eyes. "I told her I didn't want to go to jail for breaking and entering, and she waved that off and told me she had an excellent lawyer."

"Good god!" Julian burst out laughing.

"After that, we did shots of whiskey to toast to our success."

Julian shook his head. "She's a hell of a woman."

"A week later we were in your family mansion under the guise of being there with the historical society," I said. "You had offered to help me search for the brooch in Leilah's rooms and then we slipped away and..."

"I remember." Julian's voice became husky. He brushed my hair aside and began to nibble on my neck.

"That was our first time together and I wanted you so badly that I..." I trailed off as he ran his hands over my breasts. I moaned as he began to tug my shirt aside and help himself. His mouth cruised gently over my bra.

"You wanted me so badly that you what?" he prompted.

"That I..." I gulped when he pushed the bra aside and began to suckle. "That I didn't give a damn that there were people right outside of the room we were in."

He lifted his mouth. "I remember that you made so much noise I had to cover your mouth—"

"Take me to bed, Julian," I pleaded.

"Soon," he said and gave his full attention to my other breast.

I threaded my hands into his hair and yanked his mouth back up to mine. "Not soon. Now." With a frustrated growl, I kissed him with everything I had. Eventually we came up for air.

"Holly," he groaned. "We can't be as vigorous as we usually—"

"I love you," I cut him off. "We'll figure this out together."

He scooped me off the couch and carried me to the bed. "I'll be gentle, I promise."

"I know you will," I said, as he laid me down.

We made love, and while it wasn't our usual intensely crazy romp, it was soft and slow, emotional and romantic. After going without him for the past few weeks, I didn't mind that he was more controlled and restrained.

It was different, that was all. But I reminded myself, as we cuddled together afterwards, that different could be okay too.

***

It ended up that renting the two-bedroom brick house down the street from Autumn and Duncan's place *was* our best option. Within a couple of weeks, we needed to move as Duncan had gotten the building permits and construction began in earnest on the expansion of our cabin.

We hired movers to take all of the furniture and

personal items from the cabin, and I arranged to pick up a few pieces of my old furniture from the manor. They fit into the brick house and made it feel much homier.

I missed the quiet and privacy of the woods. In fact, the first night I slept at the brick house in town, I woke up constantly every time a car drove down the street. I also missed leaving the curtains open. There'd been no one to see in the windows at the cabin, but here in town, we made do for the first few days by draping sheets over the windows. Perhaps not the classiest solution, but it would work until we could get curtains.

It almost felt like I was living in a dorm again. Maybe it was the leftover energy from the last trio of students that had lived there. The small, two-bedroom one bath house had white interior walls, hardwood floors, and was very basic. The lone bathroom had yellow and black tile, which was probably original to the home. The kitchen cabinets were painted plain white, and the kitchen floor tile was so hideous that it was sort of charming. On the plus side, it was a spotlessly clean house and would certainly work for now.

Thomas had wanted us to move into the Drake mansion during the construction, but both Julian and I agreed we would be happier having our own space. I didn't want to live in the same place where I was working, and I had relished the quiet and solitude of the cabin. There'd be none of that living in the mansion. Besides, now that Julian's family knew about the pregnancy, I couldn't lift a finger without someone jumping to help me while I was working in the office.

Thomas made it a point to pop into the offices on the third floor every day. He either brought me a bottle of juice, a piece of fruit, or cheese and crackers. He'd ask how the babies and I were doing, pat me on the head, and encourage me to stay hydrated.

They all watched over me like a hawk, and while it was certainly kind, it was starting to make me twitchy.

At least, I thought, *one side of the family gives a damn.* I'd never heard from Bran or Ivy. I knew Aunt Faye had talked to them. She'd sent me an email and told me she had, but she didn't say how the conversation had gone.

But so far neither my brother or sister, or either of their spouses had made a move to reach out in any way. Julian had told Olivia and Vincent, and a few other people at the museum. I was sure that Vincent had told George...meaning George had told Candice. And well, soon everyone would know. There was no hiding the pregnancy now.

It seemed my belly popped a bit more every couple of days. Julian talked me into taking baby bump progress photos each week and seeing the difference in the photos was thrilling and a little freaky all at the same time.

Right after we moved into the brick house, Autumn made it a point to walk down with Emma and Erin. While I was happy to see her, I didn't want to put her in the middle of the family feud, but it didn't seem to bother her.

Our first weekend at the rental house, Julian had made a run to the hardware store, and I was standing in the living room eyeballing the newly installed curtain rod. I was trying to figure out if I could raise my arms high enough to hang the new curtains I'd ordered, or if I'd need to stand on a chair.

"Nope." I shook my head. That curtain rod was just out of reach, and I certainly wasn't going to risk climbing up on something. As I stood there scowling at the rod, I saw George and Vincent walking up our front sidewalk. With a smile, I went to open the door. "What a nice surprise!"

George kissed my cheek. "Brought you a housewarming gift."

"Thank you," I said.

Vincent gave me a peck on the cheek too. "Look at you! You're bumping right along." He gave my belly a light pat.

"Come in." I held the door open for them.

Once they were in the house, Vincent handed me a big wicker basket filled with pretty kitchen towels and a box of decaffeinated black teas. There was also a variety of baked goods, courtesy of George. I saw cookies, scones and cake pops.

"Where's Julian?" George asked.

"He ran to the hardware store," I answered as I looked over the basket. I spotted oatmeal raisin cookies and my mouth watered.

I placed the basket on a side table while Vincent asked if he could nose around the rental house. I told him to feel free.

George poked his head into the kitchen. "How do you cook anything on this old stove, Red?"

"It's fine for cooking," I said. "I have a crock pot too."

George shuddered. "You are so brave."

I smirked at his humor. Before I could blink, he looped his arm through mine and directed me to the rocking chair in the living room.

"Let's get you off your feet," he said.

"I'll sit if I can have an oatmeal cookie."

"Deal," George went and snagged a cellophane bag of his oatmeal cookies from the basket.

"You need to have an old priest and a young priest come out and banish the yellow tiles from your bathroom," Vincent announced as he strolled from the back of the house.

I chuckled as I unwrapped the bag. "Hideous colors, aren't they?"

"You should see the kitchen floor," George said to Vincent, who immediately went to look for himself.

"Sweet tap-dancing Christ!" The horror in Vincent's voice, as he viewed the old linoleum, made me chuckle.

"Told you," George called back to him. "So..." George sat on the couch. "How long for the renovation at the cabin?"

"Three months at least," I answered and bit in. "Oh my goddess," I said around a mouthful. "These are wonderful."

George grinned as Vincent joined him on the sofa. "I knew you liked oatmeal, Red, and I figured that's fairly healthy for you right now."

"If I wasn't already married, George," I said. "I'd propose to you."

Julian let himself in the front door as I was speaking. "What's this?" he asked. "I'm gone for twenty minutes and you're ready to toss me aside to run off with George?'

I laughed. "He baked me oatmeal raisin cookies."

Julian dropped a kiss on my head and snatched the cellophane bag holding the remainder of the cookies from my hand. "Save some for later."

I wrinkled my nose at him. "Spoilsport."

"Listen," Vincent began as Julian took a seat, "one of the reasons we dropped by was to ask you about the bed and breakfast that you two went to when you eloped."

"Oh?" I began to smile.

"Yes," George said. "Vincent and I thought maybe we'd like to do a small wedding ceremony with our parents and siblings as guests there, later this spring."

"As an associate of *Magnolia Bridal and Events*, I would be happy to coordinate that for you," I said.

"I was hoping you would say that." George grinned and linked hands with Vincent.

We spent a pleasant half hour visiting with George and Vincent. We showed them our wedding photos from the bed and breakfast, and I promised to dive right in to getting things in motion for the couple as soon as I got to the office on Monday morning.

"Let me get you my card." I got to my feet and went to my purse to pass the couple my card with my work email and cell number on it. It felt good to be able to bring in new clients on my own. I couldn't wait to tell Maggie.

CHAPTER EIGHT

After a couple of weeks, I fell into a sort of routine living back in Williams Ford. On days when the temperatures were mild, I walked to the mansion. Otherwise, I would drive. Maggie was officially finished with her maternity leave, and the bridal appointments and meetings with vendors increased exponentially. I went along to some of the meetings, as Maggie wanted me to learn the ropes, but there was plenty of paperwork and office tasks for me to do with *Magnolia Bridal and Events*.

I did call the bed and breakfast venue in Hannibal that we had used, to see what dates they had available for a small wedding ceremony for George and Vincent. After a few days and a group phone meeting, they chose their date for mid-May. It was fun helping the grooms finalize all their details. Eventually I went along with Maggie when they tried on tuxes. Vincent knew exactly what he wanted. His favorite color was blue, and he pulled his choices quickly. I was surprised, however, that George was so indecisive about what he should wear.

"How about a black suit with a hot pink vest and bow tie?" I gave him an elbow nudge so he would know I was teasing. "That way you'll coordinate with the décor at *Charming Cake Pops*."

George shuddered, but my words made him smile. "I would look like a waiter."

"Now don't you worry." Maggie patted George's shoulder. "We can always take our cues from Vincent's tux."

Vincent stepped out of the fitting room looking sleek and handsome in a slim-fit medium blue tux and white shirt. His necktie was a floral pattern in shades of navy, gray and burgundy. "How's this look?" he asked me.

"You look incredible," I said. "Those brown shoes look great, too."

Maggie pulled a suit jacket from a nearby rack. "What if we play off Vincent's blue tux and put George in a dark navy?"

George glanced from the jacket and back to his fiancé. "Well, I..."

"Humor me," Maggie said and nudged him along. A male salesclerk went and found George the matching slacks in the groom's size and a white dress shirt.

While George tried it on, Maggie selected a necktie for George in a subtle geometric pattern of gray and blue. It was a winning combination. The grooms were delighted, and while George selected his shoes, Maggie snapped a quick photo of them. For fun, I went and found some patterned socks. I didn't choose anything outrageous: blue with burgundy and gray fleur-de-lis for Vincent, and gray and navy geometric for George.

The grooms loved the socks and Maggie suggested they let their mothers know that they were doing shades of blue for their tuxes. Vincent pulled out his cell and sent the texts immediately.

"My mother has been hounding me ever since we set the date, wanting to know what color mother-of-the-groom dress she should wear."

"So has mine," George added.

"I will call the florist in Hannibal tomorrow," I said to the grooms, "and make sure the mother's corsages, and the boutonnieres for the fathers, coordinate with your blue color theme.

A few days later, I was working at my desk on the third floor in the bridal offices of the mansion. My bridal cell phone rang, and I saw that it was Emily from the Smythe-Jonas wedding—the wedding Maggie had me running point on.

"Hello, Emily," I said cheerfully.

"You will not believe this!" Emily's voice was so loud, I reached for the volume button to turn it down.

"What's wrong?" I asked and pulled out a notepad.

"Ron's sister, Mia, is refusing to order her bridesmaid's dress. She says she wants a different style or color!"

While Emily vented her frustration, I pulled up my

notes. The bride had finally chosen a soft muted shade of purple for her August wedding, called wisteria.

"If I remember correctly," I said, "there is a darker, complimentary color called plum that was also available in the same style—"

"There is," Emily said. "But I want everyone to match."

"I understand," I said soothingly.

"Mia says the dress makes her look humongous. She wants to wear black or the dark plum color instead. What am I going to do?" Emily wailed.

I sat back in my desk chair and checked my notes. Mia hadn't been with the other attendants the day they'd chosen the dresses. In fact, today was the day the remaining two attendants were to be fitted and place their orders.

"We're down here at the bridal shop," Emily, the bride said. "His sister and my other attendant from out of town were supposed to order their dresses today, but Mia's totally digging her heels in. Ron's mother is trying to talk some sense into her, but it's not working. Do you suppose you could come down here *now* and help?"

"Sure," I said. "Give me ten minutes." I hung up the phone, grabbed the wedding file and my purse, and headed out. Maggie was out of the office meeting with a rental company for an upcoming event. I shot her a quick text, to let her know I was going out. But I knew what Maggie would do in a situation like this; she would go straight to the local shop and see if she could defuse or solve the problem.

Ten minutes later, I was walking with my umbrella through a light rain to the bridal shop. I waved at the shop manager, hung up my jacket, and went directly to Emily and her mother.

I'd had weeks of watching and listening to Maggie work her mojo. So to begin, I had the groom's mother distract the bride by looking at some wedding accessories on the other side of the shop. Next, I went to the fitting room where Mia was holed up.

"Hi Mia," I said, tapping on the door. "This is Holly, the bridal coordinator."

"Are you alone?" She sounded desperate.

"I am."

The door unlocked. "Get in here."

I eased my way inside and faced Mia. She was a gorgeous, plus sized woman, with dark hair and striking blue-gray eyes. I estimated her to be in her mid-thirties. "How can I help?" I asked.

"Look at me!" Mia held her arms out to her sides. "This style of dress looks awful!"

It was true; the crepe satin, spaghetti-strapped dress was extremely unflattering on Mia. It was far too revealing for her bust line, and the back was much too low. "I see," I said.

"I mean the color is great, but I need to wear a bra, a *regular* bra," Mia insisted. "My boobs are way too big for me to be comfortable in a low-backed strapless bra."

"I know that the wisteria color of bridesmaid dress Emily has chosen comes in several different styles," I said.

"Well thank you god," Mia breathed a sigh of relief.

"Let me pull a different dress for you." I gave her my best soothing smile. "What size?"

"Eighteen. A twenty if it runs small," Mia said.

I nodded. "Okay. Sit tight."

Mia blew her bangs out of her eyes. "Emily thinks I'm trying to be difficult, but it's not that. The other attendants are practically ten years younger than me. This sort of bodice isn't appropriate for a plus sized woman, especially when I'm going to be riding herd on my four-year-old son at the reception."

"I'll do my best to find something more flattering," I said.

"I'm honored to be an attendant," Mia said, "but I will *not* have my boobs—" She grabbed them and made them bounce. "—flouncing all around or falling out on my brother's wedding day."

"I agree." I couldn't help but grin. "Flouncing is bad. Let me see what I can conjure up."

I walked out and Emily pounced. "Well?" she demanded.

Motioning the manager over, I asked her to pull a few other dresses. Then I spoke to Emily. "I'm thinking we can find a more appropriate and flattering cut of dress for Mia."

"What?" Emily scowled. "Mia's gorgeous. She looks

great in everything. Why is she being difficult now?"

"Have you seen her in that spaghetti strap dress?" I asked gently.

Emily rolled her eyes. "No. She refused to open the door."

"There's a problem with adequate coverage in the bust line," I said, trying to be diplomatic.

"I *have* seen it," Mrs. Jonas chimed in, "and that's putting it mildly. The girls were out and free range."

Emily's eyes grew wide. "*Oh no.* I never thought about that."

"Yeah," Ramona, the attendant from out of town, said. "I'm not as well-endowed as Mia but I'm going to be pretty boob-a-licious in my dress, too."

Emily was on the verge of tears. "But the style of dress looked fabulous on Ava and Justine," she said.

"We can keep the same color and fabric, but simply choose a different style," I assured the bride.

Emily's eyes were welling up. "We can?"

"Of course," I said. "The manager is pulling some dresses in the same fabric for Mia to try on. All will be available in the wisteria color you have chosen."

"I suppose that would work." Emily wiped her eyes. "Maybe."

Five minutes later Mia stepped out of the fitting room in a dark green flutter sleeve style dress. The dress had a V neck that would allow her to wear—and have the support of—a regular bra. It had the same crepe satin fabric and flowing long skirt as the other dresses, but this style had a crisscross detail at the waist that was flattering to Mia's figure.

"Whoa," I said, as Mia stepped in front of the three-way mirror. "Hello, bombshell."

Mia grinned at her reflection. "This dress is available in the wisteria color too, right?"

"That's right," the manager said.

"It's gorgeous on you," Emily said to Mia.

"If the bride approves," Mia said, meeting Emily's eyes in the mirror. "I'll get this style of dress in the wisteria color ordered immediately."

"Yes!" Emily clapped her hands. "I absolutely approve."

"Wonderful!" I said.

"Hey Emily." The other attendant spoke up. "Would you mind If I tried on that style of dress too?"

The bride turned to her other attendant. "Well, I..."

"It was boob-a-licious, Emily," Ramona gestured to her chest. "I'm not even kidding."

Emily started to laugh. "Maybe Ramona should look at the other style too."

"It's a miracle!" Ramona clasped her hands together, making Emily chuckle.

"Size twelve?" the manager asked Ramona.

"Yes, ma'am," Ramona said.

"Why don't you take a dressing room and I'll be right back?" With a nod the manager was off.

In the end, Ramona chose the same style of dress as Mia. Everyone was happy, the wisteria-colored dresses were all ordered, and the groom's mother even invited me to have lunch with them. I thanked them for the invite but declined. As I walked back to the car, I sent Maggie a text and let her know I had the dress crisis solved.

By the time I arrived at the mansion, the rain was all but over, and my stomach was growling. "I should have gone out to lunch with Emily and Mrs. Jonas," I grumbled, and then I jumped, because Thomas suddenly appeared beside me in the foyer. He had obviously been waiting for me.

"You haven't eaten yet?" he asked.

"My lunch is upstairs—" I was cut off.

"Come with me, young lady." He took my arm and escorted me to the family kitchen. With a flourish, he ushered me to a chair at the table. "It's almost two o'clock. You shouldn't skip lunch."

"I didn't mean to. I was out helping a bride. There was a dress crisis and I—" I shut up when Thomas immediately placed an apple in front of me. Absolutely starving, I grabbed it and bit in. "Thank you."

"You're welcome." He poured me a glass of water and set that beside my plate.

I took another bite. "You don't have to keep fussing over me, you know."

He smiled and patted my head. "Julian told me that the doctor recommended small meals several times a day."

I resisted rolling my eyes. "She did."

"I'm going to put together a sandwich for you," Thomas said. "Does turkey sound good?"

My stomach growled loudly in reply. "Sure."

He opened the fridge. "Swiss or provolone cheese?"

"Surprise me," I said, working my way through the apple.

Thomas nodded and went to work. "Mayo or mustard?" he asked.

"Mayo all day," I said.

"I knew you could be trusted," he said, deadpan.

I couldn't help but smile.

"Your color has been better the past couple of weeks," he said. "Is the nausea easing?"

"Yes, sir."

In a few moments, he brought the sandwich over. "I would prefer it if you called me Thomas, or if you're comfortable with it, Father."

The request made tears spring instantly to my eyes. "Well damn it," I muttered, trying to blot up tears before they spilled over.

"Here, use this." Thomas presented me with a handkerchief. "I didn't mean to upset you."

"You didn't." I took the linen and dabbed at my eyes. "That just hit me in the feels. It's probably all the hormones."

With a smile he sat in a chair beside me. "Did you walk to the mansion this morning?"

"Uh..." His question threw me. "No, I drove. It was raining."

"Well, the sun is starting to come out now," he said, glancing out the window. "After you've eaten, we can take a walk around the courtyard and look at the gardens."

"That sounds nice," I said and picked up my sandwich.

"We can talk about baby names," Thomas said innocently.

I slanted him a look.

"Thomas is an excellent name," he began.

Smiling, I replied, "I'll add it to the list."

***

Spring had arrived and the old neighborhood's show of blooming dogwoods and magnolia trees did not disappoint. The old scraggly shrubs along the front of our house ended up being forsythias. They burst into bright yellow blossoms, and it was so cheerful that it made me itch to plant some flowers. The truth was that it was silly to plant a garden at a rental, however there were some old concrete pots on either side of the front porch. Putting some annuals in them would be fun and it would brighten the place up a bit. One evening after work Julian and I went to a nursery and bought potting soil, pansies, variegated ivy, and violas to plant.

I'd been about to start on the pots when Duncan had called from the construction site with some question or issue about the cabin renovation. Julian had to go out to the cabin, and I opted to stay behind. I waved him off and sat slowly down on our small porch to consider the containers on either side of me.

I opened the first bag of potting mix and considered lifting it to dump the soil in the containers. But after eyeballing the weight of the bag—which was twenty-five pounds— I took my hand trowel and began to put heaping scoops of potting mix in the containers one scoop at a time.

"Sheesh. At this rate, it will only take five times as long," I grumbled.

In answer, I felt a strong flutter in my belly.

I smiled down at my bump. "No worries, babies, I'm going to behave myself." I was in my eighteenth week, and every week was another victory.

The sun was out, and the temperatures were in the high 50s. A strong breeze whipped around the house, and I stopped and pulled the zipper up on my oversized navy hoodie. I had on a men's large, since it was the only thing that fit around me. My bump was sticking straight out the front, and it made me appear *much* farther along. I had to roll up the too long sleeves of the hoodie, but it was soft, warm and comfortable at least.

Slowly, I filled the containers with two out of the three bags of the potting soil. Starting with a six-pack of trailing variegated ivy, I tucked a few plants around the edges of the pots so the ivy would trail down and over the sides. The fragrant violas went next, followed by the sassy, pink-faced pansies. I had the first concrete pot planted and had begun on the second when an unfamiliar car pulled in our driveway.

While I didn't recognize the car, upon closer inspection I certainly knew the driver—it was my sister, Ivy. I hadn't seen her since her wedding day three months prior. She climbed from the car, gave me a long considering look and slammed the car door with a flourish. Ivy's temper was coming off of her in waves.

She was spoiling for a fight.

Well damn it, I thought. *So much for a quiet relaxing evening planting flowers.*

I stayed where I was seated on the edge of the concrete porch. "Hello, Ivy," I said politely as she marched up the driveway toward me.

She gained the sidewalk and stopped about three feet away. Ivy stood hip shot in jeans, boots and a black leather jacket. "I was in town, and thought I'd see for myself how you were doing." After a moment, she tipped her head back and considered the brick house. "Gotta say, I was surprised to find out that you're living in the old neighborhood again."

Her words made my shoulders hitch in reaction. "It's a rental," I said, returning my attention to the flowers. "The cabin addition should be done in another couple of months or so."

She didn't respond. After a few minutes, I lifted my eyes and found that she was glaring at me. I did not want to argue with her, and so I took a steadying breath and selected an annual to plant like it was the most important thing in the world.

The silence stretched on as I planted the smaller purple violas. I figured my twin would last maybe two more minutes before she snapped. Patience had never been Ivy's strong suit.

Ivy tipped her head to one side. "You have anything you want to say to me?"

Trying to project serenity, I added a few more pansies to the container. "What do you think of the purple violas and pink pansies? I think they look pretty together."

"That's it?" Ivy's breath huffed out. "That's all you're going to say?"

"You obviously came over here looking for an argument, but honestly? I'm worn out, Ivy." I sighed. "I don't want to fight with you."

"Really?" Ivy asked, planting her hands on her hips. "You don't think that you owe me an apology?"

Tired or not, my head snapped up at her words. "What the hell do I have to apologize to *you* for?"

Her green eyes narrowed. "Let's start with the fact that you didn't bother to call to tell me that you were pregnant. Instead, you had Aunt Faye do it for you."

My temper started to bubble up. Instead of snapping back, I told myself to calm down. The breeze kicked up a bit and I worried that I was the cause. Stalling for time, I slowly brushed the potting soil from my fingers before I spoke. "Aunt Faye volunteered to pass along the news. It made her happy, and so I let her."

Ivy tossed her hands up in the air and spun away. "I don't know why I'm surprised that you didn't tell me yourself. You've become quite the expert at lying and keeping secrets."

"Watch that," I warned her.

Abruptly Ivy spun back to look at me. "Do you remember the day when I asked you to introduce me to whoever you were dating?"

"Yes, it was when you started working as a seasonal photographer for the Christmas tree farm," I said. "When you and Erik were first falling in love."

"Right." Ivy brushed her hair back. "And you refused to say who you were dating, and I told you that it didn't matter to me who it was, because you were my sister, and I loved you. I promised you that I would support you no matter what."

"I remember."

"But you never gave me the chance to support you, and you sure as hell don't want my love," Ivy argued. "Because you chose to shut me out. Again."

"That's not true," I said.

"It's what you do!" Ivy insisted. "You shut people out, Holly. You turn away, or you leave." As she spoke the wind whipped around the house and one of the empty bags of potting mix blew off the porch. Ivy grabbed it and continued. "You abjured your Craft years ago and went to a college clear across the state. We rarely heard or even saw you for *three years*. Then you came home unannounced, for some unknown reason, and that's when all of the secrets started."

"My reasons for coming home were private," I said, choosing my words with care. "I needed to heal."

"Heal?" Ivy zeroed in on that. "From what? A bad break up?"

"In a way..." I had never told Ivy about my miscarriage in my last year of college. Autumn, worried that I was ill, had scanned my memories and had pried the information out of my mind when I'd first returned to Williams Ford. It was the *only* reason she knew. I had told Julian about it after we had started seeing each other, but for almost five years that particular secret had been closely kept. Finally, I said, "It's complicated."

Ivy sneered. "*Complicated* sounds to me like a bullshit excuse to keep more secrets."

"That's not fair," I said.

"Oh, now you wanna talk about being fair?" Ivy tossed up her hands. "I suppose it was fair to exclude the family from your wedding?"

"It wasn't like that—" I began, but she spoke right over me.

"Sure as hell seems that way to me. *You* chose to exclude the family from your life now that you're married to Julian. *You* left and went to hide in a cabin in the woods on the outskirts of the county. And now you don't even have the common courtesy to tell your own sister that you are pregnant with twins?"

My legs were starting to cramp. "To be fair, we didn't tell *anyone* about the pregnancy until I made it to my second trimester."

"Why?" Ivy demanded.

"I had my reasons for keeping it private—and news flash..." I hitched myself forward on the step and stood. "That decision had absolutely *nothing* to do with you."

Ivy got her first good look at my belly. "Whoa!" Her jaw dropped. "You're huge!"

A cramp snaked its way up the back of my leg and I tried to ignore it. "That happens when there are twins. Autumn was much the same when she carried Emma and Erin."

"Her belly didn't stick out like that so early! You have to be farther along than you said." Ivy's eyes raked me up and down, and her entire expression changed. "That's the real reason you and Julian eloped. You *were* already pregnant."

"No, I wasn't," I said through my teeth. The cramp in my leg felt like I was being stabbed with a knife.

"Still lying, Holly?" Ivy said. "Surely you recall that when a Witch lies, their magick has no power. To cast an effective spell, you need both intention and *truth* to power your words."

"I know that." With a gasp at the pain in my leg, I bent to rub at the cramp.

"At this rate, no one will believe anything you say. Not ever again." Ivy's eyes focused on mine. "I certainly never will."

"I don't give a damn what you believe," I said. "Get out."

I was rapidly losing control of my temper and my magick itched to be set free. A wild wind came shrieking around the house. It seemed to wrap itself around me, and without design, I tapped into its power.

"So..." Ivy raised a single eyebrow in derision. "I catch you in yet another lie, and your response is to invoke the element of air?"

My hair swirled all around my face and the power from the element filled me up and made feel taller and stronger. "I won't say this again. Go home, Ivy, before I really lose my temper."

"I'm not afraid of you, Holly. I am, nevertheless, extremely disappointed. Clearly, being married to Julian Drake has taken your magick to a darker place." She shook her head. "I should have known this would happen."

That did it.

The extra unused bag of potting mix resting beside the porch exploded. Ivy was sprayed with the soil, and I don't know who was more surprised, her or me. It happened so quickly that she had no time to counter the magick. The peat moss mixture had all gone straight towards my sister, and she was absolutely covered in it.

The wind died as suddenly as it had been conjured. I stood there, stunned at what my temper and magick had done.

Ivy spit potting soil out of her mouth. She bent over, coughed, and spit dirt out again. "That was a dirty trick," Ivy managed to say, wiping dirt from her face.

Bag of dirt. Dirty trick. My lips twitched at the unintended pun. *Don't laugh. Don't laugh!* I thought desperately. Unfortunately, as Ivy spit out even more dirt, a very inappropriate giggle slipped out of my mouth. "I'm sorry," I said immediately and did my best to turn the rest of my laughter into a cough.

"Bitch," Ivy said calmly, and shook her head, sending more peat moss flying.

"Ivy," I began, "surely you know that I didn't intend for that to happen."

She glared. "Just like you didn't intend for the water cooler to explode all over your co-worker?"

I had been about to apologize again for the dirt, but after that remark, I thought better of it. Instead, I crossed my arms. "Listening to all the campus gossip these days, are we?"

"You're the one who got vindictive and retaliated with magick when I called you out on another lie."

"Oh, come on!" I said. "It's only peat moss and vermiculite. You did worse when we were kids. I can't count the number of things you broke or blew up when your PK first emerged."

"Unlike you," she said, brushing her clothes off, "I have never used my magick in retaliation against my sister."

"Stop being so melodramatic." I rolled my eyes. "The only thing that got hurt today was your pride."

Ivy shot me a look. "I shouldn't have come here."

"You know what?" I said. "You shouldn't have."

"At last," she said, "a truth on which we can agree."

"The *truth* is, Ivy, you rolled up spoiling for a fight." I stepped closer and poked her shoulder. "You made rude accusations and insulted both me and my husband. Now because you didn't win the argument, you're trying to play the victim."

"I'm the one that was hit with a bag of potting soil," she said and stomped off toward the driveway.

"I could send another shot of air your way," I called after her. "Might help clean you up a bit before you get all that potting soil inside of your car."

Ivy opened the door, climbed in, and slammed the car door behind her. She backed out of the driveway in a hurry and her tires made an angry squeal on the pavement when she drove away.

"Sonofabitch," I said, as she tore off down the street. Another cramp hit the back of my leg and I winced. "This won't be pretty. She's going to run straight to Bran and Lexie." Putting all my weight on the cramping leg, I hoped that would ease the pain. I recalled that Autumn used to do that.

I shook my head, annoyed at myself for getting sucked into a fight in the first place and aggravated that she'd goaded me into losing control of my magick. Grabbing up the remaining gardening supplies, I hauled it all to the back of the house and limped my way inside.

I tried taking a warm bath, but the cramping in my legs only grew more frequent. By the time Julian got home they were worse. He found me wearing a big nightshirt, standing up, and swearing a blue streak at the leg cramps. Julian called the nurse hotline, and they suggested drinking more fluids, massaging the calf area, and warm compresses.

"Where's your water bottle?" Julian asked me.

"I think I left it at the office." I shook my head. "It's probably sitting on my desk."

Julian poured me a large glass of water and handed it to me. "Drink it all."

"How's the cabin coming along?" I asked.

"I took some pictures on my phone and a video to show you," he said and sat beside me on the couch.

As I drank my water, I scrolled my way through the images. "Wow. They're moving right along."

"Duncan estimates another four to six weeks and we can move back in."

I handed him back his phone. "Won't be soon enough for me."

Julian frowned. "I thought you were enjoying living close to the mansion where you could walk to work with Maggie."

"That part is fine," I said. "Ivy dropped by while you were gone."

"I take it by your tone of voice that things didn't go well?"

I folded my arms over my belly. "She came over spoiling for a fight. We argued."

"*And?*"

"She accused me of lying about how far along I am. She thinks the pregnancy is the reason we got married."

"All you had to do was show her the first ultrasound photos." Julian laid a hand over the mound of my stomach. "The gestational date is literally printed on them."

"She never got into the house, Julian."

"You argued with her out in the front yard?"

"She started it." I heard the petulance of my own voice and winced. "Damn it." I dropped my head back against the couch.

"What else happened?" he asked and crossed his feet on the coffee table.

"She made a cheap comment about you. I lost my temper and invoked the element of air."

Julian gave me side-eye. "You did?"

I blew out a long breath. "I did. We exchanged a few more pleasantries and the final bag of potting mix blew up...and it sprayed all over Ivy."

"Angel." Julian shook his head. "That probably wasn't the wisest course of action."

"No shit?" I glared at him. "Thanks for that amazing insight, Captain Obvious."

"You must be exhausted," he said. "You only get sarcastic like this when you are very fatigued."

"Cracked the code, have you?"

He laughed at my snark, and it was everything I had not to hit him over the head with a lamp...or an end table.

"Holly, between the physical strain of carrying twins, working all day, not drinking enough water... then getting into an argument with your sister *and* the physical toll of invoking an element, you are likely dehydrated and exhausted." He patted my thigh. "It's all right." Julian stood up and held out his hand. "I think you need to go to bed."

I batted his hand away. "Swear to goddess, if you keep up this patronizing, mansplaining tone I *will* kick your ass."

He raised an eyebrow. "Now you're just trying to turn me on."

"Damn it, Julian," I swore, but didn't manage to stop the laughter. "I'm edgy, bitchy and wound up. It's been a while since I called an element. I'm still juiced by the power."

He grabbed my hands and helped haul me to my feet. "Let's get you to bed, anyway, warrior woman."

"Okay." I gave in. Calling an element was big magick; it could knock any practitioner down, energetically. The other drawback was that even though I was keyed up, it would take me hours to wind down. I probably wouldn't sleep at all tonight, and so I sat in our bed propped up on the wedge bed pillow while Julian massaged the back of my calves for me.

"Better?" he asked.

"You have one hour to stop that," I joked.

He bent over and kissed one of my raised knees. "Is that right?" He lingered over my knee and began to slowly kiss his way up my thigh. "Are you feeling better now?"

I groaned. "I will be if you keep going."

"I should probably let you rest," he said, even as he continued along the inside of my thigh.

I ran my hand over his hair. "You know it doesn't work that way. I'm too wired from the elemental magick to sleep."

"Well, perhaps I can find a way to help you relax." He pushed my nightshirt higher. "Mrs. Drake." He sounded somewhat shocked. "What happened to your underwear?"

"Are you scandalized, Mr. Drake?" I teased. "Maybe I was hoping to get lucky toni—" I gasped as he ran his tongue along the inside of my thigh. A moment later, I was clamping my fingers in his hair and holding on for dear life as he dipped his head and helped himself.

Only after I reached completion did he strip off his sweatpants and join me. He eased inside of me, and we moved together slowly. We never broke eye contact as we made love face to face. Julian held himself up on his arms to keep his weight off my baby belly, and his care only turned me on more. Afterwards we lay spooned together.

"Love you," I said.

"And I love you." He pressed a kiss to the top of my head. "Now get some rest."

"Bossy," I said and wriggled my backside more snugly against his front.

"Holly, cut that out," he said. "Lie still."

Feeling his interest peak, I tilted my head back far enough to see his face. "What are you going to do if I don't?" I settled back more firmly against him.

"Don't." His voice was close to a growl. "You shouldn't start something you won't be able to finish," he warned.

I reached back and wrapped my hand around his length. "Who says I can't *finish*?"

"You need to rest." His voice, I noticed, sounded more than a little strained.

"Can't. I'm still too wound up." I sat up, slid a leg over, and straddled him. "Maybe you can help me with that."

Julian moved, rearranging us slightly, and began to ease his way up inside. "We need to be careful, and not be too rough," Julian said.

I leaned forward and grabbed his hands. Playfully, I pinned them on either side of his head. "I'll be gentle," I promised.

"Angel," he groaned as my hair spilled all around him.

Afterwards he helped me lay down beside him. I started to drift off right away and smiled when I felt him pull a cover up and over us.

"I love you, Julian," I whispered, and I was out.

CHAPTER NINE

Two weeks had passed since Ivy's drive by—which is how I'd come to think of it—and I hadn't heard from her at all. I had half expected for Bran to show up and read me the riot act, but I didn't see my brother either.

Lexie walked by with the kids a few times for short visits, and Belinda and Morgan loved running around the backyard. The kids were mostly curious about our house being added on to so Julian showed them the progress photos and invited Lexie and the family out to the cabin to see the construction. I also offered to babysit—since we were so close by—if she and Bran wanted to go out for a date night, but they never took us up on that either. I missed Morgan and Belinda; I hadn't been away from them for so long for years.

Still, I saw Willow and baby Phillip every day at the mansion, and Isabel too. Willow wanted to know why I had two babies in my tummy, and I tried to explain to her that twins ran in the family. I wasn't sure how much about that a seven-year-old could understand, but she'd taken to carrying two of her baby dolls around with her everywhere she went.

Autumn and Duncan were still a part of our lives, and I appreciated Autumn's support so much. Her experience as a mom of twins was invaluable. It also made me wonder what my mother, Gwen, would have thought about all of this.

Would she have been excited about the twins and happy that Julian and I were together? Or would she, too, have been disappointed with me? I reminded myself that I still had support from a few members of my side of the family. Aunt Faye sent me emails regularly, and my father and stepmother called every weekend for an update.

Ruth was so excited about the quilts she was making that she had called to video chat, showing me the fabric she'd purchased. My stepmother was set on making woodland animal themed baby quilts for us. The ivory fabric had foxes, deer, and bunnies on it and was in colors of sage green, tan, and peach. She and my father were thrilled with the prospect of becoming grandparents.

I only hoped that nothing would go wrong—I didn't want to let them all down. With that in mind, I followed the doctor's guidelines carefully, and prayed to the goddess every day that I'd be holding those babies in my arms in only a few more months.

Work on the cabin was moving right along, and wall color and bathroom tile decisions needed to be made.

I'd been out to see the addition a few times and I was amazed at how much larger the cabin was going to be. Thomas went with us to meet Duncan at the cabin the day we went over the tile choices for the primary suite's bath and the Jack and Jill bathroom between the two bedrooms downstairs.

When we arrived, Duncan immediately asked me what colors I'd like the nursery to be painted, and I clutched at that. I stammered out some half-assed reply that it was too soon to be decorating the nursery, and that we still had plenty of time.

Worried that I had overreacted to his question, I walked around the newly drywalled rooms on the first floor on my own and tried to take it all in. It was hard not to feel overwhelmed. Sweat began to roll down my back and I tried to breathe slowly and remain calm. But I could feel the anxiety creeping in.

Duncan called me back to the bathroom. All of the men were there looking at the final choices. I shook myself off and went to join them. "Can we keep a sort of wood, stone, and rustic theme in the bathrooms?" I asked Duncan. "Or would that be too kitschy?"

"Why don't we combine a more modern look with the rustic?" Julian suggested.

In the end, it was white subway tiles with dark gray grout for the Jack and Jill bath. The floor we selected was shades of pale gray, and the tile was plank shaped with the look and texture of hardwood. The bathroom's vanity cabinet and the top would be white. And we chose a warm, soft gray paint for the walls.

Upstairs, in the primary suite's bath, Duncan suggested a rustic stone for the wall around the tub and shower stall and a floor tile in the same gray wooden plank look as the downstairs bath. The toilet, tub and vanity top would all be white. The primary suite's bath maintained its cabin vibe with exposed beams in the ceiling, the stone walls, and a gray-toned wooden double vanity. We decided to paint the walls in the primary suite and bath a bright warm white.

"Go ahead and paint all of the bedrooms and the office on the top floor the same shade of white," I said to Duncan. "I can always add an accent wall or choose a final color later."

We all went down to the main level and into the expanded kitchen next. Duncan and his crew had saved the sturdy, original barn-red cabinets. The island had been pushed back and new cabinets and an apron sink had been worked in to extend the workspace in the kitchen by a few more feet.

Here, the new cabinet colors had been paint-matched and antiqued with a tea-stain finish to make them look the same age as the original red cabinets. Now it was down to new countertops and a backsplash.

I had chosen a natural looking stone cut in a subway tile shape. There were many variations in the stone, and with the neutral countertop, the deep red cabinets, and the old wood walls, the kitchen would still retain its rustic cabin feel. In fact, I had been picking up vintage pieces and antiques to decorate the entryway and our refurbished kitchen. Currently they were being stored for us at Autumn's house in her basement.

A while later I was standing on the grass at the edge of our clearing, looking over the back of the house. The exterior of the addition had been wrapped in stone. There was no way to quickly do the build in logs, however the natural stone was complimentary, and as I viewed it from across the clearing and took the two-story expansion in, it felt exactly right.

It was quiet and peaceful here, and the birds sang in the woods surrounding our house. I felt myself relax; I belonged out here away from the town proper. And while it was a relief knowing we would be moved back with plenty of time to settle and decorate...I wasn't going to make any decisions on the nursery décor until we knew the genders of the babies and *after* we hit viability.

Most of the time I was able to stay positive, but there were still times that I struggled against fear of losing the pregnancy. I still was going to therapy, and tried to remain upbeat.

If things go well, I thought, *I might end up playing off the colors in the baby quilt fabric*

That woodland fabric Ruth had chosen was sweet. She'd sent me a swatch last week, and I had been secretly carrying it in my purse as sort of a good luck charm. I hoped to do neutral walls with pale peach accents for girls or soft sage green accents for boys.

They felt like they would be very good options. If we ended up with one of each, I thought I'd probably use all of those colors.

I felt a good kick, and it shook me out of daydreaming over the future nursery. With a wistful sigh, I rested my hands on my baby bump and spoke to the twins. "What do you think about your new, bigger house?" I asked and took a seat on the grass.

In answer I felt a kick and a squirm, and my heart lifted. Every kick or movement from the babies helped keep me steady...or steadier.

"I figured I should ask, since you two are the reason for all of this. Look, there's your Daddy and Uncle Duncan discussing the future landscaping," I said to my belly. "Should we go tell them that Aunt Autumn already has massive plans for perennial beds and a fenced vegetable and herb garden?"

I felt a second kick.

"I like the idea of growing my own vegetables," I said to my belly. "I could grow heirloom tomatoes, squash and beans. Maybe a few pumpkins and ornamental corn for fun."

While I sat daydreaming over the garden, Thomas walked over. To my surprise, he sat in the grass beside me. "Julian tells me he's been feeling the babies kick."

I felt another kick. "They are currently showing off, if you want to feel."

Thomas smiled. "May I?"

"Of course."

He laid one of his elegant hands on my belly and waited. Nothing happened.

"Hey, you two," I said, giving my belly a soft poke.

In answer there was a flutter and a kick.

Thomas' whole face lit up. "Wonderful."

I leaned back in the grass against my elbows. "You're going to ruin your image sitting in the grass, you know."

"I enjoy feeling the earth beneath me," Thomas said, mimicking my pose.

"I bet your dry cleaner will pass out when you drop those slacks off to be cleaned."

Thomas raised one eyebrow. "He's made of sterner stuff than that. Between Willow's paints, Isabel throwing food, and baby Phillip spitting up on me, he's well used to it."

I smiled over at him. "The kids all adore you, Thomas."

Thomas smiled back at me. "Your mother would have been *thrilled* to see all the babies. Bran's children, Autumn's twins, and now yours."

"I'd like to think so."

Thomas stood and brushed off his slacks. "I know so." He held out a hand and I accepted it. "I'm sorry to hear that you are still estranged from your brother and sister."

I stood with his help. "I'm very grateful that the Drakes and company have rallied around us."

"There was a time," he began as we walked around

the clearing, "that I wondered if the Drake's were doomed to be alone and unhappy forever. My father Silas abused his powers and his brother paid the price for it. At that point, my sister Rebecca became obsessed with trying to earn Silas' respect, when he never had any to give. Her obsession with the dark path, in the end, destroyed many lives, including her own."

I gave him an elbow nudge. "The way I heard it, it was you who stopped her and saved Duncan in the process."

"I played a role that night," he said, "just as Julian saved your Aunt Faye and Autumn."

"You were both heroes," I said, meeting his gaze. "I'll never be considered a hero, Thomas. To be honest, I always wondered if you hated me, because I once used magick and called on the element of water against your daughter, Leilah."

"No, I have never hated you." Thomas waved that away. "That was so long ago. You were teenagers. Children."

"I was old enough to know better," I argued. "I caused her lungs to fill up with water and would have let her drown if Autumn wouldn't have stopped me."

"Yes, that is true," Thomas said blandly, "and besides a cough, Leilah walked away unharmed. Unfortunately, when Leilah used her magick to attack you at the antique store a few years later; you were injured badly enough that you were hospitalized."

"That was the day Julian came to my rescue." I

smiled, remembering. "My own dark knight."

Thomas studied my face. "Is that the day you two began to fall for each other?"

"Yes," I said, "it was."

"Interesting isn't it, how all those seemingly random events drew us together?" Thomas said. "First Autumn and Duncan met and fell in love. Julian became friends with Diego and Nina. Julian was on hand to help you, and the two of you fell in love. Nina became our chef and house manager. She, Diego, and Isabel moved onto the estate, and they quickly became a part of our lives. We found Maggie and Willow and brought them home. Maggie met Wyatt and he joined the family next."

He'd left Leilah out of that conversation, and I didn't comment. His daughter was still incarcerated for abducting Maggie's daughter, Willow. I'd been there to help Maggie the day she squared off with Leilah. In the end Maggie's magick was much more powerful than Leilah's, and justice had been served.

Thomas continued. "In the past few years Erin and Emma were born, and a few months ago, baby Phillip. Now there's your and Julian's babies on the way."

"We seem to be a prolific bunch," I said, trying to keep the conversation upbeat.

Thomas smiled down at me. "The mansion is filled with family and laughter as it never was before. It makes me so happy as a father to know that Julian has well and truly found his partner; and that my son will soon have a family of his own."

"You're not upset that we chose to live here at the cabin?" I asked him.

"No." He tucked my arm in his. "The mansion should rightfully pass to Maggie and her children. They are the descendants of the eldest Drake male after all."

"Oh," I said. "I never thought about that."

Thomas nodded. "My brother, Phillip's, heirs should inherit control of the family mansion."

"That's a very generous thing you're doing," I said.

Thomas glanced over. "I see it as more of a balancing the scales. The feud between the Bishops and Drakes barred my uncle Phillip and Irene Bishop from openly being together. They never had their chance to raise their child. Irene was right to hide Patricia's existence from my father." Thomas sighed. "The world became a better place when Silas Drake passed away."

I didn't comment on that. I remembered reading about the man from my mother's journals. Silas Drake had been an evil man. After Phillip's untimely death, my Aunt Irene had run away to have Maggie's mother, Patricia, in secret. Even her own family hadn't known about Irene's child.

Discovering the truth had led to the search for Patricia. By the time Thomas' detectives had tracked her down, Patricia had sadly passed away, but there had been her daughter, Maggie. When Thomas first met Maggie, she was recently divorced, dealing with a mountain of medical debt from her mother, and raising Willow on her own. Maggie had been shocked to learn the truth of her mother's legacy.

"I can't imagine Maggie and Willow not being here in Williams Ford," I said. "They brought a special kind of magick with them when they moved here."

"Maggie, like her grandfather, Phillip, is a powerful magician."

"It's nice that she named the baby after him," I said.

Thomas' head whipped around at that.

"Don't get ahead of yourself," I warned. "It's a tad early for us to be thinking about names. Especially as we don't yet know the gender."

"I'll be thrilled no matter what the gender." Thomas grinned. "And I've never seen Julian so settled and content. Plus, you are obviously happier when you have your space and privacy out here in the woods. I understand that."

Arm in arm we started to walk over to Julian and Duncan.

"We're only a twenty-minute drive outside of Williams Ford," I said. "You can zip over easily enough to visit."

He patted my hand. "I'd like that."

"So would I, Thomas," I said and meant it. "So would I."

***

Our gender confirmation ultrasound was the following week, and Julian's family and our friends were all very excited. There were times the baby name suggestions made me anxious, and other times when it made me hopeful. The list of possible names had gotten so outrageous that Maggie had a white board up in the office with names for two boys, two girls and names for one of each.

I had mixed feelings about that board. On one hand it was sweet and funny, and it was comforting to know how invested in the pregnancy Julian's family was—on the other it made me feel a lot of pressure to not let anyone down.

I sat back in my desk chair and took a sip of water. My eyes landed on the baby name board and I saw the most recent additions for names written in a child's hand. I swallowed wrong, coughed and ended up thumping a hand to my chest. "Dare I ask who added the Disney princess names to the board?"

Maggie spun in her chair to grin. "Willow thought that *Merida* and *Ariel* would be wonderful names for the twins."

"Because of my red hair?" I guessed.

"Bless her heart," Maggie said. "She's expecting those babies to pop out with long red hair. That way she can brush and braid it."

"Aww." I teared up a bit. "That's so sweet."

"What's your guess, Mama?" Maggie asked me with a smile.

I shrugged. "We'll have to wait and see."

"What's Julian say?" Maggie asked.

"He says that all he wants are two healthy babies and a healthy me."

"Have you considered doing a gender reveal party?" Maggie asked.

I had been in mid-turn back to my computer monitor, but stopped at the question. "No," I said, "I had not." I was still worried about the pregnancy. Every ultrasound appointment was an emotional roller coaster for me. I couldn't imagine casually handing over the results to someone else to have it announced to us at a later date. Just thinking about uncertainty of *any* kind regarding the babies had my heart rate speeding up.

"I casually mentioned it to Julian a few weeks ago," Maggie said.

"What did he say about it?" I managed to say while struggling to keep a pleasant expression on my face.

"He said it would be up to you. But I don't understand why you wouldn't want to celebrate. You should throw a party," she urged. "It would be fun!"

"Our ultrasound is in six days," I said carefully, trying not to offend her. "We couldn't possibly pull off a party that fast."

"Oh, ye of little faith." Maggie opened a drawer and pulled out a file. She stood, walked over, and dropped a folder in the middle of my desk.

It was marked: *Twin Gender Reveal*. My stomach rolled. It was all I had not to flinch.

"I spoke to Nina," Maggie began. "She's all set to handle the food."

"Maggie, I—"

Maggie spoke right over me. "I'll call her up here so we can talk about it."

I opened the folder, and my heart sank. They had been obviously working on the plans for a while. "Maggie," I began, "while I appreciate the thought..."

"We didn't get to celebrate your wedding," she pointed out. "So, let's blow the roof off and have an epic gender reveal!"

"Hold on. Let's not get too carried away," I warned. "My brother and sister aren't even speaking to me. I can't imagine the problems this would cause if we invited—or if we did *not* invite them..."

I trailed off as Nina appeared in the doorway. "Are we finally talking about the gender reveal party?" she asked.

I blinked. "How'd you get up here so fast?"

She winked. "I used magick."

I opened my mouth to speak, but Nina launched into a pitch for food and fancy pink and blue iced cupcakes. Maggie was pulling out pages from the folder to show me different balloon arches, and I sat there silently.

She and Nina were so pumped up about it all that they didn't notice my lack of reaction. When Maggie launched into gender party themes, I went from anxious to a full-blown panic attack. It was a nasty one too.

My breath began to hitch, and I gripped my hands together hard under the desk trying to stay calm. The mug on my desk that held pens and pencils began to shake. When Maggie started talking about pink or blue exploding confetti guns, I snapped. "No!" I cried. "It's all too much!"

The ceramic mug cracked from the force of anxiety and fell into pieces on my desk. The pens unfortunately went flying out and across the room. Startled by my outburst and the uncontrolled magick, Maggie and Nina flinched and turned to me simultaneously.

"I'm sorry," I said. "I know you both mean well, but...just...*no*." I stood up quickly, intending to walk away, but it was too sudden of a movement. The room seemed to slide to one side. I grabbed for the back of my chair, but it shot away from me and crashed against the opposite wall. As I stumbled a bit in surprise, black and white spots appeared before my eyes.

"Holly!" I heard Maggie's voice as if from far away.

My stomach roiled, and a rushing sound filled my ears. Then everything went black.

***

"There you are," a calm male voice said.

Slowly, I opened my eyes and focused on the face of my father-in-law.

I was lying on the floor of the office; Thomas sat by my side, holding my hand. There was a lot of activity in the background. "What happened?" I asked.

"You got upset, used your powers of psychokinesis, and fainted," he said.

"I did?" I asked, my face flushing in embarrassment.

"You sure as hell did." That was Maggie's voice and she bent over Thomas' shoulder to peer at me. "But Nina and I managed to catch you when you fainted."

I tried to sit up, but Thomas and Maggie kept me where I was.

"Stay put," Thomas said. "The ambulance is on the way."

I pressed my hands over my belly, hoping to feel some movement, but the twins were quiet. My heart rapped hard against my ribs in terror. "Call Julian," I said.

"We have," Thomas said, giving my hand a squeeze. "He will meet us at the hospital. So will your doctor."

I didn't argue. I kept waiting to feel movement from the babies, and I wasn't feeling anything. "The babies aren't moving," I whispered to Thomas. As I spoke, the lights overhead began to flicker.

"Try to stay calm," he said soothingly. "Your magick is fueled by your fears, and it's become angry and chaotic."

But I couldn't stay calm. My heart was racing, and terrified tears rolled down my face. Across the room, the white board with the baby names on it shook and fell to the floor with a loud clatter.

Maggie was suddenly in my line of sight. "Give that negative energy to me." She clamped a hand on my arm, and I felt the chaotic energy swirling within me begin to fade. Maggie's eyes morphed to a deeper blue as she took it into herself, and, as I watched, she grit her teeth.

"Maggie?" Thomas asked, concerned.

"I've got it." Maggie lifted her hands and pressed them to the floor to ground the unwanted magick. She shook her head and blew out a long cleansing breath.

"I'm sorry," I said as I continued to cry.

"Hush, now." Maggie ran her hand over my hair. "It's going to be fine; you'll see."

"They're here!" Nina's voice came from the hallway. "Diego is showing the EMTs upstairs."

***

A few hours later, I was sitting on the bed in a treatment room in the ER. I was currently working on relearning how to maintain my breathing at a normal, easy pace. The babies had decided—after a terrifying hour and a half—to begin to squirm around again. The Doppler monitor had picked up both fetal heartbeats and they were strong and within the expected range. But until I felt movement I didn't even begin to relax.

My blood pressure was elevated, and the general medical consensus was that between the panic attack and standing up too quickly, it had caused me to pass out. Since I hadn't hit my head—thanks to both Nina and Maggie catching me—and had no symptoms of a concussion, they were going to send me home with orders to push fluids, rest, and to work on my stress.

I was told by the ER doctor to follow up with my obstetrician, and to my surprise Dr. Anderson popped into the treatment room to check on me personally.

She explained that she'd been about to head home after a delivery but had wanted to see how I was. She assured me and Julian that she'd looked over the attending physician's notes and was comfortable with releasing me. With a wave, she left, reminding us that a nurse would be in with discharge instructions. Before that discharge nurse could come in, Thomas walked straight into the treatment room.

"I've spoken to your Dr. Anderson," he began.

I could only shut my eyes. Julian's father was on the board of the hospital directors. I was surprised we'd managed to keep him out of the treatment room for this long.

"Father," Julian began, "perhaps we could speak at a..." Julian's words trailed off as Thomas pulled up a chair and sat at the opposite side of my bed and made himself comfortable.

"I'm satisfied with knowing the doctor thinks you and the babies are well and can go home to rest." Thomas reached over and took my hand in his. "What I am concerned about is that Holly's anxiety over the pregnancy is so severe that she's having panic attacks, high blood pressure, bursts of uncontrolled magick, and fainting episodes."

"Her medical information is private—" Julian began.

"I did not look at her medical records," Thomas said,

cutting off Julian. "Her symptoms are clearly *obvious*, son."

I shut my eyes, embarrassed all over again.

"How can I help you, my dear?" Thomas patted the back of my hand. "Talk to me."

I felt tears begin to roll down my face. I badly wanted to have the respect of Julian's father. "Five years ago," I began, "long before Julian and I started to see each other, I got pregnant."

Thomas didn't react. "Go on."

"I was a junior in college. My boyfriend wanted me to end the pregnancy and I refused. Instead, we broke up and I made plans to come home to Williams Ford at the end of the winter semester, to raise the baby by myself." I swallowed past a lump in my throat. "But before I was able to come back home, or even tell my family, I had a miscarriage."

Thomas kept a hold of my hand. "How far along were you?"

"Around seven weeks."

"I remember when you came home," he said. "I was shocked to see the difference in your appearance. You were very pale and far too thin."

"Yes," I said. "It was a horrible time in my life."

Thomas nodded. "You were grieving."

That simple acknowledgment, with no judgment on his part, had fresh tears rolling down my face.

He smiled kindly. "I'm sure your family was a comfort to you during that time."

"I never told them," I said. "Besides Autumn, no one knew."

Thomas frowned over that.

Julian sat beside me on the edge of the bed. "Holly told me about what had happened when we were first together."

Thomas continued to hold my hand, as he listened to Julian. "Well," he said, "that would certainly explain Holly's heightened unease and worry over this pregnancy."

I wiped my eyes. "When I found out that I was pregnant only a few months after we eloped, I was completely terrified. There'd been a mix up with the dates to renew my Depo shot. And, well..."

Julian shifted beside me. "They offered us an ultrasound to determine how far along Holly was. They started the exam, and after a moment the tech turned off the monitor and went to get Dr. Anderson."

"I immediately assumed the worst," I said.

"You must have been very frightened," Thomas said to me.

"I was," I said. "I thought the pregnancy wasn't viable, and they showed us that there was not only one baby on board, but *two*."

Julian smiled. "It took a while for that surprise of the pregnancy, and then the shock of there being two babies to sink in."

Thomas gave my hand a gentle squeeze. "Which explains why you waited a while to make any announcement."

"I asked Julian to hold off telling anyone until we reached the second trimester." I blew out a breath. "It was a very long three and a half weeks."

"Holly," Thomas began, "when you share your burdens, it lessens the load. Isolating yourself from the family is not the answer. You should lean on us, let us all support you and Julian at this time."

"I got used to dealing with things on my own, I suppose," I said to his father.

"But you are *not* alone," Thomas said softly. "Not anymore. You are a Drake now."

"I didn't think you were very happy about that initially," I said, honestly.

"I was taken aback at first when you and Julian announced that you had eloped," Thomas explained, "but that was mostly because I had no idea that you two had been involved with each other for so long." He gave my fingers another bolstering squeeze. "When we talked at the cabin the other day, my dear, I meant every word that I said to you. And in case there was any doubt, let me speak plainly. I love you both. There's nothing I wouldn't do for either of you."

I sniffled. "You're making me cry again."

Thomas pulled a pristine handkerchief from his pocket, stood, and proceeded to wipe my eyes himself. "These are happy tears, I hope."

"Yes. Happy tears." I smiled through them. "Thank you, Thomas."

"Excuse me." A nurse poked his head in the door. "I have Holly Drake's discharge papers."

"That'd be me," I said.

Thomas stepped back. "I'll leave you two for now. Please call once you're home and settled."

"We will," Julian promised. "I guarantee that she will be off her feet for the rest of the day."

We were able to leave shortly afterward, and I was silent on the brief drive back to the rental house. Julian parked the car and we walked inside hand in hand. I put on my pajamas—an oversized night shirt—and went straight to bed. Not because Julian told me to, but because I was worn out from the uncontrolled PK and the emotional toll of everything.

I fell asleep for a couple of hours and woke up starving. Easing from the bed, I took a few steps and caught sight of myself in the bedroom dresser's mirror.

"Good grief." I shuddered. My curly hair was poofing out everywhere. With a sigh, I stopped and combed it out with my wide toothed comb. Next, I braided my heavy curls into a thick braid. Satisfied that I looked, if not better, then at least tidy, I tossed the braid over my shoulder and wandered into the living room to see what was going on.

Julian sat on the couch, wearing a burgundy t-shirt and old gray sweatpants. It made my heart skip a beat to see my gorgeous husband in those sweats.

Damn, I thought. *The man can wear sweats like nobody's business.*

He worked unaware of my perusal. His hair was slightly mussed, his feet were bare and propped up on our coffee table, and his laptop was balanced on his thighs as he was typing away. If it hadn't been for the day and the scare I'd had, I'd have probably pounced on him.

"Hi," I said.

He glanced up and smiled. "You look better."

"Did you call my dad?" I asked. "I don't want him or Ruth to worry."

"Yes." He set the laptop aside and patted the spot beside him. "I called Aunt Faye, and Duncan and Autumn too. Father will bring Maggie, Wyatt, Nina and Diego up to speed."

"Thanks for calling everyone." I sat beside him. "I'm starving."

He smiled. "How about a ham sandwich?"

"Yes." My stomach growled. "That sounds great."

Julian put together a sandwich, added some carrot sticks, and brought the plate to me. I stayed where I was and ate my supper on the couch.

"So." Julian took a seat beside me as I plowed through the sandwich. "I was thinking about the gender reveal party that Maggie suggested."

"Not sure how I feel about that," I said around a bite of sandwich. "For a lot of reasons. Mainly because I had an emotional meltdown about it in front of Maggie and Nina earlier today."

"Angel." He patted my leg. "It's going to be all

right."

I shut my eyes in shame, even thinking about my behavior. "Gods, what must they think of me...crying, shouting, and losing control of my magick like that?"

"They were only concerned about you—" He was interrupted by a knock on the front door. "I'll be right back." He dropped a kiss on my head and got up.

"Hey." That was Autumn's voice. "I wanted to pop over and check on you two."

"Come in, Autumn," I called out.

"It's only me," she said. "Duncan's home giving the girls a bath."

Autumn came into the living room carrying a casserole dish wrapped in a kitchen towel. "I made you a turkey tetrazzini. Thought maybe you might not feel like cooking tonight."

"The kind with the peas in it, and breadcrumbs on top?" I asked, hopefully.

Autumn smiled. "Yes, ma'am."

"I *love* you," I said, anticipating the casserole.

Julian took the casserole from Autumn. "Thank you, I'll put this in the kitchen." He stopped. "Unless you'd like some now, Angel?"

"Actually, I would."

"It's still warm," Autumn said.

"Oh," I sighed. "*Yum.*"

Autumn chuckled. "I remember hitting the second trimester with Erin and Emma. I was a bottomless pit. Always starving."

"That seems to be the case with me too," I said wryly.

From the kitchen came the sounds of Julian getting out plates and utensils.

"I don't want to stay too long." Autumn perched on the arm of the sofa beside me. "The girls had dozens of toys in that tub. Goddess knows what sort of condition the bathroom will be in when I get home."

I started to laugh at the mental picture that created.

"Anyway," she continued, "I only wanted to drop off some food, remind you we're only a few houses down if you need anything, and to tell you to *try* and take it easy."

"We appreciate it," Julian called from the kitchen.

Autumn leaned over and wrapped her arm around my shoulders. "You gave us all a scare today, Holly."

"It scared me too," I admitted.

She added a squeeze. "Eat your tetrazzini, push the fluids, and rest. I'll call and check on you in the morning."

"Okay," I said.

She brushed a kiss over my cheek. "Love your face."

"And I love yours," I said in return.

My cousin let go, popped up to standing, and spun for the door. She managed almost two steps before tripping over thin air. Fortunately, she caught herself and hardly broke stride. Autumn then blew a kiss to Julian before she let herself out the door. "Holler if you need anything," she reminded him.

"Will do," Julian said. "Be careful walking home."

"I'll be fine," she said and shut the door behind her.

"Please, keep an eye on her," I called out to Julian.

I shook my head fondly. Autumn was a talented Witch, but she was adorably clumsy. I suppose it all averaged out—amazing magickal skills paired with substandard physical coordination.

"I'm staying at the kitchen window watching her walk down the sidewalk," he called back.

"It's one less thing to worry about," I said.

CHAPTER TEN

Julian walked back into the living room carrying two bowls of the casserole and with utensils sticking out of the pocket of his sweatpants. "I watched Autumn until she started up the sidewalk to the bungalow."

"Good."

"I'm not much of a casserole person, but..." He took a deep sniff of the food. "This smells amazing."

I held out my hands for my bowl. "Gimme."

Julian passed it over. "If this tastes half as good as it smells..."

"It is good," I promised. "Trust me."

He placed his bowl on the table and added the cutlery. "I'll go get our drinks."

He came back and we dug in. I scooted over closer to him and rested my feet beside his on the table. It was homey sitting on our leather couch, in the rental house, eating tetrazzini out of bowls.

I finished the food. "Oh my gods. That was *amazing*."

Julian gave me a gentle elbow nudge. "You used to say that about me."

I slanted him a look. "The night is young."

Chuckling at that, Julian took the empty bowl from me and placed his bowl and mine on the table. He shut his eyes, rested his head back against the sofa, and let out a contented sigh.

I laid my hand on his thigh. "I'm sorry about the scare today."

Julian popped one eye open to regard me. "There is no need to apologize."

"I still feel like I should," I said. "I know that Maggie and Nina meant well, but it was all too much."

"I understand," he said, and while his tone was both gracious and understanding, I still felt the need to explain.

"I would never be able to wait for *any* information about the babies," I said. "Sure, I would like to have their gender confirmed, but I would need a bit to let that information sink in. For the two of us. Considering everything that we've been through, don't we deserve the chance to savor and enjoy the news privately for a moment?"

Julian lifted my hand and pressed a kiss to the back of it. "All right."

"Afterwards we can share the news with the family." I turned our joined hands over and kissed his knuckles. "Julian, I know it's popular to make a big announcement and to document the gender reveal for social media, but I would *never* be comfortable with that."

"How about a compromise?" Julian asked.

"I'm listening."

"We find out the gender on Thursday, and the next day we share it with the family." He slipped an arm around my shoulders. "We'll keep it simple. No elaborate party, and *no* stress."

"Absolutely no exploding confetti guns, massive balloon arches, fireworks, or smoke bombs." I pointed at him. "I mean it. That's a hard line for me. We keep it simple."

His lips twitched. "How about two big balloons. One for baby A and another for baby B. We would have them done up ourselves."

"Hmm…" I pursed my lips as I thought about it. "It would be the best way to keep the genders a total surprise for the rest of the family."

"Then we all gather together in our backyard on Friday, early in the evening. We pop the balloons and a sprinkle of blue or pink confetti comes out."

"I suppose if we did a gender reveal—even a small and intimate one—we would need to extend an invitation to Bran and Lexie, and Ivy and Erik." I blew out a long breath. "Crap, even thinking about calling them makes me nervous."

"You leave them to me," Julian said. "I'd like a few words with your brother, anyway."

"You won't turn him into a newt, will you?"

Julian raised one eyebrow. "As if I'd ever do anything so cliché."

"What was I thinking? The suave, elegant Julian Drake would never stoop to such a vulgar spell."

"Ask anyone," he said soberly. "I am known for my style and panache in *any* social situation."

"Especially when you wear those sweatpants."

Soberly he inclined his head. "Why thank you, Mrs. Drake."

I couldn't help but smile at that dry tone. "I love you."

Julian leaned forward and pressed a firm kiss to my mouth. "And I love you," he said. "I will personally speak to your brother and sister. If Bran and Ivy decide to attend, they and their spouses will have to promise not to upset you; or they will deal with me."

"My own dark knight." I gave a little shudder. "That's so hot. Maybe you could take off your shirt and say that *they will deal with me* part again? Make your voice more raspy this time."

Julian shook his head. "Behave yourself, Angel."

"Hey, you're the one wearing those sexy sweatpants and being all alpha male." I waved my hand in front of my face. "It's a lot for a girl to take in."

A slow smile spread across his face. "What am I going to do with you?"

"I have a few suggestions."

"You should rest."

I slanted him a look. "Take me to bed and we'll talk

about it."

With a nod Julian stood up. He gathered up the dishes and took them to the kitchen; I heard him place them in the sink. Then he went to the front door and flipped the lock. I hauled myself to my feet, and then let out a squeal when he walked over and scooped me up into his arms.

He kissed me. It was a hard, passionate kiss. I responded instantly and kissed him back for all I was worth. Without breaking the kiss, he carried me to the bedroom.

He paused by the side of the bed and lifted his mouth from mine. "You truly should get some rest, Angel," he said, and gently laid me on the bed.

"Take your shirt off and maybe I will," I countered, leaning back against the pillows.

Slowly he reached up and pulled off his shirt. He dropped it to the floor and stood there silently in his sweatpants. The light from the lamp on the nightstand highlighted the muscles and definition of his chest and abs.

"You are," I said softly, "the most beautiful man I have ever seen. Come to bed, Julian."

"Take your hair down for me first," he said. His voice was deeper now, with a touch of gravel.

Sitting up, I pulled the holder from the end of my braid. I combed my fingers through my hair and gave my head a shake. Taking my hair down had definitely affected him. I reached out to trail my fingers over that bulge, but instead he moved away, eluding my touch.

With one quick motion, Julian removed the sweats and stepped free of them. He climbed onto the bed and gently pulled my night clothes from me. The look in his eyes had me anticipating a good ravishing and I began to tremble with desire.

But there was no wild romp. Instead, he made love to me carefully, slowly, and took me to the edge of losing my mind. This side of my husband still caught me off guard. The wild, demanding lover I knew and rejoiced in. But this was different. He was tender, and yet somehow just as intense. When at last I reached completion, I shouted in relief. Julian followed a few moments later and afterward he pulled me close. He fell asleep almost immediately.

I lay there as my system began to settle. The moon was up and shimmering through the bedroom window. It cast its silver light over the floor, and I held my hand out to catch its cool beams in my palm.

Smiling at the radiant gibbous moon, I made a wish. *Mother goddess, watch over us. Let the babies be safe and strong.*

Julian snuggled closer to me, and with a contented smile, I drifted off to sleep.

***

The next morning, I woke up cheerful and starving. I made a big breakfast of eggs, toast, yogurt, and fruit and devoured it all. I took a shower, got ready for work and was still so hungry that I ate an apple while I did my makeup.

I confided to Julian that I was nervous about going back to work with Maggie. Would she be upset with me? Disappointed or offended that I didn't want a big gender reveal party? For a short time, I gave serious consideration to the advantages of chickening out and staying home for the day. Julian understood and even offered to walk me in, but I gathered my courage and told him that I wanted to do it on my own.

When I arrived at the Drake mansion, I paused from my walk across the courtyard and took in the spring gardens. Daffodils were blooming and the tulips were growing taller. Around me the birds were singing, and the perennials were showing new growth every day. Taking a few moments, I tapped into some of that spring energy. I imagined it as a pale spring green color, filling me up and adding energy, enthusiasm and vitality. Feeling bolstered, I let myself in the back door and found that Thomas was waiting for me.

"Good morning, Holly," he said and proceeded to escort me up the stairs.

"This isn't necessary, Thomas," I said.

My father-in-law gave me a polite smile and looped my arm through his. "Until you have gone forty-eight hours without fainting," he said, "you're not going up and down the stairs unaided."

"I suppose you coordinated with Julian?" I sighed.

"He's not letting me drive or take a walk alone for the next couple of days either."

"I did," Thomas said as we gained the second-floor landing. "Also, your Dr. Anderson agreed that it would be a good idea."

I did a double take. "You talked to my doctor about me?"

"Not like you are thinking," he assured me. "We went out for coffee yesterday evening, and I may have casually floated a few ideas about being extra vigilant with your health and safety."

"Is that right?" I asked, torn between aggravation at his high handedness, and simultaneously touched by his concern.

"Brenna is a lovely woman and an excellent physician. I've admired her for years."

"Brenna?" My brows went way up at the use of her first name. "Thomas, are you *dating* my obstetrician?"

"I wouldn't say that we are dating," he said. "We've only had coffee together and that rolled into dinner."

"Well, well," I said.

He brushed at his silver hair absently. "She may have suggested that we have dinner this weekend."

"Asked *you* out, did she?" I tried not to smile.

Sophisticated Thomas Drake, the powerful mage and shrewd businessman, had the faintest of blushes on his cheeks. He paused and met my eyes. "I would appreciate it if you kept this information confidential, for now."

"Sure," I said.

He dropped me off at the doorway to the third-floor rooms that had been converted into the offices of *Magnolia Bridal and Events*. He waved at Maggie and left.

My boss was on the phone with a bride, and by the sounds of it Maggie was trying to soothe and do damage control. I tucked my purse away, placed my water bottle on my desk, and went to slip my lunch into the office mini fridge.

While Maggie finished her call, I sat at my desk and booted up my computer to check if I had any new emails. I had started replying to the first when Maggie finished her conversation.

"Good morning," she said.

I swiveled my desk chair around to face her fully. "Before we get started on today's tasks," I began, "I wanted to apologize for the meltdown yesterday."

"Stop." Maggie held up her hand. "I thought that beyond being cousins, we were friends, Holly."

"We are," I said.

"If I would have known the anxiety you were feeling about being pregnant, Nina and I would have never bombarded you with plans for a big gender reveal party."

"I know that you and Nina meant well."

Maggie dragged a hand through her long dark hair. "You do such a good job keeping people from reading your emotions. You block others out to the point that I never even guessed that your quiet comments and 'we'll have to wait and see' remarks were hiding so much fear. I thought you were simply reserved."

"Ivy accused me a few weeks ago of shutting people out. Maybe I do." I shrugged. "After my mother died it became a way to cope. Then it became a habit."

Maggie stood up and came over to my desk. "The day Willow was abducted you were the one right there beside me when we went to go find her."

"I remember," I said. "We tore across town in Julian's sports car to the McBriar farm. Drove right through their old wooden gate too."

"You were literally my 'ride or die' that day." Maggie crouched down in front of my chair so that we were eye-to-eye. "You never once flinched back from the magick I unleashed on Leilah, and you used your healing abilities for Willow to pull her out of the thrall that had been cast over her."

"Of course," I said. "I love Willow. I'd do no less for any member of my family."

"Well darlin' you better get used to the idea that I would do no less for you, Julian, and these babies." Maggie took my hands. "You put on a good show of being composed and serene, but it's all a big front. You feel more deeply than others with your empathy and holding all that in is costing you physically, energetically and magickally."

"I am aware," I said.

Maggie rested her hands on my belly. "I've seen

these babies in my dreams, Holly. They're going to be strong, healthy, and will be crawling all around here making everyone crazy before you know it."

I tipped my head to one side, considering her words. "I didn't realize you were a precognitive dreamer."

Maggie grinned. "Normally, I'm not. It's Willow who has The Sight. Yet, despite that, I keep seeing your red-haired twins and my Phillip getting into all sorts of mischief."

"Red hair?" I laughed. "Both of them?"

"Yes." Maggie nodded. "The dream didn't show me the genders, but I have seen the two of them and my Phillip several times in my dreams over the past few weeks. In the dreams they are crawling across the carpet in the main family room or trying to get up the main staircase. In another dream they were toddlers digging up Nina's kitchen garden. But the three of them are always causing mischief together."

I smiled. "I can almost visualize that, even as you say it."

"You need to have a little more faith, cousin."

"So I've been told."

One of the babies kicked and I could see by the grin on Maggie's face that she had felt it against her hands. "There," she said. "You see? They agree with me."

"Thank you, Maggie," I said quietly.

She gave me a hug. "I love you."

I hugged her tightly in return. "I love you too."

"Are we good?" she asked.

I patted her shoulder. "You bet we are."

Maggie released me. "Good, because we need to get back to work. We have a bridesmaid and MOB dress fitting appointment to attend in a half hour."

"The Ryder–Whitmore wedding?" I remembered. "There's the mother of the bride and the stepmother to contend with, correct?"

"Yes, the bride's stepmother, who has neither sense or good taste, is planning on wearing *white*."

I shook my head. "That's unfortunate."

"The bride's mother is such a darlin' woman, too." Maggie sighed, sympathetically. "She deserves a medal for dealing with her ex-husband's new wife. So, I'll keep the bride, her maids, and the MOB happy; and you'll take point on the stepmother."

I cracked my knuckles. "You leave the step-monster to me, boss. I'll straighten her out."

"Darlin'." Maggie chuckled. "I never had any doubts."

***

Maybe I was more perverse than I thought, but I enjoyed the hell out of the bridesmaid and mother of the bride dress fittings. There was something satisfying about dealing with someone else's family drama. It put me in a good mood.

The bride had chosen a smoky gray blue for her bridesmaids' dresses. Her mother had opted for a deep royal blue dress. The MOB—mother of the bride—dress was timeless, classic and a very good choice. But when the stepmother walked out of the fitting room in her dress, a couple of the bridesmaids literally gasped in horror.

It was hard not to blame their reaction. Tammi, the stepmother, had on a skintight dress. It was very low cut and completely inappropriate. The bride, I noticed, was red in the face when she got a gander at her stepmother's outfit.

I could feel the bride's anger from where I stood from across the sales floor. As the step-monster stood preening in the three-way mirror, I took the opportunity to try and make her see reason.

"Wow," I said, making sure there was some admiration in my tone. "That's a brave choice."

"Excuse me?" Tammi frowned at me in the mirror.

"Well..." I began. "With the bride in blush and the wedding party in cloudy blue and navy, wearing bright white is a risk."

"White is celebratory." Tammi stuck her nose in the air. "Everyone knows that."

"You know..." I tapped my finger against my lip as if in consideration. "With your sense of style, I'd go even more daring."

"What do you mean?" She tossed her badly bleached hair over one shoulder.

"Pantsuits are all the rage for the more avant-garde, female wedding guest; and I was thinking, that if I had your looks..." I hooked a thumb toward the mannequin. "I'd be trying on that one shouldered jumpsuit in that silvery-gray color."

When Tammi stared at me, I rested my hands on my bump. "But that's merely wishful thinking on my part. Even before I was expecting twins, I never had the good fortune to have your pretty blonde hair or slim frame."

"Well." Tammi preened a bit, but her gaze trailed over to the jumpsuit on the mannequin.

"I mean, you could be a model." Keeping my eyes wide, I pushed a sort of wistfully envious energy her way.

"I considered modeling professionally, you know," she said importantly. "I had training."

"That explains how gracefully you move." I nodded as if in complete agreement and then lowered my voice to a conspirator's whisper. "You know, the mother of the bride could *never* pull off something so bold and sleek. But you, on the other hand..."

Two minutes later, Tammi was trying on the jumpsuit. In all fairness it did look terrific on her, and I knew the moment she saw herself in it, the white dress was no longer an option.

***

Later that night I sat at the kitchen table with Julian and told him the story about Tammi the step-monster.

Julian shook his head. "There's not enough money in the world to make me take on a mother or stepmother of the bride. How do you and Maggie deal with all that drama?"

"Not all stepmothers are bad," I said. "I hit the jackpot with Ruth. She's wonderful."

"She and your father seem very happy together."

"She sent me a progress photo of the baby quilts." I tugged my phone from my dress pocket. "Did you want to see?"

"I love these," Julian said after viewing the photos. "The warm soft colors and the woodland animals."

"I was thinking," I said. "I'd use the soft peach and sage green shades from the fabric with the neutral tan for the nursery colors. Depending on what we find out on Thursday, it might be only green and tan, or peach and tan, or both."

Julian smiled. "We could match the colors from that swatch Ruth sent. Where is it?"

"I have it in my purse," I said. "I've been carrying it around for good luck. It's probably silly."

Julian reached for my hand. "I think it's sweet."

"In a few more days we'll find out if we have one of each or two of the same."

"Yes, we will." Julian stood to clear the table. "I'm getting more excited to find out every day."

I stood to help. "I was thinking, if one of the babies is a girl..." I tried to sound casual, "I'd like her middle name to be Hope." I glanced over at him and saw that he'd stopped dead in his tracks.

Worried at his stunned reaction, I continued. "Julian, do you like that name?"

He turned back to me slowly. "We've never discussed names for the babies before."

"Well..." I tried not to fidget and failed. "It was an idea I've been tossing around."

I watched as he began to smile. It lit up his entire face. Seeing his joy made me realize that in my anxiety, I'd inadvertently deprived Julian of enjoying the pregnancy.

He held out his arms. "Come over here and bring those babies with you."

Walking right to him, I wrapped my arms around his waist. "I love you," I said.

"I love you too." He held me close. "Any other possible names you'd like to discuss?"

I eased back to meet his eyes. "If it ends up being two girls, I'd like their middle names to be Hope and Faith."

"I love that," he said, his voice thick with emotion.

"I was thinking, remembering really, how Diego said to me when we found out we were pregnant *to have a little faith*. And that first time I felt the babies move was when I saw the white hind at our cabin."

"The white hind is a traditional symbol of hope and miracles," Julian said.

"Yes, and that day I thought that if one baby was a girl, I'd like to use the name Hope. And since everyone keeps reminding me to have a little faith..."

"You are so clever, Angel." He rested his hands on my baby bump. "I think that's an enchanting idea. However, I'd like to put my own name suggestion in the mix as well."

I smiled. "That's only fair."

"If one of the twins is a boy, I'd like to name him after my father."

"I'm fine with using Thomas for a middle name," I said. "Not for a first name. It would be too confusing for our son."

"That seems fair," Julian said back to me.

I rested my hands on top of his. "By the way, what *is* your father's middle name?"

"Laurence," Julian said. "The same as mine. We were named after a Drake ancestor."

"You poor thing." I patted his hands in consolation.

Julian lifted one eyebrow. "Laurence is better than Irene."

I couldn't help but laugh. "We both got saddled with some terribly old-fashioned and formal middle names thanks to our ancestors."

Julian smiled and began to pick up the plates from the table. "I'm confident we can come up with worthy names for our children."

I gathered the used cutlery and water glasses. "Let's get the dishes tidied up and we can talk about options for a boy's name."

We cleaned the kitchen together and spent the rest of

the evening with lists and looking on the internet for baby names. It was fun, and most importantly, it made Julian very happy.

Thursday arrived along with our important ultrasound appointment. The gender results were in and confirmed for Baby A and Baby B. And for the best news of all, the babies were healthy, with strong heartbeats, and their development was right on track. I didn't sleep at all on Thursday night. I was way too excited, and I found—much to my surprise—that I was eager to share the news with the family.

We had invited everyone over for Friday. We picked a time early-evening for the reveal so, weather permitting, we could pop the balloons outside. I took the day off on Friday, the better not to spill the beans, and also to tidy our house up. A lot of folks were coming to the rental, and I wanted everything to look as nice as possible. Julian surprised me by staying home too. He dove into the housework and refused to let me help clean.

With free time on my hands, I decided to bake cupcakes for the gathering. Baking usually relaxed me, so I went to the local grocery store and picked up a cake mix, ready-made frosting, cupcake liners, and a box of food coloring. I eyeballed some small paper plates and pretty colored sprinkles and bought those too.

Once I got home, I fired up the old oven and got the cupcakes going. After they were cool, I iced the cupcakes with vanilla frosting tinted with food coloring.

While my cake decorating wasn't anywhere near the level of George's, they were still cute, and the sprinkles made them look festive. I put the cupcakes on plates and covered them with wax paper and then aluminum foil over that, so the surprise wouldn't be spoiled.

Later in the afternoon, Julian went and picked up the gender reveal balloons, two huge black balloons with question marks on them and marked with tags for Baby A and Baby B. He also got the makings for lemonade and grabbed some paper cups to serve it in.

Now all we had to do was wait for everyone to show up. I tugged a floral print jersey maternity dress on, and Julian wore a pair of dark jeans and held up two button-down dress shirts.

"Which one?" he asked. He held a pink and a pale blue.

I started to snicker. "You wear the pink or blue shirt, and everyone will think you're giving them a clue."

"A white shirt it is." He slipped the other shirts back in our closet and selected a nice white polo.

"Better," I said. "Very neutral. Why do you think I'm wearing this yellow floral dress?"

He tugged the shirt over his head. "Because you look beautiful in it."

I reached up and brushed his dark hair back into place. "You'll always be prettier than me, Julian."

He swooped in and gave me a quick kiss. "Let's get this party started, Angel."

In the end, Lexie walked over with the kids by

herself. Bran had a previously scheduled staff meeting at the university library and couldn't make it. Ivy was photographing a wedding at the farm, and she couldn't come to the house either. She sent me a polite text with her reason for not attending and asked me to text her the news after the reveal.

I let that go, because to be fair, we had only given everyone five days' notice. Autumn and Duncan walked over with Erin and Emma, and of course the entire Drake contingent was all in attendance: Thomas, Maggie, Wyatt, Willow and the baby. Nina, Diego and Isabel were there, and Julian had also invited Vincent and George.

Autumn had her cell phone out and was video calling Aunt Faye and Hal. Wyatt agreed to video call my dad and Ruth and Diego had kindly offered to record the reveal for us on his phone so we would have everyone's reactions. Once we were all gathered and both of the video calls were connected, we had everyone countdown from ten.

When we got to "one," Julian kissed me and then popped Baby A's balloon. Pink confetti rained down. Everyone cheered in delight.

Once the gang settled down, we moved on to Baby B's balloon...and pink confetti rained down for a second time.

"I *knew* it!" Autumn cheered and ran forward to give me a kiss. She bent over and spoke directly to my belly. "Hi, baby girls!" She gave my baby bump a pat, straightened, and launched herself at Julian for an enthusiastic hug and a kiss.

Eventually I was able to speak to my dad and Ruth. They were very excited for us. While I tried to talk over the babble of voices, Julian spoke to Aunt Faye and Hal.

Thomas waded his way in through the crowd and gave me a hug. "Two girls!" He was grinning from ear to ear. He gave Julian a hug next, and I tried not to get misty when they held on to each other for a bit.

Duncan was there and he clapped Julian on the back. "Brace yourself, cousin. You are going to be surrounded by pink for a long, *long* time."

Julian was beaming. "From the day we found out we were pregnant with the twins, I figured it would be two girls."

"Runs in the family," Autumn pointed out. "First Holly and Ivy, then Erin and Emma, now your girls."

Hearing Ivy's name, I reached into my pocket for my own cell phone. I tapped on the screen and selected the text I had waiting to be sent. It had the words: *Looking forward to meeting you, Aunt Ivy.* I added two pink heart emojis and hit 'send.'

I accepted hugs from Wyatt, Maggie, and Willow, next.

Willow tugged on my dress. "I knew there would be two girls."

I ran my hand over her dark hair. "Did you *see* them?"

"Yes!" She bounced excitedly. "That's why I put the names on the board in my mama's office. You should name them Ariel and Merida. They're both going to have red hair."

I grinned. "Your mama told me she dreamt of red-haired twins getting into mischief with your baby brother. But she didn't know the genders."

"What's this now?" Julian asked Willow and me.

"The baby girls, Julian," Willow said. "They're gonna have red hair."

Maggie raised a hand. "I am going to agree with Willow's prediction. Because I keep dreaming about your twins and my Phillip as toddlers. The twin's gender wasn't shown to me in my dreams. It was more of a focus on how the three of them—one dark haired toddler and two redheads—will be causing all sorts of mischief in the future at the mansion."

Thomas had been listening too. "I suppose I better see about having better and stronger baby gates made for the staircases immediately." He hadn't stopped grinning since the gender reveal. "I do hope the girls both have red hair, like their mother."

Julian pressed a kiss to my cheek. "I've been hoping for the same as well."

"Well," I said, patting the top of Maggie's daughter's head. "I hope the twins have eyes like Julian's and yours, Willow. A beautiful mixture of brown and blue."

Morgan and Belinda came up for a hug and Lexie was only a few moments behind them. "Congratulations to you both." She gave me and Julian quick embraces. "Bran asked me to video the reveal so he could see it as soon as his meeting was finished."

I smiled hearing that. *Maybe my brother cared after all?*

"We should probably get going." Lexie eased back.

"I have cupcakes in the kitchen," I said quickly, knowing Belinda and Morgan wouldn't want to leave without one.

"Can we Mom?" Morgan pleaded. "Please?"

"I want a cupcake too!" Belinda bounced up and down.

"Come on, we'll get you one." I took Morgan and Belinda's hands and raised my voice so everyone would hear. "There's cupcakes and pink lemonade in the kitchen."

Willow gave a happy shout and headed for the house. Isabel, Emma, and Erin copied Willow, but I doubted they understood what all the adults' excitement was about. The children were simply running for the promise of sweets.

Vincent appeared at my side. "Can I give you a hand feeding the troops, Holly?"

"Yes." I smiled. "Thank you, Vincent, and I love the potted hydrangea you brought over."

"I figure you can plant it at the cabin," Vincent said. "Julian said there is shade at the front."

"There is," I said. "I know right where I want to plant it."

Morgan tugged on my hand. "What kind of cupcakes did you make, Aunt Holly?"

"Cupcakes?" George asked, falling into step with me, Vincent, Morgan, and Belinda. "Are you trying to put me out of business, Red?"

I rolled my eyes at his teasing. "I only hope my humble attempts at baking will earn the maestro's approval."

Morgan was watching the exchange between George and I. "Holly bakes really good," he said in my defense.

I smiled at my nephew. "Thank you, Morgan."

"I'll be the judge of that." George wiggled his eyebrows at Morgan. "But...do you know what this means?"

"What?" Morgan laughed.

"It means that we need a taste test," George said dramatically.

"What's that?" Belinda wanted to know.

"It means," George said to my niece and nephew, "that in order to test Holly's baking skills, we may have to eat more than one cupcake."

"I could eat three cupcakes!" Morgan boasted.

"Me too!" Belinda shouted and raced for the kitchen.

"Now you've done it." I laughed looking to George.

We all piled into the kitchen. Vincent took charge of the lemonade and poured and served. The kids all lined up for a cupcake, and when I pulled the covering off the plates to reveal the pale pink frosted cupcakes, Willow gave a little squeal. "Oh, they're pink with *sprinkles*!"

"Sprinkles make everything better," George said to me. "They look great."

I passed out the cupcakes and the children devoured them. George bit into one and told me that they were excellent, especially when you took into account the dinosaur of a stove that we had at the rental.

Vincent handed me a glass of lemonade. "Take that as a compliment."

I smiled at Vincent. "Oh, I do."

"I tried baking bread the other night," Vincent whispered to me. "I used a bread machine with a timer so it would be ready when I got home from work. George was scandalized."

"Those darn pastry chefs," I said sympathetically.

Vincent straightened his glasses. "The bread tasted great to me."

"And here I was going to buy you two a bread machine for a wedding gift," I said loud enough for George to hear me.

George only laughed at my mock-threat. He was sitting at the kitchen table with the children, and as I watched, he dared them all to see who could take the biggest bite of cupcake. Morgan, Belinda, Willow, Isabel, Erin and Emma all accepted his challenge. They created an unholy mess.

I looked around the rental house at the people who were crammed inside. They were too loud, and the children were getting hopped up on the sugar. Wyatt had a cranky baby Phillip over his shoulder trying to soothe him. Lexie, Nina, Autumn and Maggie were chatting. Julian was standing with Diego, his cousin Duncan, and his father and they were all talking and laughing.

There was store bought lemonade in paper cups, and simple homemade cupcakes decorated with hot pink sprinkles. Yes, Ivy, Erik, and Bran were not there, but somehow it didn't matter. In the end, all that did matter was the family we had created.

"So," Vincent said, nudging me out of my reverie. "What baby names have you thought of?"

"I have a few ideas," I told him, "but we won't tell anyone until *after* the twins are born."

CHAPTER ELEVEN

Spring was passing into summer, and Vincent and George's wedding went off without a hitch. Julian and I ended up traveling back to the bed and breakfast to attend their ceremony and reception. George and Vincent's families were wonderful, and it was a lovely day.

Since we were still living at the rental house in town, Julian and I took walks almost every evening. Sometimes Autumn and her family joined us, and we took Morgan and Belinda with us a few times. Bran and Lexie didn't seem to mind, and I was happy to see the kids more often.

We also went to the park to watch Morgan play t-ball. Autumn and Duncan met us, and we all sat in the shade of some maple trees, watching the game...which was basically organized chaos.

I sat in a lawn chair between Autumn and Julian while Belinda picked clover flowers and brought them to Erin and Emma. Duncan had one eye on the game and the other on the girls playing on a blanket in the grass.

Bran, I discovered, was sitting alone and cheering from the stands while Lexie coached the team. He gave us a distracted wave, and I wondered why my brother was sitting up there by himself. He was definitely stressed out. I could feel it all the way from where we sat.

Before I could ask, Belinda provided the answer. "Mommy says Daddy has to stay in the stands and behave himself at the games."

I bit down on the side of my mouth to keep from laughing.

"Oh?" Julian asked, as Belinda climbed in his lap. "Why's that?"

Belinda shrugged. "Because, Daddy yelled at the coach from the other team last time."

Autumn burst out laughing. "Priceless."

I felt a prickle of awareness and shifted in my chair to discover that Bran was watching Julian and I, instead of the ball game. I tried a smile and a casual wave. He responded to that with a nod.

Belinda leaned back against Julian's chest and gave him a sweet smile. "Can I have some popcorn?"

"I think that could be arranged." He set Belinda down. "Why don't we go and get some?"

Julian had barely managed one step before Erin and Emma decided they wanted to come along as well. "Want some help with the kids?" I began to rise.

"No." He waved me back into my chair. "Belinda and I can manage the girls."

Autumn smiled. "It'll be good practice for you, Julian."

"I can help!" Belinda insisted.

Julian took one of Erin's hands and one of Emma's. Belinda took Emma's other hand and the four of them were off across the grass and headed toward the concession stand. I watched as they walked away, and my heart melted a bit. He was going to be a wonderful father.

***

The construction at the cabin was finished at last, and we were excited to move back in. Julian directed the movers, and if I so much as opened a box of dishes, Julian was shooing me aside or nudging me into a chair to rest.

Autumn and Duncan showed up at noon with sandwiches, and Autumn rubbed her hands together and dove right in, helping me put everything in place in the kitchen. I unwrapped all of my vintage blue glass canning jars and lined them up on the open display shelves Duncan had built for me. They popped against the red paint and stained cabinet back. The vintage kitchen and food theme signage that I'd had in storage, Autumn hung for me. I pointed out where I wanted everything, and she hopped up on a step stool and obliged.

The towels and accessories I'd ordered for the new bathrooms were also waiting to be put in place, and she and I started working on those next. I was definitely looking forward to lounging in the big tub in the primary bath later that evening.

Right about the time I thought things were settling down, a car and smaller truck pulled down the gravel drive. It was Thomas and Wyatt driving behind a smaller moving truck. Thomas had arranged to have Julian's old furniture, from his rooms at the mansion, delivered so that we could have it to use.

I asked the movers to take Julian's bed upstairs to the primary suite, and the original bed from the cabin we had placed in the bedroom on the first floor, right across from the nursery. Autumn and I set that third bedroom up as a guest room. One of the vintage quilts I had stashed away looked great on that old sturdy wooden bed.

I walked back into the great room and found the movers had brought in five large boxes. Inside were the two white cribs and the dressers we'd ordered. Once Julian's furniture was put in place and the movers had left, Julian, Duncan, and Thomas began to put the cribs together immediately.

"We still have a couple of months and some change until I'm due," I reminded them.

"Twins often come a few weeks early," Duncan said as he and Julian carried a box into the nursery. "Erin and Emma showed up two weeks ahead of schedule."

Thomas nodded at Duncan. "Excellent point." He and Autumn carried the second crib box into the nursery after Julian and Duncan.

I rolled my eyes and made my way upstairs. I wanted to get the bed made and have things put in place as much as I could. Autumn followed a few moments later to help me make any adjustments to the placement of the furniture.

Once we had the bed made and bathroom set up, I went back down the stairs and into the nursery to see how Julian and Duncan were getting along with the crib assembly, but stopped dead in the doorway.

The last thing I had ever expected was to see my father-in-law sitting on the floor holding an allen wrench, seriously studying crib assembly instructions. He sat silently in his reading glasses, examining the directions. At a glance, I estimated he was maybe a quarter of the way through assembly, and I couldn't quite smother my smile.

Mentally pushing my sleeves up, I went over to help Thomas. "I bet we can put this crib together faster than Julian and Duncan can build theirs."

He smiled. "They have decided they don't need to use the instructions."

"I can build this from memory," Duncan claimed. "We'll build ours faster. You'll see."

"Ah! He's issued a challenge!" I said, easing down to the floor beside Thomas.

"Okay partner." Thomas patted my shoulder. "Let's show these two who they're dealing with."

Later that evening, Julian and I were finally alone. We sat side by side on the front porch of the cabin in our Adirondack chairs enjoying the quiet. Lazily, I turned my head to regard my husband. He had his arms folded across his chest, one eyebrow was cocked, and he looked...*miffed*, I decided.

"I know you used magick against us in the crib building race," Julian said.

"I have no idea what you're talking about," I said, working to inject as much innocence as possible into my tone.

"You put a reluctance spell on those bolts. Once you knew you would win, suddenly the bolts were found, sitting there in plain sight."

"I can neither confirm nor deny that," I said airily.

Julian rolled his eyes and laughed.

"You know what *I* want to do?" I said, running my hand up his thigh and hoping to distract him.

"What?" he asked.

"Try out that huge new bathtub."

He lifted one eyebrow. "Would you care for some company?"

"I would." I smiled over at him. "But you're going to have to help me get out of this chair first."

***

Autumn arrived at our house a few weeks later for a garden planting day. I had been looking forward to it, and since Julian had a meeting with a donor for the museum, we would have some time to ourselves.

We got to work early in the morning and started out with planting the perennials in the beds around the back of the cabin. Julian had hired a landscaping company to plant the larger shrubs and ornamental trees around the foundation before we had moved in, but Autumn had drawn up the perennial gardens, and I wanted my own hands in the dirt when it was time to plant the herbs and flowers.

I was now at thirty-two weeks, and it was getting harder every day to get up and down. So I sat, liberally covered in sunscreen on a folded up old beach towel beside Autumn, and added yarrow to the raised beds that were built in interlocking stacked wall stone.

I pushed my wide brimmed hat back farther on my head. "The yarrow might be past their big bloom, but they still look pretty good."

Beside me, Autumn grunted as she dug more holes to plant perennials in. "Yeah, well first we had all the delays, then the construction workers were underfoot. Followed by a week of rain. I'm sorry we didn't get these plants in the ground a few weeks ago as originally planned."

I shifted to reach for the purple coneflowers next. Using the side of the raised bed, I pulled myself up to my knees. I added a trio of the coneflowers to the bed, while Autumn dug more holes in the prepared soil. She wouldn't hear of me touching the shovel, but I was allowed to place the plants in the prepared holes. I could also pat the soil down around the new flowers, but that was about as far as she would allow me to go.

I didn't bother to argue with her for a couple of reasons. One: She would rat me out to Julian in a heartbeat. Two: While I felt more confident now that the twins were at viability, I was still cautious not to overdo it.

"I heard you and Julian invited Bran, Lexie and the kids over for dinner the other night."

I slanted my eyes over at my cousin. "We did."

"How'd it go?" she asked as she kept digging.

I pulled the elastic waist of my maternity shorts up a bit higher. "It was stiff with Bran in the beginning, but the kids were so excited to see the house. Lexie seemed okay. They brought me over that old wardrobe and a few other pieces for me to have. Bran and Julian carried them into the guest room for me. Lexie helped me hang up the curtains in the nursery. It was fun. Afterward, Bran and Julian walked around outside discussing the landscaping, while the kids explored the yard." I smiled a bit. "At least we're all trying."

"That's good news," Autumn said. "Have you heard from Ivy lately?"

I began to stack up the empty pots the perennials had been in. "We've been texting. She's pretty busy with her wedding photography business and helping Erik at his family's farm and of course the spring plant stand. Things probably won't slow down at the farm until July."

"I had hoped that maybe you two had patched things up. Since the last time you were together and you—"

"Accidentally exploded a twenty-five-pound bag of potting mix and showered her in dirt?" I finished for her.

Autumn grinned. "Right. There is that."

"Julian and I did see her at the farm stand when we bought the hanging baskets."

"Oh, those big ferns you have out there on the front porch?"

"Yup." I tucked a long curl that had escaped back behind my ear.

"Those will do great on your shady porch," she predicted.

"It was the day after we'd moved in, and we talked a little, but I may have to accept that Ivy and I will never be as close as we used to." I sighed. "I don't know how to bridge the gap."

"Ivy has mellowed out since the wedding," Autumn said, digging another hole. "She seems content now, living at the rundown house on Erik's family's farm. They've been fixing it up, but it's going to be a big job."

"I don't think I've ever seen the house," I said.

"It's way at the back of the property. Tucked into a corner between the apple orchard and the state forest."

I scratched at my belly. "That would suit Ivy down to the ground. Decrepit, timeworn house, an old orchard *and* a neighboring forest. Very witchy."

"I think the home once belonged to Erik's great-aunt. It sat vacant for twenty years." Autumn wiped sweat from her brow. "Funny how you both ended up living in the country."

"Not when you consider that we spent every summer when we were children on a farm in Iowa with our dad and Ruth. I loved it there."

"Good point," Autumn said.

I reached out and dropped the last coneflower in the waiting hole. "These will be cheerful this year and even prettier next summer. The butterflies will love them."

Autumn shifted pots of daylilies over for me to more easily reach. "You chose a good selection of perennials and herbs to start these beds, Blondie."

"This is one of the sunniest spots against the house," I said. "I want to take advantage of it."

We planted lavender, yarrow, daylilies, tall garden phlox, autumn joy sedum, and Shasta daisies. To add more color to the large bed, since this year's blooms wouldn't fill in the raised bed, I tucked some hot pink wave petunias to grow and eventually spill over the edges.

"I love these bright colors," Autumn said, leaning on the handle of the shovel. "They're so happy all mixed together."

"Once we get these watered in, I want to start on the

herb garden next," I said.

Autumn took my arm and hauled me too my feet. I rose awkwardly and had to laugh at myself as my belly rose first.

"Steady as she goes," Autumn said.

I pulled the brand-new garden hose over and watered the plants while Autumn rounded up the discarded pots and plant containers. Once the new plants had been given a drink, we walked to the large herb and vegetable garden that was in the clearing.

The vegetable garden had been built before we'd moved in and was surrounded by a tall fence to keep out the deer and other critters from the nearby woods. The tall fence posts and cross pieces were cedar. On the inside of the posts, a green coated wire fencing would keep the animals out. In time, as the plants grew larger, the mesh would hopefully not be so noticeable.

I plopped my hands on my hips as I considered the plants that were all lined up and waiting to be planted in the raised beds within the fenced area. Inside the fence, a roll of landscape fabric and many bags of mulch were stacked up and waiting to be used on the pathways between the raised beds. I pulled Autumn's design plan from my back pocket and took a deep breath.

I tried to anyway.

"Did you want to take a break for a while?" Autumn asked. "The last two months with twins is nothing but an endurance run."

"I feel fine," I assured her. "Let's get these herbs

planted." I read over the list and my lips twitched. "You have the plants listed in alphabetical order."

Autumn tugged her gloves up higher. "Be thankful I didn't list them by their botanical name."

I rolled my eyes. "You are such an overachieving Virgo."

"Big talk from the Sagittarius on the cusp of Capricorn."

I read from the list. "Angelica, artemisia, basil, catnip, chives, dill, feverfew—"

Autumn snatched the list away from me. "Behave yourself or I'll call Julian and tell him you are lifting heavy things."

I took a swig from my water bottle. "And you would, too."

"You did the same to me when I was pregnant with Erin and Emma," she pointed out.

"Yeah, but you tried to put in a butterfly garden at the bungalow all by yourself," I reminded her. "Lexie wrestled the tiller away from you."

Autumn stuck her nose in the air. "Lies."

"Truth," I countered. "She lectured you for twenty minutes."

"By the goddess, she did." Autumn threw back her head and laughed. "I had forgotten about that." My cousin slung an arm around my shoulder. "Come on. We can lay the herbs out and then you are going to plant your cute little butt in the shade on the porch and take a break before we put anything else in the ground."

"My butt isn't cute or little. Not anymore," I groused. "I've gained thirty-five pounds so far."

Autumn tightened her ponytail. "You're supposed to gain over forty pounds when you're carrying twins. I gained almost fifty."

We had barely begun laying out the plants when the sound of a car pulling down the gravel drive was heard. I glared at my cousin. "Hey."

Autumn held her hands up in surrender. "I didn't call Julian, I swear."

"I wonder who it is?" I stepped out of the garden gate and walked toward the front of the house.

To my shock, I discovered a McBriar farm truck. My sister hopped down from the passenger side of the cab. Her hair was pulled back in a stubby ponytail and she wore jeans, a t-shirt, and sunglasses.

She gave me a casual wave and walked around to the end of the vehicle and lowered the tail gate. As I watched, Erik exited from the driver's side, pulling gloves from his pocket. He too was dressed to work in jeans, a t-shirt, and a *McBriar Farms* ball cap.

My jaw dropped. The last two people I would have expected to see at the cabin were my sister and her husband. "What's going on?" I asked.

Ivy slid a potted plant to the tailgate of the truck. "Heard you were putting in a garden today."

"I don't understand," I said.

"You got a late start on lots of vegetables. But we can help with that." Ivy pointed to a large container. It was a big tomato plant covered in blooms.

"Hey, guys!" Autumn called over. "I have a map of where everything goes, right here."

Ivy pulled down her shades and peered over the top of them at Autumn. "Of course, you do."

Erik hoisted the pot and walked past me. "Nice looking house," he said. "I like the exterior stone on the addition."

"Uh, thank you," I said, feeling like an idiot.

Ivy walked up carrying two more smaller tomato plants. "How are you feeling, Holly?"

Everyone asked me the same thing these days. "I'm okay," I answered automatically. "I get out of breath easily, but the twins are doing great."

"You're around thirty-two weeks, right?" Ivy asked.

I did a double take. "Ah yes, that's correct."

Ivy jerked her head toward the fenced garden. "Why don't you show me where you want these bad boys planted?" She took off for the garden.

"Oh wow, sure," I said, scrambling to keep up with her.

Erik dug the holes and Ivy and Autumn transplanted the tomato plants. Then Erik pulled tomato cages from the bed of the truck and carefully worked the cages over the plants. I was graciously allowed to hold the foliage back as he did so, and then they let me use the garden hose to water them in.

"Sheesh," I grumbled under my breath. Now I had two more people watching over me.

Erik had returned to the truck, reached inside the bed, and pulled out a big tray of plants. He carried them over and Ivy took them two at a time and lined up the rest of the plants. Going in for a closer look, I discovered there was a couple of cucumber plants, squash, and a pumpkin.

"Thank you for the vegetable plants," I said. "That is so thoughtful."

Erik adjusted the bill of his cap. "We had a few starter plants left over from the stand, and Ivy set those aside for you a couple of weeks ago."

"I've been babying them so you could transplant them into your own garden," Ivy said.

"Thank you, Ivy," I said.

Erik studied a plant critically. "They did okay but will be happier to be in the ground. It's way too late for beans and lettuce, but you can plant those this fall when it gets cool again."

"That's what I thought too," I said to Erik. "I want to try those purple beans that climb. I have a few seed packets put aside."

The sound of a second car pulling up to the side of the house had everyone looking again. Julian parked his SUV and climbed out with a smile on his face. He had changed his clothes and was wearing jeans with a casual shirt and sneakers.

As he walked over, he tugged on a pair of work gloves. "What's this I hear about a garden party?"

I shook my head. "You were supposed to be at a

meeting."

He shrugged. "It finished early."

"You came to check up on me—"

Before I could finish, he dropped a quick kiss on my mouth. "You're getting a bit pink, Angel."

"It's a reflection of my magenta-colored shirt."

He shook his head. "Nice try. Go get out of the sun."

"It's the curse of the redheads," I argued, glancing down at my fair skin. "It'll be fine. Besides, I've got 50 SPF sunscreen on."

He touched my bare arm. "Go sit in the shade for a while."

I set my jaw. "I wanted to put the herbs in myself."

"And you will," Autumn said over me. "*After* you go sit down and take a break. I promise we won't plant the herbs. Only lay them out in their spots."

Ivy held up a hand. "I solemnly promise to plant the veggies exactly how Miss anal-retentive—"

"Hey!" Autumn said indignantly.

"Has them drawn on the plan," Ivy finished, as if she hadn't been interrupted.

"Fine." With no other options, I went around the house, climbed up the steps, and sat slowly down in the old wooden Adirondack chair on the front porch. It was nice and cool in the shade. I hated to admit it, but I *was* tired.

I took a swig from my water bottle. The sound of their voices carried clearly to where I sat, and it was comforting. I pulled my hat off and rested my head against the back of the chair.

"Going to close my eyes," I said to myself, "only for a minute..."

"Wakey-wakey!" Ivy's voice was loud and cheerful. I opened my eyes with a start. Julian and Erik were hauling a cooler up to the porch, Autumn carried a large picnic basket, and Ivy stood there grinning at me with an old blanket in her arms.

"You look better," Ivy said, flipping the blanket out over the floor of the porch. "Not as red in the face as you were."

I rolled my eyes. "You are such a comfort to me."

Julian and Erik set the cooler down beside the blanket. "Nina made us lunch," Julian said. "I picked it up on the way here. There's barbequed chicken legs and potato salad."

Before I knew it, Ivy and Julian were dishing up the food, and Erik was passing out bottles of water or soft drinks. They all seemed so at ease with each other that it made me very suspicious. Julian had clearly set this whole thing up.

"Plain grilled chicken for you," Julian said, holding out a paper plate. "No sauce."

"Appreciate it," I said, taking the plate.

"I'd love to see the house," Erik was saying to Julian.

"Of course," Julian said smoothly. "After lunch, we'll give everyone a tour."

Autumn paused in mid bite. "I wouldn't want to get

anything dirty, with our shoes and boots."

"Take your shoes off first." I shrugged. "It'll be fine."

"You've only been here a couple of weeks, "Autumn said, "and I already miss you living a few doors down. But I know you're happier living in the country."

"It's a short drive," I said. "You and the girls are welcome to visit as often as you'd like." I heard my own words and added. "*All* of you are."

Ivy smiled at the invitation. "I'll never keep Erik from wanting to check up on the vegetables we planted today."

"I'm not even going to argue with you," Erik said. "This is a sweet garden set up. The fence is perfect for keeping wildlife out of your garden."

"Thank you," Julian said to Erik. "Autumn and our landscaper put their heads together. She designed it, he built it."

"Oh, and by the way," Ivy said. "We're going to be working with Duncan now that your project is completed."

Erik put his arm around Ivy's shoulder. "We were approved for a home improvement loan. Now we can begin restoring the old farmhouse that I inherited."

"That's great," I said. "I know how much you love DIY projects, Ivy."

"I'm looking forward to it," Ivy said around a mouthful of chicken. "But I know my limits. We'll need professional help for some of this. The old electrical work is temperamental at best, evil at worst. Our plumbing is terrifying. It's been like living in a possessed house for the past five months."

"That sounds right up your alley," I said teasingly.

"Where will you live during the reno?" Autumn asked.

"We have a few options," Ivy said. "We can either stay with Erik's parents at their place—they do have plenty of room—or we might live in his sister's RV for a couple of months."

"Cozy." Autumn scooped up more potato salad. "But you're newlyweds. It'll be fun."

"We were thinking of parking the camper beside our house during the reno." Ivy shrugged. "It's either close quarters in an RV or *no* privacy living with his mom and dad."

I tossed an idea out. "Maybe you could use the rental in town we vacated?"

Erik shook his head. "Living in town isn't practical for us. It's too far from the farm and our daily operations."

"Hence our considering living in the RV." Ivy wiped barbeque sauce from her fingers. "Personally, I can't wait to tear out our kitchen. It's awful."

After lunch was finished, Julian and I gave them all a tour of the expanded cabin. The red kitchen cabinets were a hit with Ivy. Erik loved the vaulted ceiling and exposed logs of the original cabin and the fireplace. Julian took Erik to see the primary suite and bath, and Autumn went along. Ivy lingered on the first floor in the nursery with me.

Besides the cribs and dressers, the room was mostly empty. I had taken the old rocker and added it to the room, the peach curtains were hung, and I had a rug and a few décor pieces on order.

"Getting the nursery finished is the next on our to-do list," I said.

"I like the warm peach color as an accent wall." Ivy trailed her fingers along one of the dressers. "It's cute how the white cribs are lined up against that painted wall."

"Thanks. The color matches the woodland animal themed baby quilts Ruth is making for the twins." I rested my hands on my bump. "The nursery colors will be ivory and peach, with sage green and tan accents."

Ivy nodded. "That sounds pretty."

"I have a swatch of the fabric in my purse, if you want to see it later."

"Sure," Ivy said, standing at the window.

I hesitated. There was something weighing on my sister's mind. She was struggling and trying to decide whether or not to speak about it.

Maybe it's time to reach out and try and bridge that gap, I thought to myself. I joined her at the window and rested my hand on her shoulder. For a moment we stood there, side-by-side, and looked out across the clearing and the new garden.

"Julian told me," Ivy said softly.

"He told you what?"

"Julian came by the farm a few weeks ago and asked about buying some plants for your garden. We ended up having a talk." Ivy took a deep breath. "He told us why you left college all those years ago and moved back to Williams Ford."

My face turned red. "I see."

"It made a horrible sort of sense," she said. "How energetically frail you were when you came home, and why you were so emotionally closed off." Ivy slipped her arm around my waist as she spoke. "You were barely finding your feet again when Leilah attacked you. No wonder you ended up in the hospital."

"That was the day Julian rescued me."

"Call me intuitive, but that has to be when you two began to fall for each other."

I brushed my hair back. "It was."

"Looking back over the past few years I should have figured out that you were a couple," Ivy said. "But you blocked us out so damn well, I never caught on."

"It wasn't easy. I used a lot of energy keeping up that spell."

"I'll bet," Ivy said. "I mean not only did you block the family, you blocked the Drakes, and everyone at your job."

"Nina and Diego always knew," I said. "I found out later that Autumn and Duncan came across us once when we were a little...*distracted*."

Ivy's eyes danced. "Oh, jeez. How embarrassing."

"I never knew about that until after we decided to

elope."

"I get that Julian confided in Maggie," Ivy said. "She helped him reserve the venue for the elopement."

I didn't bother to correct her. She didn't need to know that Maggie had seen us together when she first moved to Williams Ford as well...

"So, what'd you use?" she asked.

I tuned back in. "Use?"

"What sort of spell did you use to shield your relationship and your emotions from everyone?" she asked. "Was it a reluctance spell or a defensive kind of spell?"

I smiled. "A combination of both. I basically switched my empathy around. So instead of feeling everyone else's emotions—I shield my own from theirs."

"Well damn, Sis." Ivy raised an eyebrow. "You're going to have you teach me that one."

"I think that could be arranged."

"Seeing the two of you together—openly—for the past seven months..." Ivy's voice broke, and she cleared her throat and tried again. "You guys are totally, crazy in love with each other."

I smiled. "Yes, we are."

"Last year, when Julian was in Charleston for so long...that must have been very hard on you."

"It was," I admitted. "We had drifted apart, and I thought we'd broken up. When he called me in November and said he wanted to meet and to try and work things out, I gave him an ultimatum that if we got back together, we'd do so out in the open. No more secrets. No more hiding."

"And that's when he proposed and sprung the idea of eloping on you."

"That's right," I said. "He told you that as well?"

Ivy nodded. "Yes, he did. Julian wanted to make sure that I understood why you had eloped. That it had nothing to do with trying to take the attention away from us on our big day."

"I'm sincerely sorry that I hurt your feelings when we announced our marriage," I said carefully. "That was never my intention."

"I know that. Now." Ivy sighed. "I was so stressed about the wedding. Trying to pull off that big ceremony and reception right after Christmas tree season and the holidays. It was insane. It made me into a Bridezilla for a while, and I'm very sorry about that."

"Apology accepted," I said immediately.

Ivy placed both her hands on my belly. "I also wanted to say that I *do* understand what a tough time you had early in your pregnancy, you know, from you being worried about miscarrying again. I wish you would have told us."

"We found out there were twins within an hour of being told we were pregnant," I explained. "I was overwhelmed and terrified. There can be challenges with multiples, and I asked Julian not to tell anyone until we hit the second trimester."

Ivy patted my belly. "Well, let's just say that now I am a lot more sympathetic to what you went through."

"What do you mean?" I asked, taking her hand.

"It's early days, yet..." Ivy began.

I felt her pulse jump. I sensed nerves, excitement, and a bit of fear. "By the goddess." I started to smile. "You're pregnant too."

Ivy sniffled. "Everyone said it would take a year to conceive after getting off the birth control shot. Well surprise, I think it took me about a month."

"How long have you known?"

"We found out a couple of weeks ago. We were so excited, and then...I started spotting."

"Oh, Ivy."

Ivy gripped both my hands. "It wasn't much, but it scared the shit out of me. Went to the doctor and she said it was all okay. They did an ultrasound."

I pulled her as close as possible for a hug.

"We saw the baby," Ivy said. "The little bean is hanging in there and doing okay."

"How far along are you?"

Ivy laid her head on my shoulder. "We were at seven weeks, two days when they did the ultrasound."

I ran my hand over her hair. "How long ago was that?"

"About two weeks ago," Ivy said.

I pulled back to look at her. "You're sure there's only one?"

Ivy laughed. "That's exactly what I asked too. But

Dr. Anderson said there's only one."

"Dr. Brenna Anderson?" I had to laugh. "We have the same obstetrician?"

"Apparently," Ivy said. "Erik asked if we could get a family discount, seeing as how you and I are pregnant at the same time."

I tapped a finger to my lips. "Now, there's a thought."

Ivy's smile faded a bit. "It's going to be a long damn four weeks until we get to the second trimester."

I met her green eyes and held them with mine. "I completely understand."

Ivy blew out a long breath. "I haven't spotted since that day, and I don't have any restrictions. The doctor said to go about my normal activities...but it's making me worry. What if I do something wrong during the demo, or lift something too heavy?"

"I suggest erring on the side of caution and take it easy with demo and construction," I said. "Go about your normal routine. But *no* heavy lifting, and no dragging claw foot bathtubs out of the house."

"I hear you," Ivy said. "I'm still nervous though."

"Basically, after a scare, you get through the first trimester one day and one week at a time." I did my best to sound positive. "Every week in the first trimester is a milestone. At least that's how it felt for me."

"That does help," Ivy said. "Thanks."

"Of course," I said. "If you need to talk, you can call

me. Day or night." I hugged her again. "I love you, Ivy."

"I love you, Holly," she said.

We stood there holding on to each other with our midsections pressed together. While we embraced, I felt the strongest premonition about her unborn baby.

Oh wow, I thought. *This kid is going to be a handful!*

It would have its mother's powers and then some, I realized. One of the twins gave a strong kick as if in confirmation. It was strong enough that Ivy felt it and jumped in reaction.

"Okay, okay," she said, looking down at my belly. "I didn't forget about you two. I love both of you girls as well."

"Congratulations and blessed be." I reached for her hand even as we stepped apart. "You're going to be a great mom."

"Thanks," she said. "I guess once we hit week thirteen, I'll call Dad and Ruth and ask her if she's finished with your baby quilts. Because now, *I'm* gonna need one."

"Oh, she'll love that." I smiled. "That would be a great way to tell them."

A sob came from the doorway. Ivy and I turned to see Autumn standing there in the hall and crying. "I'm sorry." She wiped her nose with the back of her hand. "I didn't mean to eavesdrop, but you guys..." She walked over with her arms wide. "I love you both so much. I'm so happy you patched things up between you, and Ivy,

I'm *thrilled* for you and Erik."

"Autumn—" Ivy began.

"Now, you don't even have to ask," she finished for her. "Of course, I will keep your secret. That's for you to tell everyone else. Whenever you are ready."

"Thank you." Ivy breathed a sigh of relief as Autumn let go of the both of us.

"But let me get this over with," Autumn said.

"Get *what* over with?" Ivy wanted to know.

Autumn bent over and patted Ivy's belly. "Hi baby!"

I started to laugh. "She did the same to me when we told her about the twins, and again at the gender reveal."

Autumn straightened slowly and shook her head. "Whoa," she said with a smile. "That was a surprise."

"What'd you see?" Ivy went pale. "Oh goddess, there's not two of them in there after all is there?"

"Nah, only one." Autumn said. "But I am curious. Did you plan to find out the gender? Because I had a psychic vision when I touched your belly, and holy cats, it was powerfully clear."

I chuckled. "Leave it to Ivy's kid to exhibit powers before they're even born."

"Actually, I think I already know the gender," Ivy said with a smile.

Tears began to gather in my eyes. "I wasn't going to say anything, but so do I."

Autumn held out her hands. "We could test the theory."

"I'm in," Ivy said, and the three of us joined hands.

"On the count of three," I suggested, "we'll say the gender."

Ivy nodded in response as Autumn began the countdown. "One, two...three."

"*Boy*," we all said at the same time.

"Oh, boy." Erik's voice came clearly into the room.

He and Julian were standing together in the hall. Julian was smiling and Erik was a tad wide-eyed.

"Hey, babe." Ivy smiled over at her husband. "Come on in and join the coven."

"I was looking for you." Erik walked into the nursery. "I had a feeling something was up."

"*Intuitive*," Julian coughed into his hand.

Erik only shrugged at Julian's teasing. "We'll find out in a couple months if you are all correct about the gender, I suppose."

Julian walked directly to Ivy and gave her a gentle hug. "Congratulations and blessed be, little sister."

"Aw, *hell*," Ivy said tearfully against his shoulder. "You calling me 'little sister' hit me right in the feels."

"I apologize," Julian said. He stepped back and offered Ivy an immaculate handkerchief from his pocket. "Use this, and while you're at it...you've got some garden dirt on your face."

Ivy snatched it from his hand and wiped her eyes, and then her face. "I should have stabbed you harder in the thigh with that garden trowel all those years ago."

"Undoubtedly," Julian said, giving her the slightest

of bows. "I was a terrible scoundrel."

"God damn it, Julian." Ivy started to laugh. "Don't use that upper crust and snide tone on me. It only makes me like you better."

Julian grinned. "For what it's worth, I agree with the three of you. I also think the baby is a boy, and brace yourself, Erik. This child will be powerful."

Erik blinked. "I never considered that the baby might be a Witch too."

Ivy tucked her arm around Erik's waist. "That's adorable, McBriar. Why wouldn't he be? Your maternal grandparents are Pagan. In fact, your grandfather taught our mother and Julian's father about the Runes."

Julian's eyebrow winged up. "I did not know that."

"Yup," Ivy said. "Thomas told me about it a few years ago. Ends up all of our families' magickal legacies have intertwined in one way or another."

Julian reached for my hand, and I happily took it and tucked myself along his side. "Some things," he said, dropping a kiss on my head, "are simply always meant to be."

CHAPTER TWELVE

Five weeks later...

"I can hardly believe they're here," I said to Julian.

Julian leaned over the hospital bed I was propped up in and gave me a gentle kiss. "You were amazing, Holly."

I shifted slightly trying to get more comfortable. "Sorry for all the things I said while I was in labor; and for shouting at you before they gave me an epidural."

"Heat of the moment," he said, taking my hand. "At least you didn't blow up any medical equipment while you were in transition."

"I'm still shocked that I didn't have to have a C-section," I said. "Lucky for us, the girls were both head down."

"I'm simply grateful that all of you are well." Julian rested his head back against the high-backed chair in the private hospital room and sighed. "And to think we were worried about their lungs, since they were a couple weeks early. Both the girls were screaming their heads off as soon as they were born."

"Dr. Anderson said their weight was good."

"Five pounds and six ounces for Baby A, and five pounds two ounces for Baby B." Julian smiled proudly.

"How soon do you think they will bring them back to us?" I asked. "I didn't get to hold either of them for very long."

Julian nodded. "I feel the same. But remember, we knew that the babies would be assessed in the NICU, to determine if they need oxygen. Still, considering how loud they both were...I agree with Dr. Anderson. I'd say they'll be back in the room with us very soon."

"Why don't you go down there and be with the twins?" I gave his hand a squeeze. "I'd feel better if you were there, with them."

He got up and sat on the end of the bed. "I'm not leaving you, Angel." He laid his hand on my leg. "It won't be long now. Try not to worry."

Nodding, I took a deep breath and turned my head to look out the window of my room. High in the sky I saw the moon. It was full and shone down brightly from the July nighttime sky.

Great mother-goddess, I thought, smiling up at the moon. *Thank you for keeping all of us safe.*

There was a knock on the door and a cheerful nurse popped in. "Hi, Mom and Dad," she said. "Sorry for the delay. It's always crazy around here on the full moon."

I could hear the babies crying and the noise became louder as a clear bassinet was rolled into my room. My soreness forgotten, I sat up straighter to see them. They were snuggled together in the bassinet. The twins were swaddled and had tiny knit hats with big bows on them.

Both babies were red faced and wailing for all they were worth.

Julian rose to his feet. "Oh my goodness." He chuckled.

The nurse grinned at us. "These girls have been demanding to see the both of you, and they don't care who knows about it." She picked up one twin. "Baby A," she announced, and handed me the oldest twin.

"Hello, sweet girl." I had been able to hold her for a few minutes right after her birth, but it hadn't been nearly long enough. I gave her a kiss on the brow, held her close, and she immediately quieted.

"And Baby B," the nurse said, passing the second baby into Julian's waiting arms.

"Hello little one," he said and kissed her cheek.

The nurse began to speak, filling us in on the babies' stats and so forth. I didn't hear a word; I was too busy taking in all of the details of our babies. It hit me suddenly how much they looked like Julian. The smaller of the twins continued to cry until the nurse helped Julian and I rearrange the girls. Once we positioned them so that I held them together against my chest, touching each other, they both settled.

"They're doing great," the nurse said. "If you need anything, or have any questions, press the call button."

"Thank you," I remembered to say as she left.

"Alone at last," Julian said, running a fingertip over Baby A's hand.

She gripped it and held on.

"Lucky for us these two were born in the middle of the night," I said.

Julian smiled and sat beside me on the bed. "Your dad and Ruth started driving down as soon as I called them to tell them the babies had arrived. He told me they have had their bags packed for the past two weeks and were just waiting for the call."

That made me smile. "I'm glad you took pictures of the girls with your phone and sent them to the family."

Julian laughed. "It may help keep the Drakes and Bishops at bay for a few more hours at any rate. We should enjoy the relative peace and quiet as long as we can. Visiting hours begin at nine o'clock in the morning."

I glanced at the clock on the wall. "So we've got a few hours alone before the family invades the hospital."

"For the next five hours, I'm keeping my three beautiful girls all to myself." His handsome face was beaming with pride. "We have a family, Angel."

"We do," I said, crying happy tears.

He lifted one of the knit caps. "I think her hair is red."

"Really?" Pleased at the information, I smiled.

Julian checked the other twin's hair. "So is hers." He pressed a kiss to my brow. "You made some gorgeous babies, Angel."

"Our girls take after their father." I rested my head against his shoulder. "They may have my red hair, but they both look like you, Julian."

"You think so?" His smile lit up the room.

"I know so," I said. "I love you, Julian."

***

At precisely 9:01 AM there was a knock on my hospital room's door.

"Yes?" Julian called out.

The door opened slowly, and Thomas came in carrying a massive arrangement of pink roses, and a half dozen baby-girl themed Mylar balloons. "Good morning," he said from behind the balloons.

"Hi there, Grandpa," I said.

Julian hopped up to take the balloons, while Thomas placed the flowers on the table beside me. But his eyes were all for the babies in my arms. "There they are," he said in wonder.

"They fell asleep waiting for their grandpa to visit," I said.

Thomas went directly to the sink and made a show of washing his hands. Then he came and sat in the chair beside the bed.

Julian picked up the oldest of the twins. "Father," he began, "allow me to introduce you to Luna."

"Otherwise known as Baby A," I said helpfully.

Julian settled our oldest twin in his father's arms.

"Here you go."

"Luna," Thomas said. "What a wonderful magickal name. Have you decided on a middle name?"

"Hope," Julian and I said simultaneously.

Thomas never took his eyes off the baby. He pressed a kiss to the top of her knit hat, and when he finally met my gaze, his eyes were wet.

"Would you like to hold your second granddaughter?" I asked.

"Yes, absolutely," he said.

Julian took Luna and placed her in her bassinet. He scooped up our younger twin and handed her to his father next.

"Is she a bit smaller than her sister?" Thomas asked.

"Yes," I said. "A half inch shorter as well."

"She's beautiful," Thomas said, "and looks like Julian did when he was a newborn."

"Told you they looked like you," I said to Julian.

Thomas chuckled. "What did you decide to name her?"

"Laura," Julian said. "It was as close as we could get to Laurence."

Thomas' eyes grew large. "You named one of the babies after me?"

"After you *and* Julian. Since you share a middle name." I smiled at the stunned look on his face. "You don't mind, do you?"

A tear slid down Thomas' face. "No, I don't mind."

I reached over and handed him a tissue. "Happy

tears, I hope?"

"Yes. Happy tears." He chuckled. "And her middle name?"

"Faith," I told him.

"Luna Hope and Laura Faith." Thomas thought it over and a huge smile spread across his face. "That's absolutely perfect."

Ten minutes later, the door swung open again. Ivy and Erik came in with two teddy bears, one pink and the other purple.

"I heard there was a twin party happening up here!" Ivy shoved the bears at Julian, kissed his cheek, and ran straight to me. "Congratulations!" She kissed me and gave me a hug.

"Well done." Erik smiled and shook Julian's hand. "How are you feeling?"

"Exhausted and thrilled," Julian answered.

Ivy twinkled at Thomas. "Hey there, Grandpa Drake."

"Hello, Ivy," he said. "Look who I have."

Ivy smiled and dashed to the hand sanitizer dispenser on the wall. She hit the lever and rubbed the sanitizer over her hands. "Somebody give me one of those babies."

Julian picked up Luna from the bassinet and Ivy sat down in the remaining chair. "Hello, you gorgeous thing," Ivy cooed at her niece. "Oh, before I forget, Bran and Lexie told me to remind you they'd be up this afternoon."

Erik went and bent over Ivy's shoulder to see the baby. "She's beautiful. What did you decide to name them?"

"You're holding Luna Hope Drake," I said to my sister. "Formerly known as Baby A."

Ivy grinned. "That's a fabulously witchy name."

Julian gestured toward his father. "And over there, snoozing in her grandfather's arms is Laura Faith Drake. Formerly known as Baby B."

"Luna Hope," Ivy repeated. "Dad's going to love that."

"Hmm?" I asked, not following her.

"Don't you remember?" she asked me. "Dad's grandmother's name was Hope."

"That's right," I said. "I'd completely forgotten."

"Two new witches born on the full moon," Ivy said. "A couple of fiery Leos. They're going to be fierce, loyal and fearless."

"Of course, they will be," Thomas said. "With the legacy of magick these children carry from both the Bishop and the Drake family lines...their potential is limitless."

Julian waved that away. "They have plenty of time for that." He took Laura from his father and handed her back to me. "First and foremost, Luna and Laura will grow up knowing how very much they are loved."

"Absolutely," I said, cuddling Laura. "We can get a mini coven going for the next generation as soon as we get them all potty trained."

Ivy grinned. "There's an idea." She raised an eyebrow at her husband. "What do you think about that McBriar?"

"I think we should let the new parents and their babies get some rest, while they can," Erik said.

Ivy handed Luna back to Julian. "Congratulations again. They're both gorgeous and look exactly like my sister."

"I have it on good authority that the girls look like me," Julian said.

"Nah." Ivy shook her head. "Keep dreaming, Drake."

***

Three months later…

Three-month-old Luna Hope Drake hated having her diaper changed. She made sure everyone knew about it too. While her twin smiled and cooed in her baby swing in the living room, Luna shouted the walls down.

"I know, I know," I said soothingly. "You have such a hard life. Getting your diaper changed. The indignity of it all." I put the wet diaper in the pail and quickly fastened the sides of her fresh diaper. As soon as I began to snap up her sleeper, Luna began to settle.

"There, you see? It's all better." I picked her up and Luna snuggled close. "Now, I'm going to put you in your swing next to your sister and you two can relax for a while."

Carrying her into the living room, I slipped her in the swing and got it started. I gave Luna her pacifier and she sucked on it loudly. Next, I bent over Laura and smiled. "Hi sweetie." In response Laura kicked her feet, waved her hands, and I got a big gummy grin.

Side by side, the girls did resemble each other—as they both had red hair—but they were definitely different from one another. Luna Hope's hair was wavy, and she was our feisty twin. She was still a bit longer and bigger than her sister, and her eyes were becoming a bright aqua blue, like mine.

Laura Faith had straight red hair and her eyes were mostly brown. One eye had a small patch of blue, and the other a ring of blue around the pupil almost exactly like her father's. Laura was our easy-going baby. She currently weighed a half a pound less than her sister, but with the way she was eating, I figured she would catch up soon enough. Laura loved people, she had rolled over first, and enjoyed tummy time.

Luna *hated* tummy time, threw a fit if a stranger tried to talk to her, and only slept if she could touch her twin and had a pacifier in her mouth. The girls were as different as night and day. While they were both settled for the moment, I checked the stew I had in the crockpot and hustled prepping bottles for the rest of the evening.

I'd not had the best of luck breastfeeding. I hadn't been able to supply enough for both the girls. Laura had begun to lose weight and I'd had to supplement with formula. The whole thing became so stressful that in the end I'd switched completely to formula and felt not an ounce of guilt. The babies were happy and thriving, and now they were taking longer intervals between feedings. Which with twins, was a life saver. I had just stuck the prepped bottles in the fridge when Julian came home from work.

"How are my girls?" he asked.

Laura swung her head around at the sound of her father's voice. Her kicking grew more animated.

"They are happy in their baby swings, for the moment."

"Did you want to take them for a walk before dinner? The moon is up and it's not too chilly to take the girls out," Julian said, pausing to give me a kiss.

"Yeah," I said. "We have a few hours before their next feeding."

"I'll go change clothes and be right back." He stopped, said hello to the twins and gave them each a pat on the tummy, then headed upstairs to change.

A short time later we were walking through the October woods around our home. I carried Laura in a baby carrier, and Julian had Luna. Laura was content and smiling up at me while she rode against my chest and Luna had fallen asleep as soon as her father had bundled her against him in her carrier for our walk.

"Those cute black sleepers came in for the girls today," I told Julian.

"The ones with the ruffles on the butt?"

"Yes." I pulled Laura's knit cap back father down as we walked. "I think that's our best option for Halloween costumes for them this year."

Julian grinned over at me. "With the black and orange stretchy headbands Nina and Diego got for them, that will look great."

"They love spoiling the girls," I said.

"Godparent's privilege," Julian agreed.

"Ivy will go crazy, seeing Luna and Laura dressed as little Witches."

"You know my father will too." Julian chuckled. "How is Ivy doing?"

"Fine," I said. "The pregnancy is going well, and they should be moving back into their house before Thanksgiving."

"Did they settle on a nursery theme?"

"They're going to do a Hogwarts houses theme."

"That's perfect for Ivy. Erik doesn't mind?"

"I have it on good authority that he's as big of a fan of the boy wizard as Ivy. Apparently, they went to Harry Potter World on their honeymoon. The nursery theme was *his* idea, according to my sister."

We reached the halfway point of our mile walk and stopped to admire a small stream that ran through our property. As we watched, the sky began to turn orange from the approaching sunset. Yellow leaves floated down from a nearby tree and fell softly into the water.

"Maggie sent me some photos today of the beginning of the Halloween party set up at the mansion," I said. "I spoke to the vendors to confirm all of the details for the party on zoom calls today while the girls napped. Wait until you see the desserts Candice is making for the party."

"Is it still going well for you and Maggie, with you working from home?" he asked.

"Yes," I said, patting Laura's back. "I'm getting the hang of it."

I had been back to work for a few weeks and worked remotely part-time from our office at home on Wednesday and Friday. I went into the mansion for in-person meetings with Maggie on Sunday, while Julian stayed home with the girls.

"There are a few demanding bridal clients," I said, "but for the most part it is fun. By the way, you should know that your father is going all out at the mansion this year. He is turning the ballroom into a Halloween extravaganza."

"I think my father is more excited than the kids." Julian dropped a kiss on Luna's head.

I nudged Julian's arm. "I believe that your father has a date for the party this year."

"Good." Julian smiled. "He seems happy dating Brenna Anderson."

"Yes," I agreed, "he truly does. Oh, and in other news...I spoke to Erik about having hay bales and fifty pumpkins delivered to the mansion today."

"Hay bales?" Julian gaped at the news. "Fifty pumpkins?"

I inclined my head. "That is correct."

Julian rolled his eyes. "Well that explains the group text message Nina sent about having a pumpkin carving get-together for the family the night before the big party."

"Maybe we can chip in and order pizza," I said. "Nina will be busy enough making the food to feed a hundred people at the Halloween party."

Julian smiled over at me. "Duncan said the same. Erik and Lexie said they would chip in as well. Bran seemed convinced he could out carve everyone else..."

"Bran is extremely competitive when it comes to jack-o'-lanterns," I said. "When we were younger, he always did these amazing carvings. It took three times as long as everyone else, but they were always excellent."

"I can't believe Samhain is next week," Julian said as we headed back for the house. "The past three months have flown by."

"The loss of time is from the sleep deprivation," I said dryly.

Julian took my hand. "I'm so relieved that the girls are sleeping through the night now. Even with help from our families, the first few weeks home with the twins was hard."

I nodded in agreement. My father and Ruth had stayed with us the first few days. The rest of the family had taken turns staying for the day, or sometimes spending the night with us. Autumn, Lexie, Ivy, Nina, and Maggie had really helped us out. Even Bran, Diego and Duncan had taken turns. Thomas had popped in off and on, but he always stayed on Saturday and helped out for the entire day.

By the time the girls were three weeks old we'd been determined to take care of them completely by ourselves. It had been nothing short of a trial by fire, but we had gotten through it. Together.

I spotted the moon peeking out between the branches of the trees and pointed it out to Julian. "Let's wish upon the moon that the girls sleep all night."

Julian saluted the moon, using an ancient hand gesture. I heard him talking quietly to the goddess as we walked along the path in the woods.

I did a double take. "Did you just wish upon the moon for *another* baby?"

He glanced over, and one eyebrow was raised. "I was thinking that in a few years, I'd like to have one more. We could try for a boy this time."

My breath huffed out. "Maybe. In a few years."

"We could name him Lucas," Julian said. "Lucas Thomas Drake."

I couldn't help but smile at his hopeful expression. "Talk to me about that again when the girls are three years old."

"Deal," he said.

Hand in hand, Julian and I started down the last stretch of the path. Ahead of us we could see the solar landscaping lights around the house starting to come on as dusk grew closer. We had barely reached the edge of the clearing when I saw movement in the woods to my left.

I saw a flash of white and I squeezed Julian's hand in warning. "Look!" I whispered.

A white doe, the one I'd seen earlier in the year, stepped out of the cover of the autumn woods and began to nibble on the grass at the edge of the clearing.

"The white hind," Julian breathed. "Isn't she beautiful?"

Slowly, I eased my phone from my pocket. I hoped to get a picture of her this time, but before I could lift it completely up, two fawns stepped out to join their mother. The fawns were mostly white, with white faces, throats, bellies and legs, with large patches of speckled brown on their sides. One fawn had brown around its ears, and the other had its brown markings along the top of its back as well as its sides.

"She had two fawns," I whispered. Quickly I switched my phone to silent and snapped a few photos of the white deer and her piebald fawns.

The light began to fade, and Luna lifted her head from Julian's chest and began to fuss. The three deer nimbly stepped back into the cover of the woods, and Julian and I made our way back inside.

I didn't have time to do more than glance at the photos on my phone, but they looked pretty good to me. I thought I'd get them framed for the girl's nursery. In the meantime, Luna and Laura needed to be changed.

We had our dinner and then fed the girls. Bath time came next and as was typical, Laura enjoyed the water and Luna screamed herself red in the face.

"This child does *not* like being naked," I said over the ruckus as we bathed the babies together in the tub.

"I must say, that relieves me," Julian said dryly. "No boyfriends until you have graduated from college, young lady." Using a plastic cup, Julian deftly poured water over the back of Luna's head to rinse the baby shampoo off.

Luna kicked and fussed. By the time he lifted her out and bundled her up in a towel, Luna's bottom lip pouted out so large that Julian began to laugh.

Laura smiled through it all. While we got the girls diapered and into sleepers, Laura kicked and cooed, going on a charm offensive; and Luna glared daggers at her Daddy for daring to give her a bath.

Eventually, we had them fed again and down for the night...at least we hoped it would be for the night. Together we shut off the downstairs lights and went upstairs to go to bed. I climbed into bed and checked the baby monitor screen on my nightstand. The girls were asleep, side-by side in their shared crib. In time we would put them in their own cribs, but for now they slept better if they were in close proximity or touching each other.

With a relieved sigh, I shut my eyes, snuggled closer to Julian, and promptly started to fall asleep.

"Angel?" Julian's voice was husky and low. He was

kissing his way across my throat and his hand was sliding up my thigh.

With a sleepy smile I shifted, allowing him more access. "Listen," I began as he rolled me over to my back. "If you wake up the babies, I'm going to kick your ass."

He settled over me. "You know it only turns me on more when you talk like that."

A laugh bubbled up. Quickly we pulled my nightshirt over my head, and I flung it across the room. Julian began to kiss my breasts, and as he pressed closer I moaned.

"*Shh*," he whispered against my skin. "You'll wake the babies. If you do, there'll be consequences."

"What sort of consequences?" I ran my hands over his back and dug my nails in. His response was ragged and loud.

"Holly." His voice had become deeper and more gravelly. "Do you remember the first time you used your nails on me?"

"I do, as a matter of fact," I said. "The point I am making is that I'm not the only one who makes a lot of noise." I dug my nails in harder and he hissed, arching his back in reaction.

"Damn." He ground out the word.

I smiled. "Perhaps you *do* remember that particular time?"

"Our first time together?" Julian's smile turned devilish. "Let me show you what I remember."

***

Outside, in the October sky, the waxing moon rose steadily higher, its magick casting a blessing over the family who lived within the house in the clearing. The silvery light filtered down through the upstairs window, softly illuminating the couple who loved each other so passionately there.

Holly and Julian's wishes were granted that night, and their twins slept peacefully. The legacy of magick that had started as a curse upon Bishop women and Drake men almost three hundred years before had been broken once and for all.

As the years passed, Holly and Julian faced both their difficulties and their joys together. They would raise their girls and eventually have another child as well; and the devotion they had for each other only strengthened over time.

For although they had magick, their life was not a faery tale. It was much, much more. Their love for one another became their true legacy, and one that their three children strived to someday have for their very own.

And so, they all lived happily ever after.

The End

***

A NOTE TO THE READER

Back in 2015, when I started my first paranormal novel with the idea of it being a three-book set, I never imagined this would turn into a twelve-book series. What started with the story idea of Autumn Bishop discovering her magickal legacy had rolled into a large witchy cast of ensemble characters.

I will admit that the secondary character of the beautiful Holly Bishop always intrigued me. Beloved, kind, and caring, she was almost too good to be true. It also made me wonder what would happen if she snapped and went dark...and I couldn't resist finding out.

Then there was Julian Drake. The first editor I ever worked with lost her mind over his character. Her reaction made me seriously reconsider him and his eventual story arc. Julian found his redemption in the third book of the series, and I did have long range plans for him, until everything changed in the fifth book of this series.

In chapter five of *Under The Holly Moon*, Julian and Holly exploded off the page—or my computer screen as the case may be. The day I wrote the scene where Julian rescued Holly when she was attacked changed everything.

After that, I knew that Julian and Holly would eventually close out the *Legacy Of Magick* series. What I didn't realize was that my master plan for them would be chucked out the window once again, because they would have their own ideas of how their story should play out.

From the moment I put these two on a page together a few years ago, I've been racing to keep up with them. It's been a hell of a ride, and I thank you for spending time with me in Williams Ford. The saga of the Bishops and the Drakes has come full circle now. I hope you have enjoyed Holly and Julian's happily ever after. I know I have.

Blessed be, Ellen Dugan

ABOUT THE AUTHOR

Ellen Dugan is the award-winning author of over forty books. Ellen's non-fiction titles have been translated into over twelve foreign languages. She branched out successfully into fiction with her popular *Legacy Of Magick, The Gypsy Chronicles, Daughters Of Midnight,* and *Hemlock Hollow* series. Ellen has been featured in USA TODAY'S HEA column. She lives an enchanted life in Missouri tending to her extensive perennial gardens and writing. Please visit her website or social media:
www.ellendugan.com
www.facebook.com/ellendugan
www.instagram.com/ellendugan/

Made in United States
Troutdale, OR
07/07/2025